The 1066 from Normandy

The Funny Book Company

Published by The Funny Book Company
Dalton House, 60 Windsor Ave, London SW19 2RR
www.funnybookcompany.com

Copyright © 2019 Howard Matthews
All rights reserved. No part of this publication may be reproduced, copied, or distributed by any means whatsoever without the express permission of the copyright owner. The author's moral rights have been asserted.

Cover design by Double Dagger.

ISBN 978-1-913383-03-9

Stupendous thanks are due to:
Mary of Near Warwick
Susan Fanning
Karen Nevard Downs
Lydia Reed
Claire Ward

The 1066 From Normandy

by

Howard of Warwick

(The Superfluous Chronicles of
Brother Hermitage)

Also by Howard of Warwick.
The First Chronicles of Brother Hermitage
The Heretics of De'Ath
The Garderobe of Death
The Tapestry of Death
Continuing Chronicles of Brother Hermitage
Hermitage, Wat and Some Murder or Other
Hermitage, Wat and Some Druids
Hermitage, Wat and Some Nuns
Yet More Chronicles of Brother Hermitage
The Case of the Clerical Cadaver
The Case of the Curious Corpse
The Case of the Cantankerous Carcass
Interminable Chronicles of Brother Hermitage
A Murder for Mistress Cwen
A Murder for Master Wat
A Murder for Brother Hermitage
The Umpteenth Chronicles of Brother Hermitage
The Bayeux Embroidery
The Chester Chasuble
The Hermes Parchment
Brother Hermitage Diversions
Brother Hermitage in Shorts (Free!)
Brother Hermitage's Christmas Gift

Howard of Warwick's Middle Ages crisis: History-ish.
The Domesday Book (No, Not That One.)
The Domesday Book (Still Not That One.)

The Magna Carta (Or Is It?)

Explore the whole sorry business and join the mailing
list at
Howardofwarwick.com

Another funny book from The Funny Book
Company
***Greedy** by Ainsworth Pennington*

The 1066 from Normandy

Caput I	Visitation	1
Caput II	Nice Night for a Walk	12
Caput III	Hunt the Monk	21
Caput IV	A Very Heavy Problem	32
Caput V	Taxy	44
Caput VI	Ah, There It Is	56
Caput VII	Open the Box	65
Caput VIII	In the Nice Kind of Hovel	76
Caput IX	Dishonesty Explained	88
Caput X	Off to Church	98
Caput XI	Where Has All The Money Gone?	111
Caput XII	A Less Than Dignified Death	123
Caput XIII	Back on The Road Again	134
Caput XIV	Into the Bushes	145
Caput XV	Chesterfield City Centre	156
Caput XVI	Legs	167
Caput XVII	The Uses of a Tangled Web	178
Caput XVIII	No Smoke Without Smoke	189
Caput XIX	Killer in The Night	200
Caput XX	Escape Alive?	210
Caput XXI	A Creeping Killer	221
Caput XXII	Revealed; All	230

The 1066 To Hastings

Caput 1	Descended Upon	244

Caput I

Visitation

The lone street of Derby was silent in the darkness of a still night as two figures shuffled through its shadows. They had shielded themselves from sight with long cloaks and hoods of a dark material. They kept away from the centre of the path, avoiding the risk of even a passing fox reporting their presence.

They had also waited long for full darkness. The summer evening stretched interminably and a quarter-moon bobbed between clouds, illuminating the area with irritating regularity.

Their destination was well known in the neighbourhood; that would be enough for most people to take up lurking or even employ a professional lurker to do it on their behalf. It was also a place of some wealth, and so those who lurked about it in the dark were to be treated with suspicion.

People who went anywhere in the dark these days were usually treated with the sharp end of a Norman sword. The invaders seemed to be a very nervous people, considering their strength and military prowess. They clearly thought that everyone was out to get them; people lurking in the dark particularly so. They were right.

No one would stand up to a Norman in broad daylight, but get one on his own in the dark, preferably drunk, and there would be one less to worry about.

But this street was deserted, and the scuttling pair could make their progress without interruption.

The 1066 From Normandy

Their journey had not been long. Being close by on other business had presented the perfect opportunity to achieve their goal in one night; and it was a very particular goal.

The tapestry workshop of Wat the Weaver was home to many attractions for the ordinary man. The more ordinary, and the more the man, the more the attraction.

Tapestry was a magical form, readily accessible for the common folk. Painting was a bit of a specialist activity and was only commissioned by the truly wealthy; the church, mainly. This meant that the images were pious and worthy and not remotely interesting.

Books were a source of more entertaining pictures. The borders and scribbles in margins were very imaginative and presented ordinary, day to day activities in all their detail; the toil of the field and the games of leisure. They also reported the common facts of the wider world, such as that a manticore had the body of a lion, the tail of a scorpion, the face of a man and could shoot spikes from its mane. But then everyone knew all this and very few of them had access to a book anyway.

Tapestry, on the other hand, was on display. It showed people going about their routine business and could be seen by anyone who passed by.

People tended to either pass by the tapestries of Wat the Weaver quite quickly or loiter in a very dubious manner. Wat's works displayed normal human activities, but ones that nice people didn't talk about let alone have pictures of.

All that had changed when Wat invited Brother Hermitage to live in the workshop, but a lot of the common folk still thought of Wat as a fount of the sort of information their mother wouldn't tell them; never mind draw for them in colour.

Visitation

The old works of Wat were still out there in the world, mostly hidden under the bed, but that didn't stop people turning up at the workshop expecting to see something on display; well, everything on display really.

Arriving under the cover of darkness was understandable, but not usually at this time of night. The works of Wat had value and the less there were of them, the more that value went up. The trade in previously owned Wat tapestries was booming; a fact that annoyed Wat no end.

The lurking of the visitors had now moved on to skulking. They crept around the corners of buildings, ducked low under windows and stopped quickly at the slightest noise. They clearly knew the way; but one would go ahead to make sure the next part of their route was clear before the other joined him. Then they swapped roles.

It was understandable that people visiting Wat didn't want to be seen, but these two seemed to be going to extraordinary lengths. It might be a bit odd to see two men travelling at night, but it wasn't unheard of. Keep out of the way of the Normans, was the only important instruction. In the dark it was hard to tell friend from foe, until the foe killed you with something. Better just to keep your head down.

Once they reached the end of the town, Wat's workshop being well beyond the last house at the request of the owner of the last house, they paused to take stock.

Their way appeared clear. There were no other folk abroad at this time of night and the darkness was covering their presence most effectively. There was open ground to cover now though. The chance of discovery increased and so the two men were cautious.

The 1066 From Normandy

They waited and watched, giving the world around them time to make itself known. After a period, which seemed to be mutually and silently agreed, the first one stepped forward, still bent double, and hurried his way over to the low gate that marked the boundary of the workshop's land.

Squatting down by this and waiting yet again, the first man eventually beckoned to the second, who hurried over to join him.

From their position, they surveyed the building ahead of them. A large front door stood firmly shut and above that a window from the upper storey room looked down on them like a dark glass eye. To left and right, the building extended, the timbers of its construction standing proud of the wattle and daub infill, painted with whitewash.

Farther over to the right, other buildings could be seen peeping out from the rear. This was where most of the weaving equipment was and where the works were produced. Wat lent a hand and gave direction, but most of the actual weaving was done by apprentices.

Cwen, a fine young weaver in her own right, also gave instruction; along with criticism and complaint. But, if anyone spotted two people sneaking around the workshop in the middle of the night, it would be Cwen who tackled them; quite literally.

Brother Hermitage would stand there and look aghast, while Wat would offer helpful encouragement from some way off.

There was no movement at all from the workshop though, so the two new arrivals were emboldened to step through the gate, past the vegetable patch and up to the building itself.

Now they appeared to be uncertain for the first time. A whispered discussion concluded that they would go to the

Visitation

left first. Yes, the workshop was to the right, but the apprentices would be there as well; and everyone knew what apprentices got up to in the middle of the night. There was a chance one of them would be up and about and up to no good. Best to avoid any risk of contact.

The upper storey of the building was only one room and everything else was on ground level. Their target was bound to be through one of the windows that they would be able to reach quite easily. The problem was which one. They didn't want to climb in and be apprehended, they needed to know where they were going first.

Round the corner of the building they came to the first window. This was dark and offered no clue as to what lay inside. The two men sat themselves beneath it, breathing their recent exertion deeply until they were quiet once more.

One man nodded to the other, who slowly turned and rose to a squatting position from where he could reach the window. Putting his hands on the wall to steady himself, he lifted his head until he could see in.

Eyes adjusting to the darkness within, he peered hard until he could make out rough shapes. This was not the room he was looking for and so he ducked down again.

He shook his head to his companion, who returned an expression of some impatience. A proper Saxon dwelling would have been one large hall for everyone to eat and live in together. The workshop might have been separate, but that would be it. This bizarre arrangement, obviously preferred by Wat, where people had their own rooms was simply ridiculous. Not since the Romans had there been such extravagance. And it made the task of men in the dark finding what they were looking for unnecessarily difficult.

The 1066 From Normandy

Mind you, doing what they planned in a hall full of other people would have been doubly difficult.

With nodded agreement, the two moved on down the building to the next window.

At least this one had no glass in it. It was simply a hole in the side of the building covered with a cloth. The first man followed his process of creeping slowly upwards and lifted a corner of this to one side so that he could peer in. Holding his breath, he stuck his eyes and nose over the edge of the window and strained to see what was beyond.

He ducked down quickly as noises from the room startled him. They were the sounds of someone in their sleep, but it was still a shock. Whoever was in this room was having most vivid dreams and not happy ones by the sound of it.

The first man shook his head once more and they moved on.

The next window didn't even have a cloth over it. This was just a bare opening and the two men exchanged hopeful looks.

The first man, who seemed to be in charge of window-peeping, now stood to the side of the opening and leaned around so that he could look fully into the room.

With no cloth or glass to obscure his view, he could see more clearly what this room contained. He looked down to his companion and nodded with a horrible smile. The smile he got back was no more pleasant and the second man stood with a nod, indicating that the first could now get on with it.

Getting on with it involved climbing very carefully and cautiously through the window and into the room beyond. It wasn't a large opening, but this wasn't a large man. He lifted one leg and slid it over the low sill, ducking his head

Visitation

down to slip into the room like a snake of very bad intent.

With a raised hand, the first man indicated that the second should stay put to receive whatever was being taken.

Again, pausing so that he could see what he was doing, the first man stepped slowly and quietly forward. In front of him he saw his goal. A bundle of material was laid out on a low shelf, just ready for the taking. It would need careful handling though, but he had come prepared. Taking a length of material from his belt he stepped up to tie it around his prize.

Quickly, and with obvious experience at this sort of thing, he had the treasure secured and hoisted into his arms. He stepped smartly over to the window and leaned out so that his companion could take the weight.

With their ill-gotten gains out of the house, the two men quickly retreated into the shadows and made their escape. With any luck it would be hours before anyone in the workshop was up, let alone discovered that something was missing.

The second man now paused for a moment to haul the load up onto his shoulder and the two of them set off at a fast pace to make sure they were nowhere near Derby when the sun rose.

. . .

Mornings in the workshop followed their normal routine; mostly chaos, with Wat sitting in the middle of it doing nothing to help.

The apprentices had to be roused from their slumber by Hartle, the ancient weaving master, whose shouts and insults were their normal greeting. Bleary eyed, they

The 1066 From Normandy

stumbled about, doing their very best to fall asleep again wherever they were.

Mrs Grod, Wat's disgusting cook of disgusting food, materialised before daybreak, striding up the path from wherever it was she spent the night. She needed the whole morning to prepare the noon meal for everyone who was going to eat it; which excluded Wat, Cwen, Hartle and Hermitage. A strong young apprentice stomach was required to cope with Mrs Grod's cooking.

The apprentices spent many an entertaining evening speculating on where Mrs Grod went at night. Few of the speculations were either wholesome or actually possible.

Cwen emerged from her own chamber instantly ready for the day and critical of anyone who wasn't. She could only scowl and grumble at Wat, who just sat with his morning beer. The apprentices she could scold and harry, and they soon made their way to the workshop to pick up where they had left off.

Once she and Hartle were satisfied that they were actually doing what they were told, the two of them retreated to find Wat; and discuss whether there was any special work that required their attention today.

The oldest loom in the place was showing increasing signs of wear, and Wat's continuous refusal to pay the loom maker for a new one was getting embarrassing. A couple of the apprentices, who seemed more interested than most in loom maintenance and repair, were spending more days fixing the thing than using it.

And it was the biggest one they had. Wat and Cwen had come back from Lincoln with a commission for a very pious and very large tapestry. The client, Godrinius, had started a bit of a trend for pious tapestries amongst the well-to-do Saxons. It was one means of showing King

8

William what a wonderfully devout person you were and how there was no need to take your land and kill your family at all.

The old loom was the only thing capable of producing such works, and there was a very good chance it would collapse completely any day now.

Cwen and Hartle exchanged low whispers as they went to find Wat. Perhaps this was the day that their combined strength might force his fingers into his purse.

Hermitage would join them after his morning devotions, which seemed to go on most of the morning. Many times he had tried to get Wat to instigate prayers before the day began but seemed to know that his task was hopeless.

The three of them had often speculated that giving Wat a choice between buying a new loom or allowing the apprentices half an hour away from work to pray, might kill him.

This time, Hartle carried the latest piece of wood to fall from the loom. The fact that this was mostly dust, held together by woodworm holes, should be evidence that the time to spend was fast approaching.

Agreeing their tactics, Cwen and Hartle made their way to the upper chamber, where they knew Wat would be loitering enjoying the peace and quiet.

'Well, it's simple, isn't it?' Hartle said aloud.

'Of course,' Cwen agreed.

'We just have to tell them that they can't have their tapestries. Of course, they won't pay, but I'm sure we can manage that.'

'And fortunately we don't have to tell them, Wat does.'

'Ha, ha. Yes, good point.'

'Go on, then,' Wat said as they appeared at the top of the stairs. 'What's the latest?'

The 1066 From Normandy

Hartle held out the piece of wood. 'Heddle peg end,' he announced.

'Every home should have one.'

Hartle went over to the window, pushed open the one pane that moved, and flamboyantly crumbled the wood to bits in his hand. 'I imagine you don't want the woodworm moving on to eat the house as well as the loom.'

'A heddle peg's easy enough to replace.'

'And then there's the cloth beam, the shed bar, the crank shaft. Basically, if it isn't cloth or the stone of the heddle weights, the worms have eaten it. You need a new loom.'

'Now,' Cwen added. 'Because if you don't order it now, it won't be here in time to complete the orders.'

'The apprentices can make a loom. Be good for them.'

'They could,' Hartle agreed. 'You've still got to buy the wood though. And then take the apprentices off the work they're already doing and wait twice as long for a loom that will be half as good.'

And thus, the discussion continued. Hartle and Cwen made very good arguments for the new loom, and Wat ignored them. As they pointed out, he had no good arguments against them, apart from the fact he didn't want to spend his money.

When Cwen eventually suggested that she and Hartle might put their money together to buy a loom themselves, Wat brightened a little. When they went on to say that this would mean they owned a share of the workshop, he dimmed again.

One of the tapestry orders had come from the Saxon, Thorkill of Warwick. Along with Colesvain of Lincoln, he was the only surviving Saxon noble to retain his estates after the conquest. He had achieved this by being a sycophantic supporter of William and had even started

Visitation

modelling himself on the epitome of the good Norman. This meant that he killed people quite regularly, and a weaver who didn't deliver would be an ideal target.

The prospect of death did focus Wat's attention.

'Hermitage,' he said.

'What about him?' Cwen couldn't see what Hermitage had to do with this.

'He does arguments and the like.'

'He does arguments?'

'You know, working out who's right and wrong.'

'I suppose so. But it's mainly to do with the bible.'

'Yes, but I'm sure he could think about this one.'

'You mean we let Hermitage decide?' Cwen was very surprised at this suggestion. From her experience, Hermitage loved to consider good arguments. He loved to consider them so much that he never came down on one side or the other.

'Can't do any harm.'

Cwen was pretty confident that she could persuade Hermitage to agree with her. With a glance at Hartle, she skipped back down the stairs to interrupt Hermitage's morning prayers.

Hartle sat and took a mug of Wat's beer, doing his best to look very disappointed at this whole situation.

After some time of embarrassed waiting, the embarrassment all being Hartle's, Cwen reappeared.

'Well?' Wat asked.

'Don't know where he is,' Cwen said with a disinterested shrug. 'Perhaps someone's stolen him.'

Caput II

Nice Night for a Walk

Brother Hermitage knew that he was not as familiar as he should be with the activities of the "real world", as Cwen called it. He was frequently puzzled by the behaviour of normal people as they went about their everyday business. The things they said confused him and the things they did made no sense at all.

Even he, deep in the contemplative life of the monk, could tell that being tied up and taken from his bed in the middle of the night was unusual.

When he tried to ask just what was going on, he found that the gag stuck in his mouth prevented useful conversation. All he managed to get out was a muffled complaint, after which one of his abductors promised to "shut him up". He rapidly concluded that this would be a bad thing.

Whoever was carrying him was a strong fellow. He was bouncing around on the man's shoulder like a sack of turnips. He would offer to get down and walk but suspected that any more noise would go badly for him.

With no conversation to distract him, he tried to think this situation through. He started with who these people were before rapidly moving on to what they were going to do with him. He concluded that if he had the answer to either question it would inform the other. If he knew who they were, he might have an idea of what they were going to do. If he knew what they were going to do, it might help him consider who would do that sort of thing.

Nice Night for a Walk

All totally fascinating and of absolutely no help whatsoever.

His first concern was that they were going to kill him. He felt it quite natural that this worry should take precedence over all others. But then, why would they carry him away to do it? That thought gave a moment's relief. If these people wanted him dead, they could have done the deed as he lay in his bed. Why go to all the bother of tying him and taking him when a simple knife in the dark would have done the job in no time?

He soon argued with himself that he might have made some noise as he was murdered and alerted Cwen and Wat. Much better to take him away to where he could make all the noise he wanted, and no one would come.

Then again, these men did seem to be taking him some distance from the workshop. He felt as if he had been worrying for quite a while now. Surely, if they wanted to finish him off in peace, they would only have to step off into the nearby woods.

Trying to think like men who took monks from their beds in the dark was going to get him nowhere. He couldn't think like most of the normal people he met, so he had no chance with lurking killers.

Why would anyone take anyone anywhere? That was the question. Well it was several questions, but he felt that he had the time to consider each of them just at the moment; there being no sign of his abductors stopping.

They were after him, obviously. They would have to be pretty poor abductors if they took people they didn't actually want.

There was a thought. Perhaps they'd got the wrong person? Could they have wanted Wat, sneaked into the wrong room and taken the wrong body by mistake? If that

The 1066 From Normandy

was the case, they were going to be very disappointed when they stopped. They might even take it out on Hermitage.

He could imagine some angry people wanting to get hold of Wat. He was a very wealthy man, who had made his money by creating tapestries of a uniquely explicit nature. Disgustingly explicit, if the truth be told. Perhaps someone had taken offence and decided it was time to deal with Wat.

Mind you, a lot of people seemed to take offence and declare Wat's work to be revolting and outrageous. According to Wat, that never stopped them coming back after dark and buying one or two.

Wealthy. Wat was wealthy. Could this be a hostage situation? These men had come to Wat's workshop to steal the weaver away and then demand ransom for his release. He understood this kind of thing was quite common, but mainly amongst the nobility and their families.

If they thought there was money to be made, these men would likely be quite angry when they found that all they'd got was a worthless monk.

But if he was not the intended target, the men would have very good reason to do something horrible to him when they found out; even if the mistake was their own fault. One factor of human nature that he had discerned was that when people had their mistakes pointed out to them it made them more angry rather than less. He still hadn't worked out why.

And what if these men did want him? The question was why? Who on earth would want a monk? They weren't good for very much. And if you did want one, you only had to go to a monastery and ask, there were plenty after all.

Nice Night for a Walk

Without the slightest scintilla of pride, he rapidly concluded that he was unique.

Being King William's own personal investigator, tracking down killers and bringing them to justice was not the activity of the common or garden monk. These men had not abducted any old monk, they'd taken the King's Investigator.

He was fairly confident that telling these people he didn't want to be the King's Investigator would be no help at all. He couldn't imagine them saying "oh, that's all right then", before popping him back into bed.

Revenge. Did these men want revenge for something? From the horrible tales townsfolk told one another, he knew that revenge could be worse than death. People did simply kill one another for revenge, but he understood that they frequently took their time over it.

He acknowledged that he probably had upset a few people in the course of his investigations; killers, mainly. And who more likely to abduct someone and take them off to be murdered, than a killer? This sort of thing being routine business for them.

There had already been one concerted and quite organised attempt to finish him off, but King William's man, Le Pedvin had dealt with that. Had his old adversaries returned to have another go?[1]

Or it could be any of the other people he had exposed in his unwanted career. Did it help to make a list? No, not really. He would find out soon enough.

It was no comfort to think that King William would be very cross when he found out his investigator had been abducted and murdered. It wouldn't be that the king cared

[1] *A Murder for Brother Hermitage* goes on at length about this.

The 1066 From Normandy

half a hoot for Hermitage, it would be the principle that you couldn't go round murdering the king's office holders.

The king's revenge would be very swift but totally out of proportion to the offence. If he found these killers had come from Essex, he'd probably kill Essex; all of it.

As the night wore on, Hermitage was starting to wonder how long one man could carry a monk in the dark. He could tell the fellow was powerfully built, but even so. It was no surprise to find that he was worrying about his abductor. He didn't want to cause the man a strain or anything. They'd been going for quite some time now and he hadn't even swapped shoulders.

He did start to think that if they kept going for much longer, the dawn might arrive. Then he could get some idea where they were. He also hoped that the workshop would start to rise for the morning and notice that he wasn't there. What they could do about it he wouldn't know. Start looking, he supposed. But by that time he would be miles away.

As they moved on through the countryside, Hermitage thought that he could detect a slight slowing of their pace. He assumed there was only so far monk carrying could go before anyone would need a rest.

'This'll do,' the one who wasn't doing the carrying said.

Hermitage was in no doubt that "this'll do" was a very bad sign indeed.

The shoulder beneath him stopped as his carrier drew to a halt. There was a deep exhale as the man bent forward and he was unceremoniously dumped onto the ground. This was doubly uncomfortable as his arms and legs being tied, he had no way of breaking his fall. At least the ground was strewn with leaves and gave a relatively soft landing.

Having come down on his face, he managed to roll over

Nice Night for a Walk

so that he could look at his captors.

The one who had brought him all this way was simply huge. He looked the sort who was capable of carrying a monk all day without complaint.

He wore a loose hood over his face so there was no way Hermitage was going to be able to recognise him. Not that he knew many people in this line of work.

The second man was thin but also hooded and it was clear that the carrying duties had been appropriately shared out. The thin one looked as if he'd collapse after the first few paces.

Hermitage chanced a look around and saw that they were nowhere in particular. This patch of woodland looked much the same as any other would in the dark of night. If this was their final destination, he feared that it might be his very last ever.

'You can walk from here,' the thin one instructed.

Hermitage's heart sank as the words he had been hoping to hear did not materialise. Something along the lines of "oh my God it's a bloody monk", would have been good. "Who the hell is this", was also acceptable, followed by "we'll have to take him back."

There was nothing of the sort and so he had to conclude that these men had collected their intended quarry.

Things had got worse, then. He should have expected it really. Still, there was something to be grateful for. Being carried had been most uncomfortable and he would be very glad to use his legs. He was also pleased to hear that they were walking somewhere. That meant that he was wanted elsewhere.

The thin man bent down and pulled Hermitage to his feet. He then removed the bindings from his legs and gave him a hearty shove in the chosen direction.

The 1066 From Normandy

There was still very little light, and so it was hard to avoid the brambles and roots of the ground. It was only now that Hermitage was off the shoulder, that he realised he didn't have any shoes. Even if he hadn't been gagged, he suspected that his captors would not respond favourably to the request to go back and get his sandals.

He stepped as quickly as he could, but every now and then would have to hop and stoop as something sharp dug into his soles.

'For goodness sake, you're a monk,' the thin man complained.

Hermitage had no idea what that meant. Were monks supposed to walk on rough ground without hindrance? Were their feet specially hardened? He would like to discuss what this man's idea of a monk was, but discussion of anything was out of the question. Instead he just got shoved along some more.

He tried to tread as carefully as he could, but his progress was clearly not as fast as was wanted.

'It'll be light soon,' the larger man complained, sounding worried about being caught in the daylight.

'It's all right,' the thin one replied. 'We're nearly there.'

For a moment, Hermitage was quite pleased to hear that; it meant that he'd be able to stop walking soon. Then he started worrying once more about what was going to befall once they arrived.

Stepping out from one intensely bramble strewn pathway, which made Hermitage question why God had given brambles thorns in the first place, he saw that there were tents arranged in a clearing.

There were about six of them from what Hermitage could see. They were laid out around a central fire, which had slumped and glowed red at the end of the night.

Nice Night for a Walk

These abductors had a whole camp, did they? He couldn't immediately work out why that was interesting. He didn't know if organised abductors were better or worse than any other kind.

Even in the sight of the tents, the two men proceeded cautiously, as if they didn't want to be seen. Perhaps these weren't their tents at all, and they had come to abduct someone else. What were they doing, starting a collection?

It was not the sort of encampment that would have any monks in it. Monks went from monastery to monastery and tents were a great expense. It couldn't be that they were looking for more monks then.

The two men led him around the back of one particularly large tent and stopped before going farther. The thin one peered cautiously around the edge of the canvas, as if checking that they were not being observed.

'Right,' he hissed back, beckoning them to follow.

Hermitage did so because he didn't have any choice.

They bent low, forcing Hermitage to do likewise, and scurried along the outside of this tent until they came to its entrance.

Here, the leader indicated that they should all squat down. Whatever these men were up to, it was not something the owners of the tents wanted going on. Perhaps it was plain theft? In which case, what did Hermitage have to do with anything?

He saw that outside of the tent a man was standing. It was still too dark to make anything out plainly, but the figure appeared to be just loitering. It could be that he was just taking a breath of fresh air. A bit late in the night for that sort of thing.

The three of them simply watched without moving or saying anything. It was clear that the thin man's eye was on

The 1066 From Normandy

the one outside of the tent.

After a few moments, the lone figure wandered off away from them perhaps adding a stroll to his fresh air.

'Right,' the thin one instructed, and sneaked his way around towards the entrance of the tent.

Hermitage was pushed along by the larger of the two, and the thin man carefully held the entrance flap of the tent to one side so that they could pass.

Once inside, they all stood straight and the two men seemed to breathe more easily.

Hermitage saw that this was a very comfortable tent. There was solid furniture inside, and a wall of canvas towards the back obviously separated off the sleeping area.

The sinking feeling he had had since leaving his bed now became even more horrible.

The thin man gave a light cough.

There was quick movement from the back of the tent and the canvas was thrown aside as a large, imposing and instantly recognisable figure emerged.

If Hermitage hadn't had a gag in his mouth, he would have been sick.

'Ah,' the new arrival called brightly. 'You got him then? And no one saw?'

Both abductors bowed. 'Oh, yes, Your Majesty. Just as instructed.'

Caput III

Hunt the Monk

'Well, where is he?' Wat asked.

Hartle had gone back to his work while Wat and Cwen wandered the workshop with little concern, knowing that Hermitage would turn up somewhere. He had probably found some quiet spot for prayer, away from the interruptions of the apprentices; the apprentices who seemed to consider it an amusing game to find Hermitage's latest quiet spot, and then disturb it.

'I don't think we'd be looking if we knew where he was,' Cwen replied.

After a cursory examination of each room, it was clear that Hermitage was not there; which was unusual.

Wat had even gone down to the privy, to see if he'd been delayed there for some reason. Perhaps some of Mrs Grod's cooking had sneaked onto his plate. He did find two apprentices who were loitering away from their work. They must be pretty desperate if they thought the hole in the ground that constituted the workshop privy was a suitable place for loitering.

Back in the upper chamber of the workshop they got their thoughts together. 'He wouldn't just go out,' Wat said. 'Not without telling us.'

'Of course not.' Cwen dismissed that ridiculous suggestion. Hermitage let everyone know exactly what he was doing and where he was going all the time; frequently when no one had asked.

'It's not time for church.'

21

The 1066 From Normandy

They exchanged glances. Naturally, it was not time for church as far as they were concerned. From Hermitage's perspective all time was time for church.

Cwen shrugged. 'It's the only other place he can be. It's the only other place he goes at all.'

Wat nodded his agreement to this. Neither of them moved.

'Well, I'm not going,' Wat said. 'Things to do here.'

'Like what?' Cwen folded her arms. 'Not some actual weaving, surely?'

'You can go.'

'I'm not going. Why should I? I've got apprentices to instruct; you know, it's called doing something useful.'

'You go because we've lost Hermitage and need to know he's all right?'

'There you are then.' Cwen tipped her head towards the stairs with her get-on-with-it-then look.

There was still no movement.

'We'll send an apprentice,' Wat said.

'And not see them again for the rest of the day?'

'Hartle then?'

'You can't send Hartle chasing all the way to the church; he's past it. And the apprentices would all stop work as soon as he'd gone.'

Wat released a great sigh. 'Fine,' he complained. 'I'll go then.'

'I knew you would. Think of it as doing something for Hermitage and not just because I said so.'

'I assume you have checked his room?' Wat asked wearily.

'Looked for Hermitage in his room? Now there's a thought. Of course I checked his room you idiot. Where do you think I went first?'

Hunt the Monk

'Needed to be sure. You might have missed him.'

'Missed him? In his tiny room? If we lived in a normal Saxon hall like normal Saxons, we wouldn't have lost our monk.'

'Ah, but we're not normal Saxons.'

'You're not, that's for sure.'

'I'll just have another look. Be a shame to walk all the way to the church only to find out he was hiding in his room.'

'Hiding in his room?' Cwen muttered these words with a very firm set to her mouth. 'Go on then. I'll come along, just to show you that I didn't miss the monk in the corner.'

Wat led the way, ducking his head as if to avoid a blow from behind he suspected might be coming.

In Hermitage's chamber, Cwen held her arms wide to illustrate that the room was devoid of monks. She even looked at the ceiling to confirm Hermitage wasn't up there. She lifted his straw bed sack and turned full circle in the very small space.

'Obviously, I need you to confirm this,' she said. 'But I see no monks.'

Wat didn't look convinced and stepped over to peer out of the window.

'You think he climbed out of the window instead of using the door?' Cwen snorted.

Wat didn't reply for a moment. 'Someone did.'

'What?' Cwen quickly brushed him aside as she looked out at the ground below Hermitage's window.

'Footprints, see,' Wat said.

'Probably one of the apprentices sneaking around instead of getting on with their work.'

Wat squeezed next to Cwen and stuck his head out of the window once more. He looked left and right and off

23

The 1066 From Normandy

into the woods. He pointed out the crushed and damaged undergrowth. 'Sneaked off into the woods then, rather than round the back of the workshop. And there were at least two of them by the look.'

'Fascinating. Now, if you could go to the church we can stop fretting about Hermitage who, it turns out, is not in his room. What a surprise.'

'I want to look at those tracks.' Wat turned and left the room.

Cwen scurried after him as he made for the front door. 'Why don't you want to go to the church?' she asked.

'It's not that I don't want to,' Wat called back. 'But we've got tracks outside Hermitage's window that lead off into the woods and Hermitage is missing; they could be connected.'

'Who sneaks up to a weaver's workshop in the middle of the night and makes off with a monk?

'And answer the question. Why don't you want to go to the church?' Cwen pouted a bit. 'Is the nasty priest being mean to you? Is he telling you that you're wicked and must pay for your sins or something horrible will happen, probably for eternity?'

'Stupid priest,' Wat muttered.

'Ha.' Cwen was triumphant. 'Don't you worry. I'll come to the church with you and tell that priest that he's got to be nice to you.'

'Getting him to be nice to anyone would be a miracle.'

They were now at the side of the workshop and were walking up towards the outside of Hermitage's window.

Wat was looking intently at the ground. 'Footprints.'

'Of course there are footprints. This is the way from the front of the house to the privy. Anyone coming back from town who needed it would walk up here.'

Hunt the Monk

'Hm.' Wat didn't sound satisfied.

'If someone had come this way, they'd have had to pass your room and mine,' Cwen pointed out as they passed the respective windows. 'People up to no good in the middle of the night are much more likely to want you.'

'Thank you very much. And why would that be?'

'Who knows? Any number of perfectly good reasons. Murder, revenge, ransom.'

'Ransom?' Wat sounded most worried about that prospect.

'It's all right,' Cwen assured him. 'We wouldn't pay.'

Wat turned his head and gave her a frown.

'They could send you back one bit at a time and we'd make sure that not a penny of your money ever got away.'

'Hm, we may need to talk about that.'

They were outside Hermitage's window now, and Wat was scouring the ground.

'Just like an investigator,' Cwen commented.

'Eh?'

'From *vestigare*, to track? You really need to pay attention when Hermitage speaks, you know.'

'All the time?' Wat sounded appalled by the idea.

'Well, maybe not that often.'

'Here,' Wat almost shouted. He was gesturing towards the low bushes and saplings just a few paces from Hermitage's window.

'Oh, yes,' Cwen said. 'Sorrel.'

'Not the sorrel. The tracks.'

Cwen bent down at Wat's side and peered at the undergrowth.

There were clear signs that someone had been here quite recently. Plants were crushed and trampled close by, and the trail of disturbance led off into the woods.

25

The 1066 From Normandy

'Probably just someone passing by.'

'Passing by?' Wat was incredulous. 'Who would be passing by the outside of Hermitage's window before they wandered off into the woods?'

'I don't know, do I? Could be one of the apprentices playing a trick. You know how some of them like to annoy Hermitage. They could have been hiding out here pretending to be God or something.'

Wat stood straight and looked at Cwen with obvious worry that she'd gone mad. 'Pretending to be God?'

'Making noises and moaning.'

'And that's what God does in the bushes, is it?'

'Doesn't have to be God. Could be a spirit.'

Wat said nothing.

'Don't look at me like that. A couple of apprentices come out here, make horrible noises outside Hermitage's room to frighten him, and then run off.'

'Sounds like you put them up to it.'

'What are you suggesting then? Someone came here, climbed in through the window, took Hermitage and then went off into the woods with him?'

Wat clearly agreed that that was ridiculous. 'I don't know, do I? It's just odd. Fresh footprints and tracks leading away from Hermitage's room when Hermitage has just gone missing.'

'Perhaps some friends came and he went out with them?'

Wat just gaped. 'There are so many things wrong with that idea. Why would he go out of the window? Why would he do it in the middle of the night? And what friends does he have anyway?'

Cwen nodded that this last point was a very valid argument. 'Maybe some other monks took him?'

'For what?' Wat sounded quite exasperated at this

Hunt the Monk

desperate thinking.

'I don't know, do I? Probably some monk stuff.'

'Come on.' Wat shook his head as he pushed his way into the woods.

'Hadn't you better go and change?' Cwen said.

'What?'

'We know how precious you are about snagging your fine garments. Haven't you got some old chase-the-monk-through-the-woods clothes to put on?'

'Very funny.'

'On your own head be it,' Cwen said as she followed him into the woods. 'Don't come moaning to me when you want snags in your leggings sewn up.'

Wat pressed on through the woods, following the trail around him. It was a good job that this was no sort of footpath at all, as the disturbances of someone passing this way were obvious, even to an untrained eye.

'There must have been more than one,' Wat observed. 'One man alone wouldn't barge through the woods like this.'

The growth in the woods was vibrant and lush which also helped the weavers track their quarry.

'We're heading north,' Wat said.

'You don't say?' Cwen was unimpressed by this statement of the obvious. 'Honestly, you wouldn't go to the church and see if Hermitage had gone there, but you'll tramp off into the woods.'

'If the trail led to the church, I'd go there. But it doesn't.'

'This could be badgers, for all we know.'

'Badgers,' Wat scoffed. 'If this was a badger trail it would be much more worn.'

'Oh, regular old man of the woods, aren't we?'

'No, just not stupid.'

The 1066 From Normandy

They pressed on in silence, apart from the cracking and brushing of their passage.

When they had gone some distance from the workshop, Wat paused on the trail and examined their surroundings. They had come to an obvious path now, one that came from their left and went on to the right.

'The path to the river,' Wat said. 'They could have gone either way.'

Cwen came forward and looked at the ground. 'I think they went straight over.' She pointed to where the greenery on the far side of the path was flattened.

'Still heading north, then.'

Cwen nodded and they carried on. After more moments of silent progress, she spoke up. 'Are we seriously suggesting that Hermitage came all this way with someone else? In the middle of the night, into the woods? It's really not the sort of thing he'd do at all. It would have to be the Archbishop of Canterbury to get him out of the house after dark.'

'And the Archbishop of Canterbury would probably knock,' Wat said. 'It does seem a bit odd, but what's the alternative?'

'A bit odd; the perfect expression.'

'Maybe someone did come and take him.'

'They came to the workshop of Wat the Weaver and stole away a monk?'

'Not just any monk.' Wat's voice was serious and carried a hint of concern. 'The King's Investigator.'

'Oh, bloody hell.' Cwen got a look of rebuke from Wat. 'I think I'm entitled to swear. Someone's taken Hermitage.'

'Could be,' Wat sounded careful now.

'Could be? Almost certainly be.'

'Perhaps he went with them willingly?'

28

Hunt the Monk

'In the middle of the night through the window and into the woods?'

'He would if Le Pedvin asked.'

Cwen shivered at the thought of King William's cadaverous henchman turning up at anyone's window in the middle of the night.

'I think even I'd go into the woods at midnight if Le Pedvin beckoned,' Wat said. 'Better than him murdering me in my bed.'

'It could be someone who wishes him harm,' Cwen said. 'You know, like those others tried to get him.'[2]

Wat gave this a moment's thought. 'If they wanted to get him, they could have done it there and then. Climb in through the window, deal with monk, climb out again. No need to take the monk with you.'

'He's been taken away on business?'

'Investigation? Seems likely, doesn't it? I can't think of anything else that would explain it.'

'But why like this? The Normans have never been shy about simply turning up and taking him through the front door when they want him. Why sneak him out in the middle of the night?'

'For something sneaky,' Wat said. 'It could be they want him to investigate in secret.'

'On his own?' Cwen was very worried about this.

Wat also looked alarmed.

'He couldn't do it,' Cwen stated the fact. 'You know what he's like. Without us there, he'll end up dead.'

'He is a bit trusting.'

'He'd trust the man who sticks a knife in him to take it out again before it does too much damage. And he has no

---

[2] Those others being itemised in *A Murder for Brother Hermitage*

The 1066 From Normandy

idea how to be suspicious about anything. He can't question anyone because he thinks it's rude, and faced with a killer he'd probably make him promise not to do it again.'

'All drawbacks for the modern investigator,' Wat noted.

'Which is why he needs us there to do it all for him.'

'So he can come in right at the end and say "aha".'

'We're a team,' Cwen said. 'He needs us to point out the blindingly obvious and upset people, and we need him to actually work out who did it.'

'But if the Normans have taken him for their own devices, they're not likely to be keen on us turning up.'

'Let's just find him first, shall we. Then we can worry about the Normans.'

'Put off worrying about the Normans, eh? That'll be a good trick. That's what life is these days, worrying about the Normans. They didn't come all the way here to let the locals not worry about them.'

'Well, that's a good thing, then,' Cwen said.

'Oh, yes, and why's that?'

Cwen beckoned ahead. 'Because it looks like we're coming up to a whole gathering of them.'

Wat looked up from his trail-following towards the flashes of canvas that now peeked between the trees. 'Oh, marvellous.' He squatted down on his haunches. 'Now what do we do? We still need to find Hermitage and discover what's going on, but I'd rather not do it in the middle of a camp full of Normans.'

'Maybe we could sneak up to a tent and steal one? Make him talk.'

'Maybe we just do the sneaking, followed by a bit of laying low. Then we finish off with just hoping that something turns up. And we do it all quietly.'

Wat now lay full length on the ground and beckoned

30

Hunt the Monk

that Cwen should join him.

'How long are we going to stay here?' Cwen asked as she lowered herself into the long grass.

'As long as it takes.'

It didn't take long.

'What are you two doing there?' a voice barked out; a voice with a particularly Norman accent.

Caput IV

A Very Heavy Problem

'Excellent, excellent.' King William clapped his hands and rubbed them together. He waved towards the thin man. 'You can remove his gag and untie him; he won't be any trouble. And summon Lord Le Pedvin, then you can go.'

'Yes, Your Majesty.' The man bowed low and backed from the tent, tugging at his companion's arm, prompting him to do likewise.

'You.' The king pointed at Hermitage. 'Wait.'

Hermitage waited. Which was no help in trying to understand this situation, so he didn't.

All he could do was try to take in the simple fact that this was King William. That meant that he had been taken from his bed, carried through the dark woods and deposited in this tent, all at the whim of the king; and the king's whims were always quite horrible.

Most of his horrors at being made the King's Investigator centred on the investigations. All those murders and murderers and liars and deceivers were quite revolting. The rest of the horrors came directly from the king in person.

And now he was on his own in front of the man. There was no Wat to advise him not to worry or draw upon his worldly knowledge to point out what all the suspicious people, like the king, were really up to; or that they were suspicious in the first place.

Neither was there Cwen, urging them all to refuse to

A Very Heavy Problem

cooperate and to rebel against the Normans, on pain of pain.

The king on his own simply terrified Hermitage. He was the stuff of nightmares; quite regular ones in which Hermitage had to find the king's shoes, which kept walking away on their own as soon as he got near them.

Le Pedvin was an entirely different sort of nightmare. The sort that had you waking up whimpering instead of screaming.

This waiting, which seemed to be going on and on, gave Hermitage's mind a chance to start working again.

Someone had been murdered, that was obvious. He never got to investigate the nature of sin; he had to get straight into the sin itself. And it was never any of the others. He wasn't sure how he'd investigate gluttony or envy, and wouldn't even want to do lust, but a change would be nice. Finding a killer motivated by sloth might even be quite interesting.

A murder had been committed then, and William and Le Pedvin wanted it investigated discreetly. That was peculiar. Hermitage had never seen a Norman do anything discreet.

His speculations had taken some considerable time and he was starting to wonder why the king had taken him from his bed at all. A simple invitation at dawn would have been quite sufficient.

The canvas at the back of the tent eventually swung once more and the king emerged.

'Now,' he said. 'To business.'

Hermitage managed a nod and prepared to wait until Le Pedvin joined them.

He could only think that his soul had frozen when he heard the cough behind him. He spun and saw Le Pedvin sitting there, a goblet in his hand. He had no idea how long the man had been   simply sitting and watching Hermitage. All he knew was that he had very effectively climbed inside Hermitage's head and turned his thoughts into worms. There was a scream somewhere inside him, but it didn't want to come out.

'You're going to do some investigating for me, monk,' the king said.

Of course, Hermitage would do as he was told. There was no need for William to make it sound quite so horrible, though. Unless it was quite so horrible, of course. He managed another nod.

'But it's not like the others.'

"Not like the others", was no help at all.

'No dead bodies,' the king explained. 'Which makes it all a bit dull, of course. Still, got to be done.'

An investigation without any dead bodies, eh? That would make a nice change. Except, of course, that meant there weren't any dead bodies yet. Once the King's Investigator got stuck in, people seemed to get murdered simply to give him something to do.

The king now sat in one of the chairs and folded his arms. 'What do you know about lead?'

Hermitage had no idea whether they were still talking about the investigation, or whether the king had a general question about lead that he thought Hermitage might be able to help with.

'Lead, Your Majesty?' Hermitage had sent the words to his mouth but wasn't sure if it was going to cooperate.

'Heavy stuff. Goes on churches.'

'Ah, lead, yes. Indeed.' Hermitage knew nothing about lead, apart from what it looked like and that it was heavy and that it went on churches. So far, the king knew as

34

A Very Heavy Problem

much as he did.

'Tax.'

No, that was no help either. Hermitage wished that Wat was here, he might know what was going on.

'You're going to have to explain it to him,' Le Pedvin drawled. Those few words contained all that Hermitage needed to hear. Le Pedvin still thought he was an idiot. Everything was as it should be.

'I am the king, yes?' William asked with a sigh.

That was an easy one. 'Yes, Your Majesty.'

'And the king gathers taxes.'

'Of course.' This was another area where Hermitage's expertise was non-existent but agreeing with the king was always advisable.

'The trade in lead is taxed.'

Hermitage imagined it would be. Wat frequently complained that everything was taxed, lead must be no exception.

'And the English produce lead.'

Hermitage didn't know that. He did now.

'Therefore, the English pay me tax.'

Hermitage nodded enthusiastically that this was a very sound argument. What it was an argument for, he was less certain, but as arguments went, it was a good one. Lead is taxed, the English make lead, therefore the English are taxed. Quod erat demonstrandum, or hoper edei deixai, as the Greeks would have it. Most satisfactory.

'Except they don't,' William added.

Now he was just trying to confuse Hermitage.

'They don't?' He didn't know which "don't" was the problem. They don't produce lead, or they don't pay tax. He quickly concluded that it would be the tax element.

'There is more lead being traded between merchants and

The 1066 From Normandy

the church than I am being paid tax for.' William stated his problem. 'And that lead is coming from round here.'

'I see.' Hermitage did see. What he was going to be able to do about it, he had not the first idea. This wasn't what investigation was supposed to be about. Taxes? Who investigated taxes, for goodness sake? Surely the king needed a separate investigator for this sort of thing, Hermitage mainly did murder.

'You're going to investigate where my tax has gone.'

'Investigate,' Hermitage said, it being the only word that made any sense.

The king now pointed at Hermitage. 'And no one must know.'

'No one must know,' Hermitage repeated. He had not a clue how he was going to investigate tax. He didn't even know what a clue would look like if he found one. And if no one was to know he was doing it, how was he expected to achieve anything at all?

'Obviously, I could simply march in there with a force of men, murder everyone and get things on the straight and narrow again. But,' the king went on. 'I need the lead and the tax, I don't want a mine full of dead miners, do I?'

Hermitage could only agree that that sounded like a bad thing; mainly for the miners. He nodded and shook his head at the same time, and rubbed his chin in what he hoped was a thoughtful manner.

'Thinking about what to do first?' the king enquired.

'Thinking that he doesn't know what to do at all,' Le Pedvin put in.

Hermitage was actually thinking about how he could tell the king that he simply couldn't do this. He really needed some help, and the king had been very explicit that he wasn't allowed to have any. Fearing that he was about to be

A Very Heavy Problem

dismissed to get on with it, he took a breath, hoping that some helpful words might come out.

Instead, there was a disturbance at the entrance to the tent and a Norman guard walked in.

'Get out,' the king instructed.

'What is it?' Le Pedvin asked calmly.

'Disturbance, my lord,' the guard said.

'You certainly are. And why are you bringing it to us?'

'Saxons, my lord.'

That did get the king's attention.

'Saxons? How many?'

'Two, Your Majesty.'

'Two? Why are you bothering us about two Saxons? Just kill them and have done with it.'

'They say they think you've got their monk?' The guard sounded very confused.

Hermitage's heart lifted. It had to be Wat and Cwen. They had missed him and come looking. The Lord be praised.

'Ah,' Le Pedvin said. 'Those two, eh? Well, bring them in here.'

Hermitage even dared to smile.

Le Pedvin went on. 'Then we can kill them.'

After a few moments of very little struggle at all, Wat and Cwen were presented to the king. Wat was his usual optimistic, smiling self although Hermitage knew that this was all an act.

Cwen stood fierce and defiant, giving the sort of stare that would offend a blind bunny, never mind the ruler of the country and his killer-in-chief.

'You two,' the king said. 'What are you doing here?' This was asked in a very serious and piercing manner, as if the wrong answer would lead to another sort of piercing altogether.

Wat gave a bow and tapped Cwen on the back to indicate that she should do likewise. She did, but hers was a lot more peremptory, as if her waist was game, but her head was having nothing to do with it.

'We were looking for Brother Hermitage, Your Majesty,' Wat said. 'He went missing and we followed his trail.'

'And that was your first mistake,' Le Pedvin said with little interest.

Wat turned and raised a polite and inquisitive eyebrow.

'Getting caught,' Le Pedvin explained what the second was.

'And what did you hear?' William demanded.

'Hear?' Wat sounded genuinely lost. 'Nothing at all, Your Majesty. Your man just dragged us in here.'

'Doesn't make any difference what they heard,' Le Pedvin said. 'They know the monk is here. They have to go.'

'Go?' Wat asked. 'Of course. Now that we know that Hermitage is in safe hands, we can be off straight away.'

'Not that sort of go,' Le Pedvin explained nonchalantly. 'The permanent variety.'

'What?' Wat blurted the word out.

'You know too much.'

'We don't know anything.'

Le Pedvin shrugged that this was all the same to him.

'Your Majesty,' Hermitage spoke up.

'Hm?' William said, as if he'd forgotten that Hermitage was there.

'I would be most grateful if you didn't kill Wat or Cwen, I mean and Cwen. Either. Neither. Of them, I mean.'

A Very Heavy Problem

'What?' William's irritation was always close to hand.

'The truth of the matter is that I am a monk.'

'You don't say,' Le Pedvin sighed.

'Just so. And as a monk, my knowledge of trade and tax and lead is, what can we say, limited?'

"Lead?" Wat mouthed the word with a very puzzled expression.

'He doesn't know what he's doing,' Le Pedvin translated.

Hermitage was strangely grateful that someone had got it.

'It's not that I don't know what I'm doing,' he lied, which made him feel even worse. 'Investigation is fine.' He tried to sound confident. 'There is no problem at all with investigation. Discovering what is going on, unearthing facts, establishing truths, all in a day's work.'

Everyone was looking sceptical now, even Wat and Cwen. 'But the subject matter,' Hermitage went on. 'This area is entirely new to me. The very best thing I could do would be take advice from someone knowledgeable.'

'I've told you,' William pointed his finger again.

'Indeed, Your Majesty. No one must know. But as Wat and Cwen are here now, and have considerable expertise in trade, they could assist me. As they have done on so many other occasions.'

At least William and Le Pedvin were silent at this.

The king now had a frown on his face, which Hermitage took as a good sign. 'He's a weaver, yes?'

'Oh, yes.' Hermitage nodded vigorously.

William didn't sound at all persuaded about anything. 'You want a weaver and his serving girl to help you with the investigation we've already said you're not to talk about. Correct?'

'Erm, yes.' Hermitage had to admit that was a neat

39

The 1066 From Normandy

summary. He tried to ignore Cwen's quite noisy fuming.

'Er, could we know what it is?' Wat asked. 'Something about lead?'

'Tell me, weaver.' William gave Wat a horribly intense look. 'Are you an honest weaver?'

Hermitage knew the answer to that one.

'Ah,' Wat said, not answering the question. 'Honest, eh?'

'That's what I said. Do you pay your taxes?'

'Of course.' Wat sounded mightily offended at the very idea that he wouldn't pay his taxes.

'How?'

'How?'

'That's it. How do you pay your taxes? How exactly?'

'How exactly? Well, let me see. Obviously, things have changed with the arrival of, erm, that is, with your arrival. In, erm, the previous king's time, the officials would come round and you'd erm, pay.' Wat seemed to think that was enough of an explanation.

William didn't. 'Pay what, how much?'

'Well, it was the geld, wasn't it? I mean, I don't own much land, just what the workshop stands on, really, but there's geld due on the land and that's what I pay.'

'Anything else?'

'Anything else?' Wat sounded as if the geld was bad enough.

'Tax on your trade?' the king asked.

Wat suddenly went very pale and looked like he wanted to sit down. 'Tax on my trade?' he almost whispered.

'Yes. Presumably you make money selling tapestry, then you pay tax.'

'I do? I mean, I do.'

'I knew it,' William crowed a bit. 'I knew Harold was too lax over the collection of taxes. Every trade should be

40

A Very Heavy Problem

paying the crown as they make their money,' he informed a now shaky Wat.

'Oh,' Wat almost squeaked. 'That's a very interesting idea.'

'But we'll sort all that out next,' William said, which got Wat breathing again. 'And what if you didn't want to pay your land tax?'

'Oh,' Wat shook his head in a very disappointed manner. 'That would be a very bad thing.'

'Exactly,' William agreed.

'There's the record,' Wat said helpfully. 'The local king's man knows who has what and that they should pay.'

'But it's not written down anywhere,' William was stating a fact now.

'Er, no, I suppose not. He simply knows.'

'It needs to be written down.' William was obviously saying this to Le Pedvin.

'In a great big book?' Le Pedvin was rather mocking. 'With a list of everything and who owns it?'

'Exactly.'

'Ridiculous.' Le Pedvin went back to his wine.

William went back to Wat. 'If you wanted to avoid paying your tax then, you might have a few ideas?'

'Me? Good Lord, I'd never...,'

'No, I'm sure you wouldn't. But let's assume that you are a dishonest fellow, trying not to give the king what's due. Can you manage that?'

'Try very hard,' Le Pedvin encouraged sarcastically. 'Because if you can't help, we can always ask someone else; probably just after you finish dying.'

'Ah.' Wat looked as if he was only too keen to be as helpful as he could. 'Well,' he mused. 'I suppose if I was told that I had to, I might be able to come up with one or

41

The 1066 From Normandy

two thoughts.'

'I wondered if you might. And do think hard, your life depends on it.' Le Pedvin sounded as if he was quite looking forward to that bit.

'And if your land was a lead mine, say?' William was specific. 'How would you evade the king's tax on the lead?'

'Ah, well, and this is pure guess-work on my part, but I suppose you could erm, say the land wasn't yours at all? People in the king's service, or with some ancient title are occasionally exempt from tax. If one of them was to be helpful, if you know what I mean. Put the land and the lead in their name and then split the proceeds?' Wat was sounding weak at the very idea. 'Or the church perhaps?' he suggested.

William gave a hearty scowl that the church should be brought into this. 'Well.' He nodded with interest and appraised them all with quiet concentration. None of them wanted to risk breaking the silence. 'You seem to know a lot about this.' William bent forward slightly, as if he were trying to peer into Wat's head.

'Pure speculation,' Wat managed to say.

William took a deep breath. 'All right, you can live.'

They all breathed a sigh of relief, apart from Le Pedvin, whose sigh sounded like disappointment.

'You seem to know about tax, and you can help the monk sort out who's stealing mine.'

'Of course, Your Majesty.' Wat sounded as if this had been his life's dream.

'But the rules are the same. If I hear that anyone knows anything of this, I kill you all, clear?'

They all nodded that this was very clear indeed and only fair.

'Right. Get on with it then.' William waved them away.

A Very Heavy Problem

A few moments of confusion followed while they all worked out that they were expected to leave now. As they did so, Le Pedvin smiled encouragement while he sharpened one of his daggers.

'Good God,' Wat bent double once he was outside, and breathed deeply. 'This is the worst thing that has ever happened to me in my entire life.'

Hermitage wondered at that, as he had heard Wat's own tales of some pretty horrible things.

'But we live,' Hermitage encouraged.

'For now,' Cwen pointed out.

'It's not that,' Wat complained shaking his head from side to side like some dolorous bell. He raised his eyes and looked at them both with blank resignation that some great evil had befallen him. He took a breath. 'I've been made a tax man.'

Caput V

Taxy

'Wat the tax man, eh?' Cwen almost sang as they made their way back to the workshop.

'Shut up,' Wat suggested.

'I can be Cwen the Weaver and you can be Wat the tax man.'

'Very funny.'

'Can't see many people inviting you into their homes after this. "Could you do me a great tapestry, Master Wat, one showing a big pile of naked tax, perhaps". Ha, ha.'

'You heard the king. If word of this gets out, we're all dead. You can go first. And miners are a nasty bunch.' Wat sulked.

'Nasty?' Hermitage asked.

'Well, not nasty perhaps,' Wat admitted. 'Difficult. They know what they want and what they're prepared to pay for it.'

'Oh,' Cwen sympathised. 'Very nasty customers, then.'

'Quite. And they're big and strong from all that digging. No point arguing with any of them unless you want to come off worse.'

'You've dealt with miners before, then?' Hermitage thought that this would be another help in the investigation, as well as Wat knowing the first thing about tax, which Hermitage didn't.

'One or two. If they're not slaves, they've usually got money and not much to spend it on.'

'It won't be the miners themselves who are not paying

their taxes though, will it?' Cwen said. 'It'll be the mine owner. He'll be paying the miners as little as he can get away with. And he obviously wants to pay the king nothing at all.'

'I'm afraid I know nothing of mining or tax,' Hermitage apologised. 'The king simply picked me because I'm his investigator. He just assumed I'd be able to help.' He was slightly disappointed that Wat and Cwen appeared to agree that was a rash assumption.

'Don't worry about it, Hermitage,' Cwen encouraged. 'We'll sort it out. We always do. We haven't died yet.'

'We haven't dealt with tax before,' Wat moaned. 'If we don't die by the sword, we could die of shame.'

They arrived back at the workshop now, having taken the slightly longer way round, using proper paths instead of crashing through the woods. They still moved at a slow pace as Hermitage hadn't liked to ask the king if he could borrow a pair of sandals.

Wat slumped through the door and made straight for the beer barrel. Taking a large leather tankard full, he stomped up the stairs to the first-floor chamber and dropped into the large chair by the cold fireplace.

Hermitage and Cwen followed, showing some genuine concern as they had never seen Wat like this before.

Hermitage thought that perhaps discussion of mining would take his mind off the tax.

'What am I going to do when people know I'm chasing the king's tax?' Wat complained.

Obviously, discussion of mining was going to have to wait.

'No one will know, will they?' Hermitage said. 'The king's already said that he'll kill us if anyone finds out. That's as good a secret as you'll get these days.' He thought

45

The 1066 From Normandy

that was quite a good argument, although Wat didn't look convinced.

'How can we investigate the lead mine and its taxes without someone knowing what we're doing? Won't be much of an investigation if we can't ask any questions. And if we ask questions, people will know what we're doing. I'll never be able to show my face again.'

'You can't show your face in a lot of places already,' Cwen pointed out, less than helpfully.

'Two weavers and a monk turn up at a lead mine and start enquiring about the tax situation? I think the mine owner will have his men kill us themselves.' Wat took a deep draught of his beer.

'Well, obviously that's not what we do, is it?' Cwen was starting to sound a bit cross now. It was nice to have things back to normal.

Hermitage frowned at her, thinking that if they didn't do what the king had asked, there would be even more trouble.

'For goodness sake,' Cwen snapped. 'We go in disguise.'

'Disguise?' Hermitage asked. He couldn't see that that dressing up would help; unless these miners were very peculiar folk.

'Or do we think it's a good idea to walk up and announce that we've been sent by King William?'

Hermitage knew the answer to that one.

Cwen pressed on. 'We go to the mine and say that we've got some money we want to hide from the king, and we've heard that mining is a good way to do it.'

'We lie?' Hermitage was shocked.

'Do you want to explore what lying means?'

'I know what lying means, and it's not good. And why on earth would the mine owner believe that two weavers and a

Taxy

monk want to cheat the king?'

'Because we're rich weavers and we've heard the king is thinking of taxing our trade. You can be a dishonest churchman who wants to get some cheap lead for his roof.'

Hermitage was truly horrified by all this. Wat looked as if he was perking up a bit.

Cwen clicked her fingers as she had another idea. 'With Wat the Weaver's horrible reputation they'll believe every word.'

'And when we've found out their secrets, we go and tell the king?' Wat said. 'If the mine owner didn't want us dead to begin with, he will now.'

'Then look at it this way,' Cwen said in her sweetest, most sympathetic voice.

Wat raised a hopeful eyebrow.

'You don't have any choice.' She was back to normal. 'Of course, you can go and tell the king that we'd rather not investigate for him and ask if he'd like to kill us straight away. I'm sure Le Pedvin would oblige.'

'I know I don't have any choice. It doesn't mean I have to be happy about it, does it?' He dived into his beer once more.

'Where are these mines, anyway?' Hermitage asked. 'I didn't know there were any around here.'

'They're out of town a bit,' Wat replied. 'There's a big old Roman mine at Crich, we'd have to start there.' Talking about the practicalities seemed to take his mind off the tax element.

'I imagine they're like the mines of Job,' Hermitage mused. 'Where gold and silver is taken out of the earth through open shafts.'

'Fascinating,' Wat sighed. 'Lead mines aren't shafts though.'

47

The 1066 From Normandy

'Really?' Hermitage tried hard to think how you could have a mine without some sort of hole, but he was no help to himself. 'How do they get it then?'

'Well, I sold a work to a lead miner down Cheddar way.'

'Interesting,' Hermitage nodded.

'No, he wasn't. He couldn't talk about anything but mining. Hours and hours of it, there was. And I couldn't get away.'

'Go on,' Hermitage encouraged.

'Apparently, the veins of lead can be seen on the surface, if you know what you're looking for. Then, you get a load of water and wash everything away exposing the rocks with the lead in them.'

'Where does the water come from?'

'That's what a lot of people don't realise,' Wat put on a very peculiar voice and was clearly doing an impersonation of the miner. It was a nasal, whining sort of voice, full of fascination with its own subject, and completely oblivious of anyone nearby. Even this impression sounded incredibly dull.

'There's as much expertise in water management as there is in lead extraction, you know. People don't understand what a complex business it is. There's aqueducts to be built to gather the water, and that's not straight forward, oh no. And then, once you've gathered the water, you have to build it up in a holding tank before letting it wash over the selected area. Hushing, it's called.'

'Is it?'

'Yes, indeed. Oh, I could talk to you for hours of the subject of hushing alone, it's absolutely fascinating.'

Even Hermitage thought that this didn't sound very fascinating at all, and he found all manner of things fascinating that put most people to sleep.

Taxy

'And that's before we even get started on smelting. People say it's just putting some rocks in a fire and boiling them, but do they understand? Of course they don't. It's nowhere near as simple as that. There's the Galena to begin with. I expect you want to know all about the Galena.'

'Erm,' Hermitage wasn't sure that he did.

'That's where you start, with the Galena, or lead glance, if you will. That's your basic lead ore, that is.' Wat resumed his normal voice. 'Shall I go on? And on and on and on?'

'I think we've got the picture,' Cwen said. 'You wash away the ground with some water, pick up the Galena, put it in a fire and there you are, lead.'

'Oh, if it only it were so simple,' Wat went back to the miner's voice.

'I think we'll leave it there for now,' Cwen said. 'Perhaps pick it up another day.'

'Or not,' Wat said.

'Sounds like you know enough to come across as someone who really wants to hide their money in lead, though.'

'If this mine owner is avoiding King William's tax, he's going to be no fool of any sort. We need to be very careful.' Wat descended back into his gloom. 'And what if there's a whole gaggle of them?'

'A gaggle of who?' Hermitage asked.

'A gaggle of people trying to avoid William's lovely new taxes. A whole collection of very keen and very astute merchants, squirrelling their money away through this lead mine.' He paused for a moment. 'Oh my God.'

'What?' Hermitage tutted at the profanity but could see that Wat had thought of something else.

49

The 1066 From Normandy

'This is worse than I thought.' He took a deep breath before explaining. 'The merchants put their money into the lead mine, yes? They then sell the lead to the church and no one pays any tax.'

'It all sounds terribly dishonest,' Hermitage said.

'Dishonest, yes, I do believe you're right.'

'You should fit right in,' Cwen said.

'Charming. But if that is what's going on, it would be suicide to stick our noses into the middle of it. These are not the sort of people you want to cross.'

Hermitage had nothing to say.

'I might even know some of them,' Wat wailed.

'Why am I not surprised?' Cwen muttered.

'If I betray them to the king, the worst of them will come after me, hold me down and cut some of my valuable bits off.'

Cwen gave this some thought. 'We'll have to make sure the merchants don't find out. We make out that you've been caught along with the rest of them.'

Wat shook his head. 'I'm not talking about the merchants; I'm talking about the church.'

. . .

Wat's mood had not lifted with the rising of the sun the following day, when they persuaded him that they really had to go. He had said that it was too late to set off the previous day and seemed to be suggesting waiting a week or two would be fine.

Cwen helpfully pointed out that that if he didn't get on with it, there was a good chance Le Pedvin would appear at the door asking if they'd finished the investigation yet. And that would likely result in Wat's death; then he'd

Taxy

have all the time he wanted.

Hermitage was impressed by her reasoning. It was quite harsh and heartless, but you couldn't argue with the conclusions.

'Very persuasive,' Wat complained as he stood at the door with his pack on his back. 'But I am warning you both.' He raised a finger. 'It will not go well if either of you try to cheer me up.'

'Wouldn't dream of it,' Cwen said quietly to Hermitage.

As they walked along in the trail of Wat's gloomy silence, Hermitage wondered what help he was actually going to be in an investigation where there was no dead body.

But then he had to consider his role in this investigation. He was the King's Investigator and he knew what went with that title: death.

Reason told him that there could not possibly be any real connection between his presence in a given situation and the fact that people in the vicinity of the situation got murdered, but the coincidences were getting a bit hard to manage.

If tiny ducklings were skimming across the water of a pond and he sat down to watch, at least one of them would drown; probably murdered by a sibling.

'What are you thinking about, Hermitage?' Cwen disturbed his reverie. 'You look as if you're the one who hasn't paid his tax.'

'I was just thinking about these tax evaders and the fact that the three of us are about to turn up, albeit in disguise.'

'Ah. You think at least one of them is going to get murdered.'

Cwen had never been any help at all in assuaging Hermitage's worries; any of them really. He said nothing.

'It's a very good question,' Cwen said thoughtfully. 'After

51

The 1066 From Normandy

all, if they don't know you're the investigator, or that the three of us have dealt with more murders than a Saxon on a trip to Hastings, will they still die?'

'That is the question.' Hermitage felt as miserable as Wat looked.

'We'll find out, won't we?' Cwen sounded as if she was positively enthusiastic about resolving this conundrum. 'Mind you,' she went on. 'I'm sure the king will be much happier with them if they die. Better that than not pay his tax.'

'But once they're dead, they can't pay him anymore.'

'I'm not sure William would let that get in his way.'

Hours of silent walking followed this indulgent and entirely unproductive speculation. Wat was clearly in no mood to stop by the side of the road for rest, and so his pace was rapid, and Hermitage had just kept up. And now here they were at Crich.

The place was small; there was no avoiding that. If this really was where lead was mined, there was no sign of it in the village. As far as Hermitage could see there only appeared to be six houses, all of them humble and functional. There was no great hall, or even a less than great one. No sign of a Lord of the Manor living anywhere nearby. As they walked along the road, they could see that there was a bit of meadow and some ploughed land with wheat growing in it, but not even much of that.

There were two people working the field, going over it for weeds by the look of them, but they didn't even glance up at the strangers.

Three rather ragged sheep grazed the meadow under the not-very-watchful eye of a shepherd boy and that was it. If there were anyone else in this place, they must be off in the

Taxy

forest, or working somewhere else. Perhaps at the mine, Hermitage thought.

'No sign of a wealthy mine here, or of merchants avoiding the king's tax,' Hermitage said.

'They're hardly going to lavish their riches on the peasants, are they?' Wat replied. He led the way towards the meadow and the boy who was half asleep against a tree.

'Ho, there, lad. Which way is the mine?' he asked.

The boy, startled from his reverie, leapt to his feet and gazed in wonder at the three of them, as if thinking that his sheep had suddenly turned into people. 'What, what?' he said, in a very nervous manner.

'The mine?' Wat asked. 'The lead mine. Is it nearby?'

The boy looked left and right up and down the track, still unable to believe where these three strangers had come from.

'The mine?' he asked, as if not understanding the word.

'Yes, the mine,' Wat was impatient. 'The lead mine. This is Crich, yes?'

'Oh, yes,' the boy was confident of that.

'And Crich has a mine. Has had since Roman times.'

The boy now looked as if he thought these three might be Romans, and he'd been expected to look after their mine for them while they were gone.

'A big hole in the ground where metal comes from?' Wat explained slowly and carefully.

'Oh,' the boy sounded hugely relieved. 'The mine.'

'That's the one. Well done.'

There was a pause.

'So, where is it?' Wat went back to his very first question.

'You want to go to the mine?'

'God spare me,' Wat muttered. 'Yes, that's right. I'm

asking where it is so that I can go there. Peculiar, I know, but there you are.'

'Well, it'd be up the road a way, wouldn't it?'

'Of course it would. Silly me. Fancy me not knowing where the mine is that I've been asking about. What am I thinking?'

Cwen stepped forward and pushed Wat to one side.

'Up this way?' she asked, gesturing farther up the road they had been travelling.

'That's it,' the boy confirmed. 'You carry on up the hill.'

'How far is it?'

'Be about a mile, I reckon.'

'A mile. Well, thank you. And don't mind our friend.' She nodded her head towards Wat as if sharing with the lad the secret that he was a bit mad.

They left the boy with their thanks, and half a penny that had to be dragged from Wat's purse.

The mile up the hill felt much longer. The land hereabouts was mostly flat, but their route now took them up the side of a long low hill. By the time they made the top they would be well above the village, but the climb, while gentle, seemed inexorable.

After some time, they reached a break in the woods of the hillside and walked on through to a scene of utter devastation.

Hermitage had never seen a mine before, so didn't really know what to expect. He'd imagined something like a cave entrance set in the hillside, with perhaps a few shovels and tools lying around.

He hadn't expected to see the whole of the landscape blasted away.

An area larger than he could estimate was bare of anything. There was no grass or trees, just the rocks of the

Taxy

earth, laid out before the rain and the sun.

And everything had been scraped clean. It wasn't as if the rocks had mellowed in the weather, they hadn't been given the chance. They had clearly been smashed and cracked, burned and bruised, and were lying around in exhaustion that they had been forced to give up their all.

Pathways wound through the wreckage and the charred remains of old fires dotted the land like scars.

'Big, isn't it?' Cwen commented as the three of them stood still and tried to take in the immensity of the destruction.

'It certainly is,' Wat said, sounding very thoughtful.

'I don't see anyone,' Hermitage said, scanning the site for any sign of life.

'Quite,' Wat agreed. 'And there's one other thing I don't see.'

'What's that?'

'Any actual mining.'

Caput VI

Ah, There It Is

'Do you think this is the right place?' Hermitage asked.

'The right gaping slash in the landscape?' Cwen enquired. 'I can't imagine there are many more like this.'

'I don't see any miners.' Hermitage was actually quite pleased about that.

'Let's take a look around,' Wat said. 'They're probably holed up here somewhere.'

'They must be,' Hermitage said. 'I imagine that if one wants to mine lead, one needs miners?'

'Yes.' Wat was thoughtful. 'Unless it's even more devious than that.' He wandered off into the body of the mine, following a bare path that soon wound through hillocks of discarded rock.

Hermitage peered at these piles closely, as if expecting to see the lead. He knew what the stuff looked like when it was on a roof, or was being used for a drain, or gutter. After all, several of his more mischievous Brothers had put him up on the roof on more than one occasion. He'd had plenty of time to consider his surroundings before the abbot made them get him down again.

'This will be the spoil, I assume,' Cwen said.

'Spoil?'

'The rock they've dug out that doesn't have any lead in it.'

'Hushed,' Wat said.

'Sorry,' Cwen lowered her voice.

'No, I mean it's hushed. I've told you all this once.' Wat

Ah, There It Is

sounded impatient that they hadn't been listening to his fascinating lecture on mining. 'They gather a tank full of water up on the hill and then release it all in one go. It washes all the soil and material from the face of the rock. Then, once the rock is bare, they set fires on it, let the rock get nice and hot and then wash water over it again. The rock cracks and they can dig it out. Everything left over is piled up.'

'I see.' Hermitage looked again at the rock piles, content that he now knew how they'd got there. 'Hence the signs of fires all over the place.'

'That's it. And up there,' Wat gestured towards the top of the hill. 'Is where they probably put the tank.'

Hermitage could imagine the scene, and it seemed like one out of hell. Fires raging on the rock before being doused, cracking the very fabric of the earth wide open.

'I hope that we're not in the way when they do it again,' he said, always willing to take on a brand-new worry when it presented itself.

'There's no sign of anyone doing anything.' Wat said. 'Not even the smell of a wet fire in the air. I don't think there's been any mining here for quite a while.'

Hermitage was grateful that they weren't going to be drowned in a torrent or burnt in a fire. But then he wondered about a mine where there wasn't any mining.

'Let me get this straight. I know I don't understand tax at all, but I'm not clear how any tax can be due if there isn't any lead.'

'Exactly.' Wat had rather grim smile. 'That's why I think this may be even more devious than first impression.'

Hermitage's first impression had been so devious he didn't actually understand it.

'So devious that no one is actually doing any mining at

The 1066 From Normandy

all?' Cwen asked.

'Mining is an expensive business. You have to have men and tools and time. It all costs a lot. Far better to save yourself the trouble by not mining at all. That way it's much cheaper.'

'No,' Hermitage said with a shake of the head. 'I'm lost.'

'It's quite simple,' Wat explained. 'You don't pay tax because all your income is from lead. And the lead is owned by someone who is exempt.'

'With you so far.'

'But there isn't any actual lead. You simply pass your own money through the mine and take it out again on the other side. If the king's man ever wants to see the lead mine, like we do, here it is.' Wat held his arms out.

'But, erm, where is the lead?' Hermitage asked.

'There isn't any.'

Hermitage thought about this. 'I'm pretty sure there is, you know. I've seen it on churches and in all sorts of places.'

'There is lead,' Wat sounded quite impatient. 'The stuff exists. I'm not saying there's no such thing as lead. I'm just saying that there isn't any here.'

No, this still wasn't making any sense at all.

'Then where does the church get its lead?'

'Somewhere else. But they say they're buying it from here.'

'Why?' Hermitage was starting to feel disturbed at quite a fundamental level that this was all nonsense. Non-existent lead in a mine that didn't mine it, was more than he could cope with.

'Because they are in league with the merchants and are simply moving the money around to make sure the king never gets his hands on it.'

58

Ah, There It Is

'Erm,' Hermitage said.

'And the church is exempt from tax anyway.' Cwen sounded as if she was getting the idea.

Wat could see the look of total confusion that sat on Hermitage's face. 'If the merchants simply had a lot of money, the king would tax it, yes?'

'Erm, yes.' Hermitage got that bit.

'But they don't, they've spent it all.' He snapped his fingers. 'Probably given it to the church. Like alms.'

Hermitage nodded cautiously.

'And the church, which doesn't have to pay tax, gives the merchants the money back again for some non-existent lead. See? It's quite simple.'

'Oh,' Hermitage actually understood it. 'That's awful.'

'Not if you're a merchant.'

'But why does the church give the money back again? After all, they're not getting any lead.'

'Oh, Hermitage,' Wat sighed. 'Perhaps you should have brought quill and parchment to make notes. The church will give back slightly less money than they get.'

No, he was lost again.

'The merchant gives a pound to the church. No,' Wat spoke quickly, before Hermitage drew the wrong conclusion. 'Not a pound of rock or lead, a pound of money.'

Hermitage nodded. Clear enough so far.

'The church then gives the merchant nineteen shillings, say.'

'All for some lead that isn't here?'

'Now you're getting it. The church keeps the extra shilling and the merchant gets nineteen back, without the king being able to touch it. He'd want a lot more than a shilling in tax.'

59

The 1066 From Normandy

Now Hermitage got it. 'It's dishonest,' he said. He could understand the merchants doing it, that was the sort of thing they did, but the church? That was shocking.

'It certainly is,' Wat said. 'Quite clever, too.'

'I bet you wish you'd thought of it,' Cwen said.

Hermitage still couldn't really take in the complexity of what seemed to be a completely ridiculous scheme. It was an awful lot of trouble to go to, just to save a shilling. Or was it make a shilling? He was losing track again. He did know that a report back to the king about an empty mine would not be well received.

'If there is no lead, and there is no mining, how do we find out who's behind it all?'

Wat was looking around the place as they continued to stroll through the waste heaps. 'There could still be someone here. The merchants might think the king would send someone to find out what's going on.'

'Like us.'

'Just like us. They might keep someone here, just for appearance's sake. Let's just keep looking.' Wat wandered on.

Once they were in the mine itself, Hermitage felt as if he had descended into the labyrinth. The heaps and piles of rock were so high that they obscured the view of the surrounding country and even of their way out. All they could see, as the path wound its way in and out, was the next mound of rock, or the last one. He started to worry that they might be trapped here, endlessly circling towers of rock until they starved to death. The king would never get his tax if they were all dead at the bottom of the mine.

'There's nothing,' Wat said eventually. He seemed to think that they had now walked around all the areas of the mine. Hermitage had no idea where they were and hadn't

Ah, There It Is

had for some time now. He briefly considered the origin of his title, investigator; *vestigare*, to track. And he couldn't even track his way round a hole in the ground. If ever proof were needed that he shouldn't be an investigator at all, surely this was it.

'Let's try up the hill,' Wat waved an arm in a direction, which Hermitage sincerely hoped was the way out.

As he considered the ground at their feet, he noticed that it did rise up in that direction. There was a lesson in tracking for him.

Wat led the way, and Hermitage breathed a sigh of relief as they emerged from the maze of rock and could see the wider world once more.

Leaving the mine itself on their left, they carried on up the hillside path, rising now above the scar that was ripped across the land. As they did so, the ubiquitous trees re-established themselves and restored the traditional English landscape: wood.

The mine became a bit of a memory as the trees wandered down the side of the hill, jumped over the track and carried on marching to the valley below.

Before they had gone very far, a small path dived off the main thoroughfare and burrowed into the woods on their left.

'This looks hopeful,' Wat said, as he strode into the cover of the trees.

'Are we sure?' Hermitage asked, wondering what sort of hope Wat was harbouring.

'It should bring us out on the hill above the mine. Probably where the hushing tank is.'

'And if there are six or seven rough miners just waiting for us,' Cwen said, 'they'll probably be there as well.' She patted Hermitage on the back as they followed Wat, just

The 1066 From Normandy

to make him feel even worse.

The wood was thick here, but the path through it was clear. Every now and then a clearing appeared to left or right, probably where the trees had been taken for the rock-cracking fires.

The path steepened now, and Hermitage's new worry was that they would step right off the edge of mine and fall to their deaths.

'Here we are,' Wat said brightly as he emerged from the line of trees.

Hermitage and Cwen joined him and they did, indeed, stand on the edge of a cliff, looking quite a way down to the mine below.

'Plenty of height for the hushing,' Wat remarked. He scanned around the space they had come out in. 'There you go.' He pointed to a very large wooden construction that sat very close to the edge of the cliff.

To Hermitage's eye, this looked like a simple pile of logs. They'd been piled up on their sides, like a log cabin, but in this case there were no windows or doors.

'The whole thing will be sealed with daub, or something, and then levers at the back are used to tip it over when it's full. Or some of them have a door that can be opened to let the flow out.'

As they drew up to it, Hermitage saw that it was, in fact, a huge wooden box. Its sides must be at least eight feet tall and it was sitting upon tree trunks laid on the ground. These looked ready to roll it forward so that it could peer over the edge of the cliff, as if considering whether to jump or not.

'Once they've hushed away the cliff edge, and then cracked the rock after the fire, they move the whole thing back, fill it once more and start again. They've probably

62

Ah, There It Is

got wooden channels that can direct the water from a stream. Not that it looks like this one has been used for a while.'

'What a knowledgeable fellow you are,' Cwen said. 'When you can't weave anymore, you can move into mining.'

'That's what apprentices are for,' Wat said. 'No self-respecting weaver actually does his own weaving.'

'But then you're not a...,'

'Perhaps,' Hermitage interrupted. 'We should be wary about the miners?' He glanced about nervously. 'They could be watching us at this very moment.'

'There's no sign of anyone, Hermitage,' Wat assured him. 'No camp, no fire. I don't think anyone's been here for weeks.'

'Is there nothing, then? Have we come all this way for a completely empty mine? There's no sign of your tax-exempt person, or the mine owner, let alone any miners. Could it be that the king is wrong?'

They all seemed to reach the same conclusion about that. If there was no cheating of the king's tax, they would all be in serious trouble.

'King William didn't send us out to come back with nothing,' Cwen gave their worries life. 'If we go back and say, "sorry your Majesty, we couldn't find anything," I don't think he'll be pleased. We've got to find some tax cheats. And fairly quickly, I'd suggest.'

Wat didn't seem happy about the developments either. 'I suppose we could go back to the village and see if they know who owns this mine. Or who owned it in the past.'

'Some Saxon, probably,' Cwen said. 'Who might have had a short trip to Hastings not long ago. Hence the absence of any actual mining.'

The 1066 From Normandy

Hermitage felt a new despair now. It was wonderful that the mine wasn't full of dishonest merchants and churchmen, but the king had other ideas. 'Are there any other mines around here?' he asked. 'Perhaps ones where there is some mining and some tax evasion going on?'

'Probably,' Wat sighed. 'But it could take weeks to find them. William tends not to be that patient.'

Cwen wandered, in a desultory manner over to the wooden water tank and gave it a pointless kick.

Hermitage twitched slightly at that. The sides of the thing towered over her and if it was still full of water, but was in a fragile condition, it might break and wash them all over the cliff to their deaths. Of course, it could be empty and harmless, but not in the world of worry that Hermitage inhabited.

'Cwen, do you think that's sensible?' he called over, as he saw her put a hand up on the wooden wall and set a foot up as if to start climbing.

'I just want to have a look,' she said. 'Be interesting if the thing is full of water.'

Hermitage kept half an eye on her, as if expecting the wall to collapse as soon as she put any strain on it.

'If there's nothing at this mine, there could be another one,' he said. 'After all, the king didn't tell us exactly where it was. Perhaps we've just started at the wrong place?'

'And the king will be reasonable about that, will he?' Wat asked. 'Like he's reasonable about everything else?'

'Probably not,' Hermitage acknowledged.

'Ah, there it is,' Cwen announced, sounding very relieved about something. 'It's not the wrong place,' she called to the others.

'What makes you say that?'

'The dead body in this water store.'

Caput VII

Open the Box

Hermitage just sat where he was and looked at the water store, with Cwen still clinging to the side. He didn't really know what to feel. He found that what should be horror that some poor individual was lying dead close by, was being brushed aside by a rather annoyed resignation.

Where was his human sympathy? Where was his fellow-feeling? Was he really starting to find dead bodies a bit of an irritation instead of an appalling reality?

Instead of his mind filling with the words, "Oh Lord, how awful", he found, "well, that's typical", springing to the fore. He had a strong, yet simultaneously unreasonable conviction that this whole situation was all the corpse's fault. What had the fellow been doing getting himself killed just here? Had he done it on purpose, knowing that Hermitage was in the vicinity to be bothered by yet another murder investigation? Was he to get no peace?

And if it wasn't the deceased's responsibility, it was King William's. If that wretched man hadn't made him King's Investigator in the first place, people wouldn't be getting murdered whenever he sat down for a rest.

And he was in a disused mine half-way up a hill, for goodness sake. If it was the middle of a thriving town, he might understand someone being killed nearby, but here? He felt as if the whole of God's creation was spread around him and he was an insignificant dot; an insignificant dot where all the murders got done.

All he could do was cast his eyes to the sky, silently

65

The 1066 From Normandy

pleading with the Lord to make this sort of thing simply go away.

'Murdered, I expect,' he said, with a weary sigh.

'Hard to tell,' Cwen called back. 'We'll have to get in and have a look at him.'

Yes, of course they would. It wasn't sufficient that there was a body close at hand, Hermitage would have to have a long hard look at it.

'Is there still water in the store?' he asked, thinking that an old corpse that had been floating for a while would not be a pretty sight. Not that he deserved pretty sights, of course.

'No, quite dry. And has been for some time, by the look of it.'

Well, that was something. Hermitage stood now and wandered over towards the water store. At least the bodies were coming in boxes these days, and not being strewn at his feet.

'How does he, erm, look?' Hermitage asked, hoping that the sight was not going to be too revolting.

'Not bad, actually,' Cwen said. 'I mean, dead, obviously, but not been that way for long, I'd say. Doesn't smell much.'

Hermitage sighed. It was bad enough that he had to deal with such matters, but dragging Cwen and Wat into this was unfair somehow. Not that Cwen seemed to see it that way. One of his newest worries was that she was quite enjoying dealing with murder and death. It couldn't be healthy.

'Can you see how he died?' Wat asked. 'It may not be murder, perhaps he lives in there and just died.'

'Lives in a water box?' Hermitage asked, surprised at the very idea.

Open the Box

'Easier than building your own house.'

'But houses tend to have more in the way of a roof. What's the point of living in an open box?'

'I don't know, do I? Perhaps he was an idiot.'

'Or drunk?' Cwen suggested.

'Yes,' Wat agreed. 'Could be a drunk. Came up here after too many beers, thought he'd climb into the box for a rest, fell and couldn't get out again.'

Hermitage shook his head at this fantasy.

Cwen was now making her way over the wall of the box and started to lower herself into it.

As they looked on, she vanished from sight.

'Perhaps we should try to get the fellow out,' Hermitage said.

'Don't know how we'd manage that,' Wat said. 'Lifting a dead body over an eight-foot wall? We'd probably need ropes and a pulley.'

'How do they get the water out? When they want to do their hushing?'

'You should have paid attention when I explained all this. A lever at the back to tip the whole thing up, or a door in the front that slides up and the water rushes out.'

Wat adopted the boring miner's voice once more. 'Do you know that the smaller the stream of water coming from the tank, the stronger it is? Who'd have thought that, eh? You'd think more water all at once would do the job, but oh, no. What you need is a narrow stream to blast away at the ground. Rather like a river that gets faster as it gets narrower. Now rivers, there's a subject I could tell you all about...,'

'Fascinating,' Hermitage said.

'Isn't it?' Wat didn't sound as if he agreed.

'Could we find the door, then? Get the body out that

The 1066 From Normandy

way?'

'And why do we want to get the body out? Exactly?'

'Well, erm, we need to see what happened.'

'Do we? Really?'

'Of course. There is a dead body in the water box,' Hermitage pointed out.

'So we're told.'

'By Cwen.'

'Yes, by Cwen. She is quite trustworthy, I suppose.'

'The dead person could be a tax evader.'

'We'll probably never know; dead people being less forthcoming than the living ones.'

'What if he was murdered?'

'Murdered?' Wat sounded as if he thought Hermitage was getting carried away. 'We have nothing at all to tell us that he was murdered.'

'He was murdered,' Cwen called from inside the box.

'There you are.' Hermitage was rather alarmed that he found himself feeling quite pleased at this news.

'Well, the hole in his back is certainly knife-shaped.'

Hermitage simply gave Wat a knowing glance as he looked around the box. 'Ho, Wat,' he called. 'The door is here. Come and see if we can get it open.'

Wat shambled along as if he'd been made to do some unpleasant errand. Hermitage positioned himself on one side of the wooden panel that was plainly the door to the box. Wat took the other and together they heaved. With no body of water behind it holding it in place, it moved quite easily.

'Hello.' Cwen stuck her head out of the doorway.

The space created was certainly large enough for anyone to crawl through, so Hermitage could see how the dead body could have got in there; dragged through the hole,

Open the Box

rather than thrown over the wall.

'Come on then,' Cwen instructed. 'Let's be having him.'

Wat gestured that Hermitage was perfectly welcome to help, and he would wait outside.

With more disappointment, Hermitage bent and crawled into the box to join Cwen.

The inside was actually quite comfortable. The walls protected the place from the wind, and the sun overhead created quite a warm little pocket inside.

Warm pockets were not really the best location for a dead body, but now that Hermitage could see the one in question, he agreed with Cwen that it had not been dead for long. With a nod of agreement they both bent and turned the body onto its back. Hermitage thought it best to check that the fellow was actually dead.

Despite his apparent disinterest, Wat stuck his head in through the door. 'Oh no,' he sighed.

'Do you know him?' Cwen asked

Wat breathed deeply. 'I do. And I might have known.' Wat now seemed to be terribly angry with the cadaver. 'I might have bloody well known. Durwin, you idiot,' he reprimanded the face staring up at him.

Hermitage asked, 'This is Durwin?'

'It was.'

'And you knew him?'

'I did.'

'What does, erm, I mean did he do?'

'He was a glass worker.'

'Glass worker?' Hermitage had no idea where glass came from or how it was made to fit windows or to be shaped into jugs. He thought it had something to do with sand, so perhaps the sand had to be mined. Although, come to think of it, sand really was lying around on the ground.

69

The 1066 From Normandy

'I think we'd better get him out,' Hermitage said. 'This is hardly a decent resting place.'

Wat and Hermitage exchanged looks and bent to take Durwin by the shoulders. Heaving hard, they dragged the rest of him through the opening of the water box and out onto the slope of the mine.

'Durwin the glass, eh?' Cwen said once they were standing by the corpse.

'You know him as well?'

'Only by repute.' Cwen nodded thoughtfully.

'His glass was of high quality then?'

'Probably. But most of his repute was for dishonesty. Wasn't it, Wat?' She folded her arms at this point, making it quite clear that anyone who knew Durwin was probably dishonest as well.

'He was creative,' Wat replied.

'Creative! Pah. He was a thief.'

'A thief? I thought he was a glass worker.' Hermitage couldn't understand why anyone with a craft would need to steal.

'A thieving little glass worker. He'd steal anything, sell anything and offer to buy the straw from your bed if he thought he'd get a good price for the fleas.'

'Surely glass working is a reputable trade? And a flourishing one, what with all the new churches wanting glass for their windows.'

'True. But you have to get the glass before you can work it.'

'Get it?'

'From overseas merchants. Apparently, we don't have the right stuff here to make our own glass. We get lumps of it in from abroad. Then people like Durwin shape it into what's wanted.'

70

Open the Box

'I must say,' Hermitage had to say. 'With Wat's knowledge of mining and yours of glass, I am learning an awful lot.'

'I suppose when he couldn't get the glass, he took up thievery,' Cwen speculated. 'And then discovered it was a lot more profitable than his own craft.'

'Just the sort of person to be involved in a scheme to avoid the king's tax,' Hermitage suggested.

'Exactly. Although I wouldn't be surprised to find out that Durwin was killed by his own people when he tried to steal their purses.'

'Surely he wouldn't.'

'Couldn't help himself anymore, from what I heard. If it wasn't attached to you, Durwin would steal it.'

Hermitage shook his head at a sad life brought to an abrupt conclusion. Durwin must only be thirty years old or so, judging from his mortal remains. To have come to such an end so early was deplorable.

'Specialised in stealing church silver,' Cwen said.

'What?' Hermitage now glared at dead Durwin, thinking that the deplorable wretch had got all he deserved.

'Melted it down in his glass furnace and sold it on at half price. If you wanted cheap silver, Durwin was your man.'

Hermitage shook his head in sadness and disappointment. 'What was he doing in the box?'

Cwen just looked from the corpse to the box as if the answer to that was obvious.

'I mean, how did he get in the box? Was he killed in there? In which case why on earth would he go into a large box with his killer? And if he was killed out here and then thrown in the box, someone went to a lot of trouble. Someone quite strong who could throw people in boxes.

Oh, there's a thought.'

Wat and Cwen looked on with interest while Hermitage got down on his hands and knees and stuck his head in through the water box door.

'Find anything interesting?' Cwen asked when he emerged again.

'I did.' Hermitage wondered what was coming over him; he was looking for clues, weighing up possibilities in his head and drawing tentative conclusions. Just as he imagined a real investigator might do. If there even were such a thing.

'There is a good layer of old silt on the bottom of the box, doubtless washed in with years of stream water. And it shows footprints.' He left them to see the significance of his find.

'Good Lord,' Cwen said. 'You mean Durwin had feet?' She glanced down. 'Look, he's still got them.'

'What I mean,' Hermitage sighed, 'is that he was not thrown in. If he had been, there would be a great disturbance in the silt. A mess where he had landed and not much else.'

'Unless he wasn't quite dead,' Wat suggested. 'He got up and had a bit of a walk about before dying?'

'There are only footprints and the single impression where Durwin lay. There is no sign of anyone landing from the height of the wall. And there's more.'

'I can't wait,' Cwen said.

'The footprints are not all the same.'

'Some are animals?' Cwen was puzzled.

'No, not animals.' Sometimes Hermitage wondered where she got her ideas. They are prints from different feet. I think that if we took Durwin's shoe, we could match it to some of the footprints.'

72

Open the Box

'I was just in there,' Cwen said. 'And I used my feet.'

'Your prints are clear and fresh; these others are older.'

Cwen looked genuinely impressed now. 'That is clever.'

'And the other prints would match someone else's shoe.'

'The killer.' Cwen seemed very satisfied that they now knew the killer's shoe size.

'Although the prints are odd. They look as if someone was standing on the tips of their toes.'

'Which they would be if they were sneaking up to stab someone in the back,' Wat said.

Hermitage tried to ignore the pair of them. 'Which further leads us to conclude that Durwin went in the box willingly, and that he knew his killer. There is no sign of a scuffle.'

'Good heavens.' Cwen was looking quite surprised now. 'All that from some footprints.'

'The question remains why on earth anyone would willingly climb into a water box.'

'Could be a meeting place,' Wat offered.

'A meeting place?' Meetings in boxes did not sound at all right to Hermitage.

'Out of sight, nice and private. Durwin goes into the box for a meeting and doesn't come out.'

'Who has their meetings in boxes?' Hermitage's mind was starting to spin.

'People who don't want to be seen having meetings.'

Hermitage still wasn't happy. Coincidental murders in boxes were just not natural. 'It must be connected,' he said. 'We've come here following a trail of tax-avoiding merchants and what do we find? A dead thief in a box. He must be involved in this somehow.'

'It could be that our killer needed him dead in the box, not wanting him to be found,' Cwen suggested.

The 1066 From Normandy

'Hide the body, you mean.' Hermitage nodded wearily. 'Very sensible. They probably didn't know that the King's Investigator was going to come this way and would need a dead body.'

'Quite.' Cwen followed her own thoughts. 'Durwin was involved in the tax scheme somehow. Someone wanted him dealt with and out of the way. So they killed him.'

'Who knows how the dishonest mind works,' Hermitage ruminated.

'Wat probably does,' Cwen suggested.

'Not at all,' Wat protested.

Cwen narrowed her eyes. 'Why did you call him an idiot when you saw the body?'

Hermitage had been wondering about that.

Wat gave a shrug, but it was a rather shifty one. 'No reason. He's simply a rather stupid thief who has obviously got into something too big for him.

'I liked Durwin. Yes, he was awful and you wouldn't leave him alone with a used loaf of bread, but he was harmless. And now he's got himself stabbed in the back. Probably for being an idiot.

'And what need would he have to cheat tax? I mean, the king hasn't started taxing theft, has he? If he did, the whole world would collapse. He'd have to tax all his friends for one thing. And what sort of leader does that if they want to stay leader?'

'We must go back to the village,' Hermitage said. 'We can ask if anyone has been seen coming up here. '

'Come on then,' Wat grumbled as he started off.

'What about Durwin?' Hermitage asked.

'What about him?' Wat didn't seem to think there was much they could do for the man now.

'We can't just leave him out here. Animals might come.'

Open the Box

'I am not putting him back in that box.'

'Just put some logs on top of him,' Cwen suggested. She nodded towards some reasonably large timbers that were lying close by, probably spares for the water box.

Hermitage wasn't happy, but it did seem the best he was going to get. There were certainly no tools here to dig a grave.

He went over and helped Cwen lift the first log, which they laid at Durwin's side. With a few more placed properly, they could build a covering that would at least protect the body from the elements and the wildlife.

Wat joined in, and he and Cwen fetched the next timber.

They were just placing it on the other side of Durwin, when Hermitage noticed a movement down the hill. He glanced up and saw the boy from the village wandering up the path. Doubtless he was curious about these visitors and wanted to see what was going on. Life was probably very dull most of the time.

Hermitage nodded an acknowledgement, indicating that they were no threat to the boy. Then he went to help Wat with the next log.

'Murder!' the boy screamed when he got close enough. They all stood and considered him.

'Foul murder,' he yelled as he turned on his heels and ran back down the hill.

'Oh, marvellous,' Cwen moaned. 'Now we're the killers.'

Caput VIII

In the Nice Kind of Hovel

They finished providing Durwin with his modest mausoleum and Hermitage said a few words over the makeshift grave. They were all in Latin so Wat and Cwen just mumbled incoherently to show willing.

Then they started the walk back to the village. Hermitage wondered if they ought to go quite quickly. The boy was doubtless taking word that there were killers on the hillside, and the village might be preparing a warm welcome.

Wat and Cwen didn't seem at all concerned. They ambled down the hill as if they had not a care in the world.

'Do come along,' Hermitage urged.

'What's the rush?' Cwen asked.

'What's the rush? The rush is to get to the village before that boy prepares the place to receive three killers. Probably in a most unfriendly manner.'

'Judging from the size of the place, I'd think three people wandering down the hill will prompt almost instant surrender. And you're a monk. Monks aren't killers.'

'They don't know that.'

'Well, they should.'

'If they think we're horrible hardened killers, they might answer a few questions,' Wat suggested.

'I am not pretending to be a killer monk just to get some information,' Hermitage informed him. 'We will simply explain the situation and ask for what help they may give.'

'Ha.' Both Wat and Cwen seemed quite amused by that

In the Nice Kind of Hovel

idea.

The return to the village was quiet and trouble-free. Much to Hermitage's relief, there was no band of violent peasants waving their tools in the air or brandishing burning sticks. Although he was pleased about that, he thought that it was a bit of a paltry response to the alert that killers were on the way. Were murderers regular visitors in these parts? Perhaps the whole village was made up of killers and three more wouldn't make much difference.

No, the boy had been quite alarmed at the sight of the body. If the young lad came from a family of murderous persuasion, he would just have been interested.

There was no sign of any activity at all, which puzzled Hermitage. Surely a boy screaming murder would have got some reaction, even if it was only an adult clipping him round the ear for his impudence.

'Where is everyone? They aren't even out there weeding the crops anymore.'

'And the sheep have gone as well,' Cwen pointed out.

'Probably all run away from the band of merciless killer monks coming down the hill,' Wat said. 'Perhaps the sheep led the villagers to safety.'

Cwen glanced at the sky. 'More likely it's the noon meal and they've all gone to eat together.'

Hermitage was relieved at that piece of common sense. Not that he believed for a moment that the sheep would really be involved.

There was nothing for it but to wander the small collection of houses to find out where the people had gone.

Rounding the side of the first modest hovel, there was nothing to see, but the smell of cooking wafted towards them. Quite wholesome and appetizing cooking from the

The 1066 From Normandy

odours that drifted about.

'They're having something nice, then,' Cwen observed.

Wat sniffed and smiled. 'Not bad for a collection of hovels. Perhaps they decided time was up for one of the sheep.'

Hermitage scowled at that. Such a poor village was unlikely to slaughter their source of wool and the trade it delivered.

Following their noses, they came to a house towards the back of the village. This was one that had been invisible from the road, shielded as it was by its crowding neighbours.

And they could see that it needed shielding. Far from being the worst example of the peasant's hovel, that needed to hide away in shame, this was quite a magnificent place.

It was not large or grand in any way. No landowner's house this, but it was far better than anything that deserved to be in this place.

The walls were wattle and daub, of course, but they were straight and true. This sort of construction was only usually achieved by people who knew what they were doing. And this did not look like a village of master builders.

The thatch on the roof was neat and well ordered, with very few signs of rot, or invasive moss taking the thing over and turning it into a soggy mess within a couple of winters.

The door was solid wood, a remarkable feature. And it didn't even look as if was made up of left-over bits of wood that had been stuck together and called a door.

Even the ground outside was neat and well ordered. A few tufts of vegetables grew in neat rows and the smell of some of them cooking wandered from a proper chimney set in the roof.

In the Nice Kind of Hovel

The three of them looked to one another for some sort of explanation for this peculiar and out-of-place construction.

'The village head man?' Hermitage suggested.

Cwen snorted, 'There are only six houses, not much of a job being head of this lot. In which case how do you get such a nice house? And more importantly, who paid for it?'

'Perhaps we simply knock and ask?' Hermitage took his courage in his hands and stepped up to the door.

There were sounds of conversation coming from inside, so this was clearly where everyone had gone. He couldn't hear any sheep though.

His rather timid knock dropped a silence into the room, the sort of silence that said the people inside were hoping that they hadn't been noticed, but probably realised that it was too late.

After slightly too long a wait, there was a shuffle behind the door, and it opened the tiniest bit.

'Yes?' a voice from the darkness within asked.

'Hello,' Hermitage said.

'Yes,' the voice confirmed. 'What do you want?'

'Ah, yes.' Hermitage hadn't been prepared to get straight into explanations. He thought a spell of pointless conversation would come first. 'A boy,' was all he could come up with.

'We haven't got one,' the voice said and sounded as if it was keen on closing the door now.

'No, no. I mean we met a boy on our way up to the mine. He followed us and saw something unusual. He came running back here.'

'All right.' The voice seemed to think that this was the end of the discussion, as if Hermitage had knocked on the door simply to tell them about boys who ran up and down

The 1066 From Normandy

hills.

'And we probably need to explain.'

'No, that's fine. Thank you.'

The door started to close again.

'And we need some explanations as well,' Cwen spoke up as she strode to the door and stuck her foot in the closing gap.

'Oy!' the voice protested.

'Yes. Mind my foot. There's a body up at the mine and we need to know about it.'

'Body? What body?' There's no body.'

'You'd better go and tell him that. Durwin the glass?'

The collective intake of breath that came at the mention of the name should have been enough to slam the door on its own.

'Dead Durwin,' Cwen specified. 'The stabbed in the back Durwin. That one.'

'Never heard of him,' the voice in the house said very unconvincingly.

'Yes, you have,' Cwen informed him. 'And you didn't know he was dead, let alone that he'd been murdered. And now you all think you'll be next. Whoever you are. The boy is probably in there warning you about killers coming down the hill, and you think they've come for you.'

Hermitage thought that was quite a leap of deduction. He wondered if investigators were supposed to make leaps of deduction like that. If they were, then it was ever more reason why he shouldn't be one. He wouldn't leap anywhere, let alone with anything as important as a deduction.

'Who are you people?' the voice asked.

'Not killers,' Cwen assured him. 'We didn't finish off Durwin, but we'd like to know who did. As well as just

In the Nice Kind of Hovel

what is going on here.'

'Mind your own business,' the voice suggested.

'But it is our business; that's the problem. We found a body in a box. What are we supposed to do walk away?'

'Yes.' The voice clearly considered that to be the proper response to body finding. 'You've got a monk,' it observed astutely. 'What are you doing with a monk?'

'He's the one who's got to find out what's going on. You can't have monks finding bodies and then expect them to move on. And we're helping him.'

'Well, help me close my door and then go away.'

'Help you close the door on the nicest hovel for miles around? Why would I do that?'

'Because if you don't there will be some trouble. And I don't think one girl and a monk are going to do much about it.'

Hermitage was at a loss what to do next. It was clear that Cwen didn't have the strength to force the door open, or she did, but didn't want to try.

A heavy sigh wandered over from Wat. 'Come on, Burley, open up.'

There was no immediate response from the house to this.

'Is that Wat?' the voice inside asked eventually. 'Wat the Weaver?' It now sounded quite relieved.

'I might have known,' Cwen muttered as the door opened wide revealing a small, squat, but very well-dressed man of middle age.

Behind him, in the interior of the house, a table was set with food and wine, and it had another half-dozen people sitting around it, including the boy, who was munching on a very appetizing loaf of bread.

The furniture inside looked well-made and comfortable

The 1066 From Normandy

and the fact that there was wine at all, confused Hermitage no end.

'Friend of yours?' Cwen asked Wat.

'Acquaintance,' Wat confessed. 'I didn't know he was here though.'

'Of course you didn't.'

Wat came over and joined them at the door now and Burley, the owner of the voice, beckoned extravagantly that they should all enter. He did give a rather confused glance at Hermitage, as if having a monk in the house was not at all comfortable.

'Nice place you've got here,' Cwen observed as they went in.

The people already in the room gave them very wary looks and some of them appeared to be positively worried.

'It's all right,' Burley assured them. 'This is Wat. Wat the Weaver.' He held an arm out, as if introducing Wat at a fair.

The name seemed to make everyone relax. Two of the people released snorts and guffaws and indulged in some nudging of ribs.

'One of you then, is he?' Cwen asked.

'No, I am not,' Wat insisted. 'I just happen to know Burley. He's a wool merchant and we've done business before. I have no idea what he is doing here.'

Burley just smiled.

'And what's a very well-off looking wool merchant doing sipping wine in a hovel of remarkably fine condition. All just down the road from a lead mine with a dead body in it?'

'Shush,' Burley urged. He hurried them all to take seats at the table while he closed the door behind them. As he did this he took a look outside, as if expecting them to

In the Nice Kind of Hovel

have been followed.

'The boy came running down here saying there had been murder and that a monk had done it. Obvious nonsense. Children will say anything to get attention. But what's this about Durwin being dead?'

'It's about Durwin being dead,' Cwen explained. 'Stabbed in the back in a water box.'

Burley sat down and wrung his hands. 'This is awful. Who would do such a thing?'

'We thought you might know. Whoever you are?' She cast her glance around the table. It simply bounced off one couple, who were clearly used to being the most important people in any room. The boy and two others cowered under its weight.

Hermitage saw that these two were the man and woman who had been weeding the crops. They sat close to one another, as if for protection What on earth were they doing sitting at a fine table with fine people eating fine food; eating any food at all, come to that? It was they who had snorted at the mention of Wat's name.

The better dressed pair were clearly Burley's equals. A man and woman, they were very well presented indeed, and were not touching anything from the table, it clearly not being good enough for them.

There was one more presence in the room, that of a very old man. He looked to be of peasant stock, not being as finely attired as Burley and his friends. This man was not exactly at the table but sat in a comfortable looking chair by the fire. He took very little notice of proceedings as he was fast asleep.

At least, Hermitage assumed he was fast asleep and not dead. The head was lolled backwards and the mouth hung open, revealing the hideous space where this ancient used

The 1066 From Normandy

to keep his teeth. There was no chance of him doing anything with a loaf of bread. Probably not even pick it up, looking at his condition. Fortunately, just at that moment, he released a ghastly gurgling snore, and so Hermitage concluded that he wasn't quite dead yet.

'What would we know about it?' Burley asked, sounding worried and offended at the same time.

'You obviously know him, knew him, sorry. And he is dead just up the road from where you're having a nice meal. And we think he was killed by someone he knew. There you are.' Cwen seemed to consider that quite sufficient.

Burley looked to the others around the table for any help. The two well-dressed folk looked like they wouldn't offer help to a drowning man if they didn't know his family. The peasants simply cowered some more.

'He was fine when we last met.'

'And when was that?'

Hermitage thought that Cwen was doing all this questioning very well indeed. He always found it very awkward and rather embarrassing. The only concern he had about Cwen was that she seemed to be enjoying it a bit too much.

'This morning. First thing.'

'That would explain why it looked as if he hadn't been dead very long.'

'Oh my.' Burley resumed his hand wringing. He looked as if he were struggling to come up with an explanation for any of this. 'But what are you doing here?' He asked this of Wat. 'How come Wat the Weaver is finding dead bodies on hillsides?'

'It's a very long tale,' Wat said.

'Come to join, I expect, and what do you find? Durwin dead. It's awful.'

In the Nice Kind of Hovel

'Join?' Cwen asked very quietly in the silence provided for just that purpose.

'Join the Associamus.'

Cwen looked to Hermitage.

'Erm, associamus?' He tried to understand what on earth Burley was talking about. 'Join the *we join*? What does that mean?'

'It means we are a joint venture.'

'Ah,' Hermitage understood now. 'You don't want associamus then, that's the plural verb, we join. You want consociatio…,'

'Let's worry about what they call themselves later, shall we?' Cwen interrupted. 'And why would Wat want to join your whatever-it-is?'

'It's an excellent plan.'

'Excellent at getting people murdered. Dare I assume that this plan of yours is to avoid giving our new king his tax?'

Burley looked absolutely horrified at that. 'For God's holy sake,' he cried.

Cwen seemed quite taken aback by the reaction.

Burley looked around his companions, his face expressing his alarm at Cwen's words.

'Don't say it so loud,' he instructed. 'You never know who's listening.'

'Aha,' Cwen said with a rather triumphant look at Wat.

'I'm surprised you didn't join us earlier, Wat, old boy.'

'Yes, old boy,' Cwen asked. 'Why didn't you join them earlier? Or perhaps you did, and we just didn't know about it.'

'Why won't you believe me?' Wat protested. 'You've heard from Burley himself that I have not been involved in this. I'm not in his plan and I didn't even know he had

The 1066 From Normandy

one.'

'But now you're here, you can come in,' Burley smiled.

'Replace Durwin, perhaps?' Cwen suggested grimly.

Burley had the grace to swallow hard at that.

Wat shook his head. 'From what I know, King William takes his taxes very seriously. Anyone trying to evade them is going to bring down the sort of trouble the Normans do best. You know, death.'

'Oh, no need to worry,' Burley smiled. 'There's nothing wrong with what we're doing. It's all completely legal.'

'I'm not sure the king will see it that way.'

'Ah, but he doesn't know about the gesith of King Edward, does he?' Burley nodded to the old man, dozing in his chair.

'I imagine not.' Wat clearly didn't understand what was being said.

'A gesith?' Hermitage asked, frowning at the use of an old Saxon title. 'A companion of the king?' He couldn't believe that the old man slowly decaying in front of them could have had anything to do with King Edward. He had fallen on very hard times if that had been the case.

And judging from the age of this fellow, King Edward must have been a boy at the time.

'King Edward's gesith is living in a hovel outside Derby?'

'Not that Edward. Edward the Elder.'

'Edward the Elder?' Hermitage must be losing his mind. 'Edward the Elder died a hundred and sixty odd years ago. I don't think even this man is that old.'

'Of course not, he's a descendant. His great-great-grandfather was King Edward's gesith, and it was a hereditary appointment.'

'Family gone down a bit in the world?' Cwen grimaced at the state of the old man in the chair.

86

In the Nice Kind of Hovel

Wat nodded his head knowingly. 'And along with the title, the old man here inherited his great-great-grandfather's right to be exempt from the king's taxes.'

'Got it,' Burley smiled broadly. 'And as he's in our associamus,' (Hermitage shivered at the word), 'we can make use of his rights.'

'Very handy,' Cwen agreed. 'And it's all going so well, isn't it? Only the one dead body so far.' She smiled at them all. 'Let's just hope for your sake that the gethis inherited some exemption from being stabbed in the back.'

Caput IX

Dishonesty Explained

'I've got to ask,' Wat asked. 'What on earth was Durwin doing in a box?'

Hermitage was intrigued by that as well. As the consociatio had a nice hovel in the village, why would they meet in a box?

'No idea,' Burley said. 'We certainly didn't send him there.'

'Where did you send him, then? Presumably he was on some errand for this associo.'

'Consociatio,' Hermitage corrected. He thought that if he told them the right word every time they used the wrong one, they'd soon get the hang of it. He did recall trying this approach with some of his brothers in the monastery of De'Ath's Dingle once; that had gone very badly indeed. But then most things in that awful place tended to go badly.

Burley replied, trying to sound nonchalant, but coming across as plain dishonest. 'Just running an errand.'

'Running an errand? What errand?' Wat obviously didn't believe this. 'And Durwin? What possessed you to involve Durwin in something like this at all?'

'He has a lot of contacts.'

'I know he does. He's stolen from most of them and they probably want to kill him. What errand?' Wat repeated the question more forcefully.

'He was just taking word to some, erm, people.' Burley gave cautious looks to Cwen and Hermitage, obviously not

88

Dishonesty Explained

willing to reveal too much to strangers; or anything at all if he could avoid it.

'People who might kill him, you think?'

'Oh no. Absolutely not.'

'Well, someone did it.'

Burley had nothing to offer.

'Did Durwin have anything with him?' Wat asked.

'With him?'

'For heaven's sake, Burley. You're going to have to answer some questions or you could all end up in the box with Durwin. And there's room; it's a big box.'

Burley looked nervously at Cwen and Hermitage again.

'Don't worry about them, they're with me.'

Hermitage was quite pleased with himself as he reasoned that he should absolutely not mention that he was King William's investigator. Not that anyone had asked, so he didn't have to lie anyway.

Burley's companions were no help at all. The wealthy couple bore the sort of stony looks that gave nothing away, and the peasants in the room just looked confused; apart from the old man who snored at everything.

'He was taking word to our, erm, colleagues in the matter.'

Hermitage nodded that he was happy with the word "colleague". It was an innovative use of the Latin, but not unreasonable in the circumstances.

Wat gave him a hard stare. 'The church?' he asked.

Burley made extravagant gestures that Wat should keep his voice down. 'For God's sake. They really do have ears everywhere.'

Wat shook his head in disappointment. 'You have a nice scheme to keep tax out of the king's hand and you go and involve the church.'

The 1066 From Normandy

'How did you know?' Burley asked, sounding a bit suspicious now.

'It's not hard to work out, is it?' Wat said. 'You're just down the road from an old lead mine. Why would you be here if it wasn't connected somehow. And who uses all the lead these days? The church. And who else is exempt from the king's tax? The church.'

Burley nodded that it was an entirely reasonable conclusion, but he was still suspicious of Wat's questions. 'But what are you doing here anyway?' he asked. 'This is hardly the sort of spot people pass through on the way to somewhere more interesting.' He passed his frowning look over Cwen and Hermitage. 'Let alone a famous weaver and his peculiar companions.'

Hermitage felt his stomach tighten at that question. He was only grateful that he hadn't been asked.

Wat leaned into the table as if sharing his own secrets. 'This is Cwen, she used to work for Briston the Weaver.'

'With Briston,' Cwen corrected.

'Quite. With Briston the Weaver.'

'Really?' Burley seemed quite interested now. 'Those works of Briston were positively, erm,' he searched for the word. Hermitage hoped that he wouldn't find it.

'They certainly were,' Cwen confirmed. 'All of them very…, indeed. And I made most of them.'

'Well I never,' Burley looked very impressed, and a little shocked. 'And the monk?' he asked, as if Hermitage wasn't there.

'Brother Hermitage,' Wat said. 'Since the Normans came, the market has gone very pious. It's all anyone want:; pious. Everyone's got to show the Normans how pious they are, so they need great big pious tapestries. It's one way of avoiding death by Norman. "Please don't kill me,

90

Dishonesty Explained

look at my lovely tapestry of a saint instead.'"

'And the monk makes sure you're being pious enough.'

'That's it. You can imagine that I didn't know pious from a pie up until now.'

'I certainly can. I saw that one of yours, what was it called? Had a pie in it, if I recall. But they certainly weren't blackbirds coming out of it.'

'Ha, ha,' Wat smiled at the thought. Hermitage trusted that he would keep it to himself. 'And it's not safe to travel the roads on your own these days,' Wat went on. 'We have to go out together.'

'You still haven't said what brings you up a lonely hill in this part of the world.'

'Well,' Wat began, sounding as if he was taking Burley into some profound confidence. 'Obviously, I knew nothing about what you were up to, but every merchant in the land must be thinking how to avoid giving away profit unnecessarily.' Wat smiled and Burley nodded back.

Hermitage didn't have the first idea what had just been said.

'You've heard about the king's plans for taxes, then.' Burley shook his head that anyone could come with quite so revolting an idea.

'Certainly have.' Wat looked equally appalled. 'And that got me thinking. Where could I put my money that the king couldn't get at it? It would have to be somewhere that paid no tax, so I'd the concluded that the church would have to be involved somewhere, not that I'd usually trust that lot with a worn-out shoe. But then I never thought of anything as clever as a gesith.' He nodded towards the decrepit old gesith in the corner.

'He's perfect,' Burley acknowledged. 'Master...,'

'No names,' the wealthy looking man interrupted.

91

The 1066 From Normandy

Burley nodded agreement. 'One of our number knew of the old man. Had him living on his land being a complete nuisance about him and his family not having to pay tithe because they were exempt.'

'Outrageous,' Wat commented.

Burley shook his head in weary despair. 'I don't know how peasants think the country works, but if they get the idea that they can avoid paying their dues, goodness knows where we'll end up.'

'Quite.'

'So, we hatched the plan that we could use the gesith to avoid paying the king.'

'Your dues?' Cwen suggested.

Burley scowled at her. 'You had the idea of using a lead mine as well, then?' he asked Wat.

'Just a thought,' Wat agreed.

'A good one. And we've got everything set up, so you can join now.' There was the slightest murmur of complaint from the table. 'I'll vouch for you,' Burley said pointedly.

'Well.' Wat drew the word out as if he were about to offer a penny for something worth a pound. 'I don't know. What with Durwin being dead from a knife in the back. What was he taking to the church? Just word or anything of value?'

'He did have a small token of our commitment,' Burley admitted.

'The church wanted paying up front, you mean. Typical. And you trusted someone like Durwin with your valuables? I'm not sure that bodes very well. Durwin was an idiot, we all know that. But you're the ones who put your money in his hands.' Wat left it unsaid, but it was clear he thought Burley and his conspirators were idiots as well.

'It was only a token,' Burley insisted.

92

Dishonesty Explained

'A token is enough for people these days. Durwin himself would have stolen one if he'd seen it. Anyone could have killed him. What sort of token was it?'

'Just a small purse.'

'Not just the purse. I imagine there was something in it.'

'A small piece of lead from the mine.'

'A piece of lead?' Wat seemed to find this hard to believe. 'Where did you find a piece of lead in that place?'

'Obviously it wasn't going to be a real piece of lead.'

'Obviously.'

'It was symbolic.'

'A symbolic piece of lead.' Wat thought about this for a moment. 'You mean more like a rock.'

'It could be a rock with lead in it.'

'Or not?'

'Or not,' Burley admitted. 'It was the symbol that mattered. We were handing over the produce of the mine.'

'And the church was paying for it?'

'That's it.' Burley seemed very happy that Wat understood the whole business.

'How much? Symbolically, that is.'

'A pound.'

'A pound!' Cwen blurted out. 'A pound for some old bit of rock?'

'A pound that can't be taxed,' Wat explained. 'The church is paying for this lead so there's no tax on it.'

'Exactly.' Burley nodded. 'Clever, isn't it.'

'If you say so.' Cwen didn't seem able to spot the cleverness.

Wat's face was creased in thought, and he even tipped his head over slightly. He slowly raised one finger as whatever he was trying to work out, was coming to him in its own sweet time.

The 1066 From Normandy

'And,' he said very carefully. 'The church is hardly going to give you their own money for this piece of rock. You have to give them the pound first.'

'A charitable donation,' Burley sounded solemn.

'This sounds very wrong,' Hermitage said. He didn't understand it, but from what he had heard, he was pretty sure it was sinful.

'It's brilliant,' Wat said. 'You donate your profit to the church, so you don't pay tax on it. The church then uses your own money to buy some lead from you and they don't pay tax either. Then, the lead mine is in the name of the gethis and so he doesn't pay tax. The money ends up back in your pocket and the king is none-the-wiser.'

Burley held out his hands to demonstrate that Wat had just explained the whole thing.

'Not only did Durwin have this piece of lead in his purse, the one that the church was buying, he also had the pound for them to buy it with.'

'I don't understand.' Hermitage was now completely lost.

'A single pound, as a token, that's all.' Burley said.

'A pound!' Cwen exclaimed once more. 'There's half the country would kill for a pound these days. You could live a comfortable life for months with a pound.'

Burley and the wealthy couple at the table looked very confused about how anyone could manage that.

The peasants looked very disappointed that they weren't seeing any of these pounds that were floating around.

'And you sent him off on his own carrying a pound of silver?' Cwen gaped. 'I'm not surprised he was murdered, lugging that lot about with him.'

'Ah, that was the clever bit.'

'There's a clever bit?' Cwen sounded very doubtful about

Dishonesty Explained

that.

'We didn't send silver, far too heavy and obvious.'

'What then?'

Burley leaned forward and whispered so that the walls wouldn't hear. 'Gold.'

'Gold?' Cwen blurted loudly. 'And that was the clever bit? I sincerely hope there isn't a stupid bit.'

'And I wouldn't put it past Durwin to go boasting about how he had a pound in his purse,' Wat said, shaking his head. 'Just inviting the man with the knife to take it from him. Where was he supposed to be taking this pound? Not to a meeting with a bishop in a box, I imagine.'

'Of course not. He was going to Chesterfield.'

'Chesterfield?' Cwen asked. 'Never heard of it.'

'Everyone's getting the names of places wrong these days,' Burley complained.

Hermitage sympathised with that.

'It's actually Caester Feld, an old Roman fort.'

'Still never heard of it.'

'Well, that's where our church contact wanted the meeting. Probably convenient for them.'

'And what was he supposed to do when he got to this place?' Wat asked.

Burley lowered his voice. 'There was to be an exchange. A ritual exchange.'

'A ritual exchange, eh?'

'We hand over the pound and the piece of lead. The church keeps the lead and hands the money back to us.'

'Except it won't be a pound, will it? How much were the church actually going to pay for this pound's worth of rock-that-might-be-lead?'

'Two hundred and thirty pence.'

'Keeping ten for their trouble. Ten pence in every pound,

95

The 1066 From Normandy

eh?'

'I really don't understand,' Hermitage insisted.

Wat sighed. He turned to Hermitage and held up his hand, counting each step off on his fingers.

'One; Burley has a pound profit from his wool, yes?'

Hermitage nodded that he understood. He wasn't sure he approved, but his approval seemed completely irrelevant to anything that was going on.

'If he does nothing about it, the king will come along and take his tax. And who knows how much that could be? A lot, I expect. After all, William has a conquest to pay for.'

Hermitage nodded that he was with it so far.

'Two; Burley donates his pound to the church.'

'Very good.' Hermitage did approve of that.

'Three; the church gives Burley two hundred and thirty pence for some lead.'

'Which isn't real,' Hermitage said.

'Of course it's real. There's a whole mine of the stuff if anyone asks.

'Four; Burley doesn't have to pay the king any tax on that because the mine belongs to the gethis.'

Hermitage had followed all of that. Now he knew that he didn't approve. 'And what does the gethis get out of it?'

Wat and Burley both looked very puzzled, as if they couldn't understand the question at all.

The two peasants looked as if they'd quite like an answer to that one.

'It's terribly complicated,' Hermitage said. 'Why doesn't Burley just hide his pound and not tell the king he's got it?'

'Brother Hermitage, I'm shocked,' Wat said. 'That would be very dishonest.'

Hermitage wasn't sure he knew what honest meant anymore.

Dishonesty Explained

'If Master Burley wanted to spend his money on a fine house, or a tapestry say, the king would get suspicious and ask where it had come from. Unexplained wealth always attracts the most suspicious types. This way, it's all quite proper.'

'Hardly. I don't think greed and avarice on this scale warrants the word *proper*.'

'It's a very sophisticated and entirely legitimate scheme.' Burley said.

'Oh yes,' Cwen agreed. 'The knife that went in Durwin's back and killed him was probably sophisticated as well.'

Burley's face dropped, as if he'd forgotten all about that.

'You've got a new problem though,' Wat said. 'Apart from your errand boy being dead in a box.'

Burley nodded agreement. 'The church isn't going to get their pound as expected.'

'And if you think King William will be a bit testy if he doesn't get his tax, try not paying a bishop when he expects it.'

Burley swallowed. 'We have to get to Chesterfield with another pound and new piece of rock.'

'That's not strictly true,' Cwen said.

Burley looked to her as if she might have some solution to the dilemma.

'You have to get to Chesterfield. It's not our pound and it's not our rock. Let's just hope you make it a bit further than the box on the hill.'

Caput X

Off to Church

Hermitage felt quite proud of the humble peasant who just sat in the corner of the room and said nothing. From weeding the crops to deception of the king must be a huge and confusing step. That the fellow steadfastly refused all of Burley's pleadings that he should take the next pound to Chesterfield, was honest and true; and probably very sensible.

Burley even implied that there could be an extra pound in it for the man; he didn't promise, or even offer, but he implied.

The man was having none of it. He simply sat shaking his head implacably, as if he wasn't even going to start thinking about considering such a request.

'Why won't you do it?' Burley eventually demanded, implying that it was the man's duty to do what he was told. 'It's only just up the road.'

'I ain't getting killed,' the man replied, which seemed to be a very good reason.

'No one is going to get killed,' Burley assured him.

'If no one is going to get killed, you can go.' The man folded his arms, making it quite clear that he wasn't going to budge.

This too was a very reasonable argument, but Burley didn't seem to see it that way.

'Your master can order you to go,' Burley snapped, starting to lose his temper. He cast a glance at his wealthy fellow across the table. The wealthy fellow showed no

Off to Church

signs of interest, as if he was in this scheme so far, but he wasn't going to go any deeper. 'You're a bloody peasant, you have to do what you're told.'

'Can I ask a question?' Cwen interrupted.

Burley sighed and shrugged. He looked grateful to have anyone say anything.

Cwen screwed up her face and moved her mouth around as she got her thoughts in order. 'This man is the son of the older one, I assume.'

'That's right.'

'Then he'll be the next gethis once this one's gone.'

They all looked at the old man, expecting the departure to take place any moment now.

'Yes.' Burley obviously couldn't see the point of this.

'And the lead mine is in the name of the gethis, so that there's no tax to pay, yes?'

'Of course,' Burley sighed as he had explained all this once already.

'In which case, isn't the peasant here a landowner and not a peasant at all?' Cwen asked this very sweetly, as if she had not the first idea about the implications.

'What?' Burley barked.

'I mean, if the mine is in his name, that means it's his. His land. He's a landowner. Landowners aren't peasants. If the mine is as big as five hides, he might even be a thegn.'

The peasant looked quite pleased about this.

Hermitage considered it to be a very interesting argument. 'In fact,' he put in. 'It was quite common for a gesith, once he had served the king, to be given land.'

'There you are then,' Cwen smiled that she was pleased to have been so helpful. 'He's not peasant at all so doesn't have to do what anyone tells him.'

From the fact that Burley's fists were so tightly clenched

The 1066 From Normandy

that his knuckles had turned white, Hermitage concluded that he was not very happy about this. 'The mine is only in his name, it's not really his.'

'What's the difference?' Wat now asked. 'How can anyone own land other than it being in their name?'

'You are not being helpful,' Burley ground his words out.

'Don't think we're here to be helpful. And I'm really going off this tax scheme of yours.'

Burley was getting no help from anyone and was obviously feeling quite alone in the middle of his problems.

'The pound and the rock must go to Chesterfield.' He seemed to say this more to his well-off companions than anyone. 'If the church doesn't receive what they're expecting, there will be questions for all of us to answer.'

That did seem to prompt some worry on the two faces. The man and woman drew close into whispered conversation. 'We will just step outside and consider the situation,' the man said after they'd hissed at one another for a moment or two.

'Oh no, you won't,' Burley said. 'You're staying here until we get this sorted.'

'I've had another idea,' Cwen said brightly.

'Another one?' Burley asked with some despair.

'Yes, we can come with you.'

'What?' Wat asked. 'Why would we do that? This is Burley's problem, let him sort it out.'

'Thank you very much,' Burley expressed his disappointment.

'You still need somewhere to put your money,' Cwen said to Wat. 'And mine, come to that. Or you could give it to the king in tax?'

Hermitage thought that they had been in the presence of dishonesty for too long. It was starting to affect Cwen

Off to Church

and it was confusing him. One moment she was arguing that the peasant was entitled to do what he wanted, the next she was suggesting cheating the king of his tax.

'That's right,' Burley agreed with a smile and a nod.

Wat glared at Cwen. 'Perhaps we can just discuss this for a moment? In private?' He nodded towards the door.

'Of course,' Burley agreed.

Wat subtly gestured that Hermitage should follow as he stood.

The wealthy pair got up as well.

'Oh no, not you two,' Burley said. 'You're not going anywhere.' They sat again.

'What the devil?' Wat hissed at Cwen once they were out of the door. 'What do you mean, we'll go with them? Are you mad?'

'I'm thinking ahead, that's what I'm doing.'

'Thinking ahead to us all getting our own personal water box in which to be stabbed.'

'What is it you're thinking?' Hermitage asked, seeing that Wat was in no state to consider any rational argument.

Cwen addressed Hermitage but pulled Wat by the arm to make sure he was close and listening too. 'The king sent us to find out about his tax evaders, yes?'

'And we have,' Wat said. 'It's Burley and those two.'

'And the church.'

'Oh well, he can hardly do anything about the church, can he?' Wat shook his head at Hermitage, as if the church was his fault.

'Yes, but you do know what William is like.'

'I certainly do. Big fellow with a crown and a very sharp sword.'

'And is he going to be content with us going back and

101

The 1066 From Normandy

saying that Burley and some people whose names we didn't get, are evading his tax with someone from the church? Oh, who? Well, we didn't stay to find out?'

Hermitage's heart sank as he realised that King William would not be content with that at all. He wasn't content most of the time anyway, but such a vague report would not help his temper; apart from help it to get worse.

'The best we can hope for is that he tells us to turn around and start again. The worst is that he tells us to turn around so that Le Pedvin can stab us in the back. And he wouldn't even insist on a water box to do it in.'

Wat had no answer to that, but his shoulders sagged and he released a very heavy sigh. 'Oh, God,' he moaned.

'We have to go with Burley to find out who these church people are.'

'And discover who killed Durwin,' Hermitage said.

'Who? Oh him, yes, I suppose so.' Cwen didn't seem concerned about Durwin.

'Probably just some passing robber who found out he had a pound on him,' Wat said. 'We'll never get to the bottom of that. And William won't care anyway.'

'I know William won't care, but a murder has been committed.'

'If you like.' Wat waved the murder away as a minor distraction from more important worries.

'And what do we do when we get to Chesterfield and find out who the church representative is?'

'Smile nicely and walk away slowly,' Wat suggested.

'Then we tell the king?'

'If we have to.'

'We do have to, surely. That's why he gave us this task.'

'It is. But I don't want the church knowing that it was us told the king about their business. Especially if the king

102

Off to Church

decides to do something about it. There should be something separating church and state, and it shouldn't be us.'

Cwen quietly nodded her agreement to that. 'Right. We tell Burley that we'll go with him to Chesterfield. But only if the others come as well.'

'The peasants included?' Hermitage asked.

'Hardly. If we don't deserve to be caught up in this, they certainly don't.'

Burley was very happy that they were prepared to go to Chesterfield. He was so happy that he thought they might like to go on their own and he could wait here for them.

Wat made it quite clear that that was not going to happen. He was also insistent that the two quiet rich people should go as well.

They were very reluctant indeed, insisting that this was never part of their arrangement. They said that they had had enough of this nonsense and would simply go home again. They did let slip that it was their pound that had gone with Durwin, which caused Burley to study the intricacies of the floor for a few moments.

The thought of losing another pound appeared to motivate them to keep a better watch on the next one.

To drive the motivation home, Wat speculated whether the Castigatori might be representing the church in this business. That band of very strong and fit brothers wandered the country making sure that church discipline was enforced; or any other discipline they fancied at the time.[3] They always had the best interests of the church at heart and would enforce their discipline on anyone within

---

[3] *The Tapestry of Death* sees encounters with the Castigatori; nasty!

103

reach; rich, poor, clerical or lay, it made no difference to the Castigatori.

From the swallowing and nervous looks that followed, it was clear that the Castigatori were known of and were to be avoided.

It was agreed that a journey to Chesterfield was just the thing. The day had drawn into afternoon though. Finding bodies and discovering conspiracy had taken most of the day, and there was little point leaving now.

'We'll set off tomorrow morning,' Wat said. 'This is a nice comfortable spot for the night.'

Both the peasants and the rich couple seemed united in their horror at this suggestion.

'Where will we sleep?' The woman asked in a shrill and contemptuous voice.

'Ask the gethis to move over,' Cwen said. 'He seems quite comfortable.'

There was more hissed and intense conversation between the couple and Burley before they appeared to be reluctantly persuaded that they had to stay. They still looked pretty disgusted by the prospect but found a corner of the room where they might have a little bit of privacy. The thought of conversation with the new arrivals was clearly quite revolting.

'I need to step out for a moment,' the woman said as if there would be no question about this.

'Oh really?' Burley's suspicion of her motives was clear.

The woman repeated her words slowly and clearly. 'I need to step out.'

'Oh, right,' Burley blushed and flustered as he realised the purpose of the stepping out.

Hermitage knew that asking the rich to share a privy with the poor really was going too far.

Off to Church

When the woman returned, brushing her skirts back into order, Burley took a seat by the door. Hermitage suspected that this was to make sure no one got out. He couldn't imagine where else the rich couple thought they were going to sleep? Perhaps there was another rich person who lived nearby, and they all put one another up when they were travelling.

With conversation painful by its absence, Hermitage thought he might pass the time by letting everyone know of his latest considerations concerning the post-Exodus prophets.

Before long he found that he was talking to himself as everyone had settled to private tasks such as repair or reorganisation of their packs. The rich couple were even sitting together reading a small book they'd got from somewhere; how rude.

The afternoon wore on as afternoons do when everyone wants them to come to an end; they took an interminable amount of time about it. Eventually, as the sun showed the very first signs of calling it a day, everyone decided that they could really do with an early night and settled for sleep.

The following morning started before dawn had fully made it as far as the hovel windows, which was not surprising, considering how early they'd all gone to bed.

Preparations for the journey were short and quick, simple packs being slung on backs: apart from the rich couple who appeared to be looking around for someone to carry their pack for them. They were truly puzzled when it became obvious that the pack wasn't going to move itself and that one of them would have to touch it. It didn't look like they'd done it before. The man approached the simple

The 1066 From Normandy

bag of his own belongings with some curiosity. This turned to surprise when he felt how heavy the thing was.

Hermitage wondered how it had got here in the first place. It had doubtless been carried by some servant who had then been dismissed. Not only did these rich people not do their own work, they didn't think things through, either.

'We must attend to Durwin before we leave,' Hermitage said as they all stood at the doorway.

'Isn't he dead?' Burley asked.

'Of course. But we have left him on the hillside simply covered in logs. That's not suitable at all.'

Burley looked as if he couldn't see the problem. 'I'm sure the locals can deal with Durwin.' He looked expectantly towards the peasants, who appeared to be quite pleased that the awful people were about to leave, and so were prepared to agree to anything. The man nodded, although Hermitage suspected it was a nod that they could deal with Durwin, not a nod that they would.

Stepping out of the house onto the road back to the mine, sent on their way by the cheery waves of the peasants, the party set off.

The rich couple, whose names they still didn't know, seemed to be almost puzzled by the whole process. They looked about the open countryside as if seeing it for the first time.

'Don't usually travel without a retinue, I expect,' Cwen said to the woman. The look that was returned said that this was a rich woman who didn't expect to be bothered by her inferiors, let alone spoken to.

'We've got a dead body to look forward to,' Cwen offered with a disturbing smile.

The woman moved over to her partner and clutched his

Off to Church

arm tight.

At the top of the hill once more, Hermitage was grateful to see that Durwin's resting place had not been disturbed.

'Is it worth checking for the pound?' Wat said. 'We didn't know anything about it when we found him, so didn't bother looking.'

Hermitage was horrified at the thought.

'I suppose we should,' Burley said. 'It's unlikely that whoever stabbed him would leave a pound behind, but you never know.'

'We can't,' Hermitage said. 'Searching the dead for money? It's unthinkable.'

'I just thought it,' Wat pointed out. 'In fact, we probably must do it.'

'Why, for heaven's sake?'

'Because if it's gone, we'll know it was robbery. A nice clean, what do you call it, motive?'

'Motive, yes,' Hermitage confirmed.

He looked away as they stopped by the log mound and Wat and Burley moved the top of the pile away.

It seemed to be an inordinate time before Burley confirmed that there was no pound. No purse either.

'The robber is going to pretty confused when he finds he's stolen a rock,' Cwen said.

'Ah, a rock,' Burley said quickly. 'We must take another rock from the mine with us. Good heavens, I almost forgot.' He stooped and picked up a random bit of the ground and put it in his own purse, which was tied at his waist.

'Lead from the mine, eh?' Hermitage said accusingly.

'It certainly is.'

'Who is it from the church that we're going to meet?' Wat asked as they walked along, leaving Durwin to his

107

The 1066 From Normandy

wooden resting place.

'No idea,' Burley said.

'Then how will we know who to talk to?' Hermitage asked. He didn't understand much about this scheme, but knowing who you were going to give your money and your rock to seemed pretty fundamental.

'There won't be many expectant looking churchmen loitering in Chesterfield,' Burley explained.

'How did you arrange the meeting then?'

'How do these things ever get arranged?' Burley asked, which was no help whatsoever as Hermitage didn't have the first clue.

'A quiet word,' Wat explained, with a knowing nod.

'That's it,' Burley agreed. 'A quiet suggestion to someone who you think might be trustworthy. They have a discussion with someone they know, who passes word on to people who deal with this sort of thing.'

'Then word is sent that someone might be available for a discussion, without making any promises, of course.' It sounded as if Wat had done this sort of thing before.

'News comes down the chain that a meeting in Chesterfield might be arranged for the exchange of principle.'

It all sounded positively unprincipled to Hermitage.

'But this meeting was supposed to be yesterday?' Wat asked.

'That's right.' Burley sounded and looked worried. 'Durwin should have been there by end of day and everything done by sundown.'

'Is your contact going to stay?'

'I don't know. Obviously, the church is interested in this or they wouldn't have agreed to meet at all. I'm sure they'll wait at least a day; you never know what inconveniences

Off to Church

get in the way of travel these days.'

'Knives in the back,' Cwen suggested. 'That sort of thing.'

'Robbery,' Burley corrected. 'It's all very well the Normans keeping order, but they only keep it for themselves. The very roads of the country are not safe. I don't think anyone expects to be on time when they set out these days.'

'Let's hope we don't meet any Normans on the way, then,' Cwen said, which gave everyone pause for thought. 'If they see a group like us wandering along, they aren't just going to pass the time of day.'

'Perhaps we should spread out a bit,' Burley suggested, apparently genuinely concerned at the prospect of bumping into a Norman or two.

'You mean not travel together having gone to the trouble of travelling together?' Cwen asked.

'Just don't look as if we're going together. I'll bring up the rear, you three go in the middle and the other two can lead the way.'

'I'm not sure they're going to be too keen on that.'

'They're not keen on anything, those two,' Burley complained. 'Apart from getting money for nothing.'

'How shocking,' Cwen said. 'Just imagine.' She rolled her eyes and shook her head.

Burley walked on to impart the news to the couple, who weren't walking with the others anyway.

'Suits them,' he reported when he came back. 'They really don't want to be associated with tradespeople anyway, apparently.'

'Tradespeople?' Wat sounded mightily offended. 'I'm a craftsman, I am. And I bet that if I knew who they were, I'd have a few tales to tell. There's not many families of

The 1066 From Normandy

their type who don't have a work of Wat the Weaver in the closet somewhere.'

'Let them go ahead,' Cwen snorted. 'If there are any Normans on the road, they can be the first to bump into them.'

Caput XI

Where Has All The Money Gone?

'They've run off,' Burley complained loudly. 'They've bloody well run off.'

There was certainly no sign of the wealthy couple anymore, but Hermitage thought that they weren't the type to run anywhere. They had moved out of sight round a bend in the track, and when the rest of them followed, the path was empty of rich people.

'Perhaps they've stepped into the woods,' Cwen suggested. 'They seem the type to be all shy and private about routine business. "Stepping outside",' she mocked, as if the pot in the corner was good enough for her.

Burley stood in the middle of the roadway and turned full circle, looking for any indication of where the couple might have gone. 'They've run off. They've been trying long enough, now they've managed it.'

'Why would they run off?' Wat asked. 'They're in the scheme as well, surely?'

'Yes, yes.' Burley wasn't really paying attention, he was still rather frantically searching for any trace of the missing pair.

'Or are they?'

'Are they what?'

'Part of the scheme?'

'Of course, they are. Fundamental to it.'

'In which case, why run off?'

Burley did now turn to face Wat. 'Because those two never lift a finger to do anything themselves, they have

The 1066 From Normandy

people for that sort of thing.'

'What sort of thing?'

'Any sort of thing. Even dressing themselves, as far as I can make out.'

'Why are they in this with you at all, then?'

'Because the idea of anyone taking what's rightfully theirs gives them the shakes.'

'Like the king taking some tax off them.'

'Exactly. And you probably gathered from all the sideways glances and sighs that the lead mine is actually on their land.'

'Not theirs anymore,' Cwen said. 'It belongs to the gethis now.'

'Oh, I don't think so.'

'What? You said yourself that it's in his name.'

'You don't think those two are going to let something like that bother them. When they want it back, they'll take it, gethis or no gethis. When it suits them for it not to be theirs, it isn't.'

'And they're passing some of their wealth through the church so that good King William can't get his hands on it.'

'My, you are sharp today,' Burley sighed. 'It's one thing for them to get their money cleaned up like this, it's quite another for them to actually have to walk anywhere or talk to anyone to get it done. They've been trying all along to get me to do it all for them.'

'Why don't you?'

'Because I need them in the thick of it.'

'Aha,' Wat nodded knowingly.

Hermitage hoped that he would pass some of that knowing on fairly soon.

Wat saw Hermitage's confusion. 'If King William turns

112

Where Has All The Money Gone

up at their manor, which I imagine is quite a nice one.'

'Very nice,' Burley confirmed.

'Thought so. And if said King William asks where his taxes are, our rich couple will be able to say that they gave it all to Burley. By this means they stay the living loyal subjects of the king, while Burley doesn't.'

'They'll express their shock and outrage that I could turn out to be such an untrustworthy wretch.' Burley sounded as if he was reciting.

Hermitage could only shake his head that even the dishonesty he'd already come across had further depths of dishonesty within it. 'Is this really how people of substance behave?'

'Only the people of substance,' Cwen said. 'If you've got nothing, there's no point going to extraordinary lengths to hold on to it.'

Burley looked frustrated by this sort of thinking. 'It's only people of substance who keep the rest of the country in work and food.'

'And as little of both as possible,' Cwen gave Burley one of her harder looks.

'The point is that they have gone, and the question is where.'

'Home again to keep their heads down and pretend all this is nothing to do with them,' Wat suggested. 'Durwin coming to his untimely end must have been a real shock. Made everything a bit too personal.'

'They could be on their way to the king,' Burley speculated morosely. 'Show their loyalty to the crown by telling him what we're up to.'

'That would be pretty stupid,' Cwen said. 'It is their land in the middle of all this.'

'That's right,' Wat agreed. 'For all we know, William is

The 1066 From Normandy

already suspicious of people with lead mines.' He shrugged as if this was an entirely nonchalant and irrelevant bit of guess work.

Hermitage felt quite alarmed that he was in danger of giving too much away.

'And they signed it over to a Saxon king's gethis? That won't go down well,' Wat concluded.

Burley did not appear to be encouraged by any of this. 'I want them where I can see them.'

'They didn't strike me as the type to go running off into the woods,' Hermitage said. 'They seemed a little, what can we say, delicate for such an adventure?'

Burley did seem to consider this a reasonable argument. 'Where have they gone then?'

'It could be as Cwen said, they've simply gone to attend to the business of nature.'

'Can't think they'd like doing that in the woods either,' Cwen observed.

'Nowhere else to go round here,' Wat said, looking as if he might take advantage of the break to do the same.

'Perhaps they've been taken by robbers?' Hermitage suggested.

'Taken by robbers?' Burley clearly thought Hermitage's imagination was carrying him away; he didn't know that Hermitage's imagination couldn't carry the weight of half a dead sparrow. 'I think we'd have heard the commotion if they were taken by robbers, they were only just ahead of us, for goodness sake.'

'Anyway,' Wat chipped in, 'if this is their land, the robbers round here probably work for them as well.'

Burley nodded his agreement to that.

'Any chance we could know who they are now?' Cwen asked with a weary sigh. 'Or were, if they're lying dead in a

114

Where Has All The Money Gone

ditch somewhere.'

Burley frowned, clearly not convinced that would be a good a idea.

'You might as well,' Wat said, sounding largely disinterested. 'If this does all go horribly wrong, we'll be able to tell the king's men who was involved. Back up your side of the story, that sort of thing.'

It was clear from Burley's expression that his overwhelming self-interest was battling with promises made.

'And they have just run off,' Cwen prompted.

Burley now looked around the wood, as if checking that no inquisitive squirrels were listening in. 'You've got to swear to keep this to yourselves.'

They all nodded.

Still, Burley didn't seem happy. 'I can trust a monk. If he swears, I'll know he won't tell, but you two? Well, you mainly, Wat.'

'Me?' Wat's offence at the question was obviously over-blown.

'Yes, you. You're a first class and successful merchant, so I wouldn't trust you with a bucket of dung in a farmyard.'

'I am mortally offended,' Wat sniffed. 'But it's up to you. If you don't want help finding these two, that's fine. And if we can't explain anything to the Normans, so be it.'

'All right,' Burley huffed. He dropped his voice to impart the information. 'Hendor and his wife,' he whispered.

Wat shrugged. 'Never heard of them.'

'That's because he didn't used to be called Hendor.'

'Very mysterious, I'm sure.'

Burley became even more cautious and careful. 'He used to be called Aluric of Yelling.'

115

The 1066 From Normandy

'Aluric of Yelling?' Wat cried out.

'Quiet!'

'The Aluric of Yelling who was definitively killed at Hastings?'

'Obviously not.'

'Not that Aluric, or not killed?'

'Not quite as killed as people believe.'

'Not quite as killed as everyone was told.'

Even Hermitage had heard about the death of Aluric of Yelling. He wasn't a significant figure in the country, just a minor landowner, really, and no sort of fighter at all. His death seemed to be taken as a real blow. If unimportant folk such as Aluric were gone, what hope was there for the remaining Saxons? The great and the good were expected to die, after all, that was what they were for. If death started working its way down to the ordinary man, it really was the end.

But if this was Aluric of Yelling, he didn't seem to be very ordinary.

'Why is he not dead?' Wat asked, as if criticising Aluric for not getting killed properly.

'He never was,' Burley confirmed.

'I imagine not.'

'Apparently, when everyone started reporting his death, he didn't like to contradict them.'

'Who can blame him,' Cwen said. 'After all, if the Normans think you're dead, they're less likely to try and kill you.'

'He simply vanished from the field of battle and reappeared as Hendor.'

'He doesn't seem the sort to manage well on the field of battle,' Hermitage commented. He had no expertise in fields of battle or the sort of the people that went there,

Where Has All The Money Gone

but he imagined they'd be a bit more, well, aggressive, than Aluric/Hendor seemed to be.

'And he wasn't,' Burley confirmed. 'A force of Harold's men came through Yelling on their way from the north, gathering every man of fighting age.'

'Not necessarily worrying about fighting disposition,' Wat said.

'Or ability,' Cwen added.

Burley just shrugged at that.

'I can picture the scene,' Wat said. 'Aluric of Yelling is loitering in one of the less battle-like areas of the battle, when someone shouts that Aluric of Yelling has fallen. "Oh no," says Aluric, "how awful, and he was such a nice man. Thank heavens that Hendor is still alive to return to the bosom of his family."'

Cwen grunted at such self-serving behaviour. 'Perhaps it was Aluric himself who shouted.'

Wat nodded. 'Good plan.'

'Not content with keeping his life out of King Harold's hands, he wants to keep his money out of William's.'

'And now he's vanished again,' Burley complained. 'He's making a habit of it.'

'What do we do then?' Hermitage asked. He really didn't want to spend time looking for someone who had run away. As far as their mission was concerned, they knew who the conspirators were. Once they found out who from the church was involved, they could go home again. He didn't like to think about reporting all this back to William, knowing that the king would be keen on making sure Aluric was really dead this time. And that would be Hermitage's fault.

Still, he knew what to do in situations like this; not think about it and hope it all turned out all right in the

The 1066 From Normandy

end.

'We carry on,' Wat said. 'If Aluric or Hendor's chief skill is avoiding responsibility or anyone who wants to hold him responsible, we're hardly likely to find him. And the church is still waiting, we hope.'

Burley grumbled incoherently but didn't have an alternative to offer. 'If this does all end up in trouble, I might suddenly remember that Aluric of Yelling isn't quite as dead as King William likes his Saxons.'

With no one having anything more useful to offer they resumed their walk along the track. Burley continued to look left and right, as if hoping to spot Aluric and his wife hiding behind a tree. He even looked up into the canopy in case they'd climbed one.

Hermitage really couldn't see either of the Saxons climbing a tree; certainly not without a bevy of servants and a ladder.

'What does Aluric think is going to happen if this all works out?' Wat asked as they strode on. 'The Normans are going to turn up in Yelling at some time. How does he explain that he's made it back from Hastings after his death?'

'Aluric is dead, isn't he?' Burley said. 'It's Hendor now.'

'And he hopes no one recognises him.'

'Who would? I'm sure Duke William of Normandy, King of England, wouldn't know a minor Saxon landowner from the back end of his horse.'

'But the people of Yelling must know that their lord and master is looking remarkably well considering he's been killed in battle.'

'And they're going to betray him to the Normans, are they?'

That made Hermitage feel very awkward.

Where Has All The Money Gone

'Hendor's a distant cousin of Aluric,' Burley said. 'Heard about the poor fellow's death and has come to take over.'

'And the resemblance to old Aluric is remarkable,' Wat suggested.

Cwen sounded uninterested in Aluric's problems. 'Hendor can have his land taken off him by the Normans instead of Aluric then.'

'But if he has a sack full of money from this little deception, he'll be comfortable enough,' Wat said. 'Probably doubly important for him to have some wealth the king can't tax.'

'Why worry about him anyway?' Cwen asked. 'If he wants to run away just let him. Deal with the church without him.'

'He's the one with all the money,' Burley complained. 'The church isn't going to be interested in this with only my paltry fortune.'

'Paltry?' Wat coughed. 'The Burley I know wouldn't have a paltry anything.'

'Compared to Aluric, I'm a pauper.'

'How's that possible?' Wat seemed confused. 'A minor Saxon landowner has a great fortune? How did he get that?'

'Funnily enough, I never asked.' Burley obviously thought asking where the money came from was a very stupid idea.

Wat frowned his doubts. 'Aluric of Yelling was no one of significance, that's why his death was a bit of shock. If he wasn't that wealthy before he went to Hastings, where did it come from?'

Burley indicated that he wasn't even interested in hearing someone else's discussion about where the money came from. It was here, that was the important bit.

The 1066 From Normandy

'Are these church people expecting to see him?' Wat asked.

'Oh, it's all too discreet for any names, let alone dead Aluric of Yelling. All that's been arranged is a meeting between interested parties.' Burley was thoughtful. 'There is one thing we do need to think about before we get there.'

'What's that?' Wat asked.

'You.'

'Me?'

'Exactly. They won't know who I am, and the name of Aluric will never be raised. Wat the Weaver though? It'll be helpful to have your money in the pot, but if the church thinks they're working with Wat the Weaver we might not be able to run fast enough to keep up.'

'You'd be surprised how much business people in the church have done with Wat the Weaver.' Wat gave a knowing smile, which worried Hermitage no end.

'Are they likely to recognise you?' Burley asked in a very worried tone.

'How would I know? I don't even know who it is we're meeting.'

'No need to mention the name then,' Burley said.

Wat shrugged that he had no problem with that. 'If it is someone I know, they might be persuaded to do an even better deal. After all, the Normans are a strangely pious lot, between the battles, killings and theft. The church folk will want any sins of their own kept quiet.'

Burley now nodded that this could be useful.

Hermitage was positively fretting that the deceptions were getting increasingly complicated. 'How do we explain me?'

'You?'

'What's a monk doing involved in this frankly sinful

Where Has All The Money Gone

business?'

'I know a few monks...,' Wat began.

'The business is not only sinful,' Hermitage ignored him. 'There's sin under it, through it and coming out of the other end.'

Burley was looking at him carefully. 'You're not a monk.'

'I can assure you I am,' Hermitage was offended by the suggestion.

'Not as far as the meeting is concerned. I'm not going to use my name; we're not mentioning Wat the Weaver and so you needn't be a monk.'

Hermitage just held out his arms pointing out the fact that he looked very much like a monk.

'You're in hiding. You could be a noble who escaped Hastings and has taken on the guise of a monk.'

'Dishonesty upon dishonesty!'

'What's a little bit more?' Cwen asked. 'I think I'd like to be a noble lady who encouraged her husband to go to Hastings. Support the king, defend the land and the rights of the Saxon people; and with any luck not come back.'

'Oh, really.' Hermitage despaired.

'Excellent,' Burley said. 'Now that's all sorted we can press on to Chesterfield.'

Hermitage followed reluctantly along, shaking his head. He turned quickly as he heard a plaintive shout from behind.

Running along the track was the dishevelled figure of the wife of Aluric. It took Hermitage a moment to recognise her, probably because she was the last person he expected to see coming towards them. She and her husband had gone to the trouble of running away from them. Why would she be coming back?

With a sudden descent of his stomach, he knew what

121

The 1066 From Normandy

was coming next.

'Murder!' the woman cried.

He was right.

Caput XII

A Less Than Dignified Death

'Lord Hendor is dead,' the woman's noise sounded as if the moon had suddenly decided to howl back at all those dogs.

'Again?' Cwen asked quietly. 'Can we trust him to be really dead, that's the question? Perhaps there's another cousin in the woods somewhere.'

Hermitage gave her a very harsh glance. Lady Hendor was obviously in great distress. As she drew up to them she collapsed into Wat's arms, where she sobbed loudly.

He staggered under the onslaught and managed to wobble over to the edge of the path, where he sat on a fallen tree trunk, Lady Hendor slumped in his lap.

Burley and Cwen simply stood and looked at her, as if expecting this to be a ruse of some sort.

'What has happened?' Hermitage asked gently.

'Murder,' the lady wailed again from somewhere in Wat's jerkin.

'Of Hendor, yes,' Cwen said. 'Or should we say…,'

'Most foul,' Burley interrupted quickly. He gave Cwen a fierce warning glance to say nothing. 'Murder most foul.'

Hermitage couldn't immediately think what other sort there was, but that was hardly the point at the moment. 'How?' he asked.

'He is done to death.' The lady fell into a descending stream of panting sobs. When she reached the bottom, she honked in air like a drowning woman and then started again.

The 1066 From Normandy

Hermitage had an urge to point out that death was quite common in murder, but he chastised himself instead.

'How?' he repeated.

'By villainy.'

He couldn't think that saying "how" again would be any help. Perhaps he wasn't making himself clear.

'Can you tell us what you have seen?' he tried. 'Who did it? Where? How did it happen?' Perhaps adding some detail would get the information required.

Lady Hendor now raised her head and simply looked at him as if the questions were too much for her to bear. Her face was wet with tears and contorted by grief. In reply she simply waved an arm back down the track.

Wat took the opportunity to get Lady Hendor a bit more upright so he could get her weight off his knees. After some gentle wrestling, he managed to sit her on the log beside him.

'Back there,' Hermitage confirmed. He'd been pretty sure that would be the case, but every little helped. 'On the track? In the woods?'

The lady nodded.

'Well, which?' Hermitage was never driven to impatience, but if anyone was going to manage it, it would be someone who couldn't answer a simple question.

'The woods?' he tried.

The lady nodded again.

'You were in the woods and someone attacked you?'

Another nod.

'What were you doing in the woods, then?' Cwen asked. 'Instead of on the track with the rest of us.'

'Cwen,' Hermitage reprimanded. 'The poor woman has just seen her husband murdered.'

Lady Hendor sniffed the sniff of a congested peasant

124

A Less Than Dignified Death

and seemed to be shocked into a response by Cwen's question. 'We were only attending to our business.'

Hermitage was disappointed by that. His gentle and sympathetic approach to a woman in distress had got him nowhere. Cwen's rudeness and insensitivity had got the first plain answer about anything. He shook his head sadly as he knew that he would never be able to do rude and insensitive as well as Cwen.

'And someone attacked while you were doing it?' Cwen asked, sounding quite disgusted that Lady Hendor allowed such a thing to happen.

'Not exactly while we were doing it, obviously,' Lady Hendor recovered a little bit of her poise; the little bit that looked down on other people.

Cwen just stared at her, clearly waiting for the rest of the explanation.

'We had gone our separate ways in the woods to attend to matters. I behind some bushes and Hendor to a tree.'

Cwen shook her head slightly in frustration at the pointless sensitivities of pretentious folk.

'When I was, erm, ready, to return to the track there was no sign of Hendor.'

'Still busy behind his tree, I expect.'

'So I thought.'

Cwen looked Lady Hendor up and down, considering the many layers of fine garments she wore, including the outermost, which was a fine, thick red skirt embroidered with intricate and delicate patterns. 'Must have taken you an age to get to anything under that lot,' she said.

Hermitage turned away and put a hand to his forehead, covering his eyes in shame.

Even Lady Hendor looked a bit put out at the detail of this interrogation.

The 1066 From Normandy

'I'm just saying that Hendor must have finished first,' Cwen explained, as if it was a perfectly reasonable question. 'Unless he had a different sort of business to attend to? You know, he needed to ...,'

'Cwen!' Hermitage had to speak up. 'We do not need to go into the details of exactly who was doing exactly what behind which bit of undergrowth. Can we skip to the bit where Hendor is dead?'

'Please yourself,' Cwen sulked.

Hermitage nodded that Lady Hendor could carry on.

With a wary look towards the young woman who appeared to want to know things that were none of her business, Lady Hendor composed herself. 'I went looking for Hendor and called him. There was no reply, so I started wandering amongst the trees. That's when I found him.'

'Dead?' Hermitage asked quietly.

'Yes.' Lady Hendor broke down into more inconsolable cries.

Cwen looked as if she had a question about the details of this discovery on her lips but was managing to keep it to herself.

'And then you ran to us?'

Lady Hendor could only nod.

'We had better go and see,' Hermitage said to the others. He was going to suggest that Cwen stay with Lady Hendor to care for her, but quickly concluded that was not a good idea at all. 'Can you guide us to the spot?'

The lady looked a bit worried about that but nodded reluctantly.

Hermitage gestured that they would go back down the track, and that she needed to lead the way.

Rising from the log, she adjusted her skirts and tried to

A Less Than Dignified Death

recover some of her dignity. She now looked rather embarrassed that she had let herself go in front of strangers. On top of that she was being asked to take them to the spot where she'd let herself go.

Wat stood as well, checking his own clothing to make sure no damage had been done by the sobbing, sniffling woman who had buried her head in his nice jerkin.

'This is a disaster,' Burley hissed, when Lady Hendor was several paces ahead. 'Under no circumstances must the church know that he's dead.'

'They don't know who he is anyway, according to you,' Wat pointed out.

'That's right. But whoever they think he is, they mustn't think he's dead.'

'Because he won't be able to give them his money now.'

'Exactly.'

'Lady Hendor might want to carry on. The money hasn't died as well.'

Hermitage passed them both a very disappointed look as they discussed such matters.

'If she knows what's going on at all,' Burley said.

'It hardly seems the time to ask,' Hermitage said quickly, before someone could decide it was just the time to ask.

Lady Hendor had stopped on the path now, and they were quickly at her side. She pointed over to the right with a shaking hand.

'Which tree?' Cwen asked, looking at the large collection that traditionally made up a forest.

The new widow waved her hand in a particular direction, turning her head away at the same time.

They followed her indication and concluded that the lady would never be able to look at an oak in quite the same way again.

The 1066 From Normandy

Leaving her on the path, they all stepped onto the crackling ground of leaf and twig. The way was easy here, the trees growing so thick and dark that their shadow and years of leaf droppings had quickly killed anything impudent enough to try and grow at their feet.

'Careful you don't tread in anything,' Cwen offered.

As so often on their travels in the past, Hermitage told himself that he really would have to have a word with Cwen when they got back. Whenever they got back, the moment seemed to have passed and he never got round to it. Perhaps he should carry quill and parchment so that he could make notes as they went.

They arrived at the mighty oak that spread its massive limbs in all directions, as if trying to push its fellow trees out of the way.

Hermitage very cautiously walked around the trunk, hoping that something would have happened that meant there was no body. Top of his list was the body getting up and walking away because it wasn't really dead.

That list shrivelled and died as he came across the mortal remains of Hendor who is also known as Aluric. Or who used to be also known as Aluric.

'Oh my.'

'That's definitely him and he's definitely dead,' Wat helpfully described the situation.

Lord Hendor was lying on his front at the foot of the tree and the dark stain on his back told the tale of how he had come to his end.

Hermitage quickly scanned the ground around them, seeing if there was any sign that would indicate more about this awful event. He didn't really know what it might be, perhaps a bloody knife?

'The same way as Durwin,' he said solemnly.

A Less Than Dignified Death

'Stabbed in the back,' Wat agreed. 'Still, I imagine that's quite common if you want to kill someone with the least amount of personal risk.'

'Should we roll him over?' Hermitage asked.

'Why?'

'Just to check that it really is him?'

'What? That it really is him and not someone else who's wearing his clothes all of a sudden?'

Hermitage saw that the hope that this was not Hendor was faint. And even if it wasn't Hendor, someone had been murdered in the woods.

'If we are going to turn him over,' Cwen said. 'Can we do one thing first?'

'What's that?'

'Pull his leggings up.'

Hermitage was surprised that he only now noticed that Lord Aluric really had been caught in the middle of his business. His leggings were around his knees, and the tail of his jerkin was the only thing covering his modesty.

'Oh, yes, yes,' Hermitage said quickly. 'We'll, erm, deal with the body. You go back to Lady Aluric.'

Cwen turned away but didn't move as the men restored Aluric to a state of decency.

Wat spoke as they worked. 'You were the one implying that the Alurics were so precious they couldn't even share the same tree. Now you look away when the man's dead?'

'I didn't know him, did I?' Cwen replied. 'It's hardly decent on first meeting.'

'Right, you can look now.' Wat stood from their labours and considered the body before them.

Hermitage couldn't see that rolling Aluric over had been much help. It was still him and he was still dead.

'Who could have done this?' Burley was in a quite a

129

The 1066 From Normandy

panic, perhaps at the thought of killers wandering the woods.

Hermitage suspected the panic was more to do with his own interests than Aluric's welfare.

'I think the question is why they would have done this,' he said, and was quite impressed with his own question.

'Why?' Burley didn't seem concerned by the distinction.

'Exactly.'

'Why would someone stab Aluric in the back?' Wat specified the problem, which Hermitage thought was pretty obvious in the current circumstances.

'He's rich.' Burley seemed to think that was a complete and adequate explanation for anyone getting stabbed in the back.

Wat looked over the body. 'He still is, by the state of him. Doesn't look like anything's been taken. He's still got a fine pair of boots on him.'

'And his leggings were already half-way down,' Cwen added. 'Would have been easy to have them away.'

'And his pack is still lying there. Hermitage, can you take that?'

Hermitage nodded and moved the pack away from the side of its deceased owner. 'He's even still got rings on his fingers.' He tried to concentrate on the more obvious features and ignore Cwen's horrible suggestion.

Burley was confused. 'Perhaps the killer didn't have time. Lady Aluric, er, Hendor was nearby. She could have disturbed him.'

'Kill her as well, then.' Cwen shrugged. 'Twice the takings.'

Burley appeared to see that was also a very reasonable approach to rich people on their own in the woods. 'Then why?'

A Less Than Dignified Death

'I think that's where we began,' Wat pointed out.

'And done to death in the same manner as Durwin.' Hermitage repeated his previous point, seeing that no one had taken any notice the first time.

'Not put in a water box, though,' Cwen said.

'There isn't one to put him in.'

'It must be connected, water box or not.'

Hermitage nodded thoughtfully. 'I fear it must. And not just because I'm here.' He quickly realised what he'd said.

'You're here?' Burley looked worried as well as confused.

'Because Hermitage is a monk,' Cwen said quickly.

'What's that got to do with anything? Does he kill people?'

'Of course not. But he has to deal with death, doesn't he? Being a monk and all. Last rites, that sort of thing.'

'You mean the killer waited until there was a monk nearby and then did it?'

'Each monk specialises in their area of expertise,' Hermitage explained. 'I have simply dealt with death quite frequently, that's all.' At least this was honest, if not the complete truth.

'People wait until you're to hand before dying, do they?'

Hermitage longed to say that it certainly felt like that, but of course, he couldn't give away his role for the king.

'No, but I am usually summoned quite soon afterwards.'

Burley spoke slowly and seemed to be carefully considering a possible conclusion. 'You found Durwin in the box and now you're here when Aluric was killed.'

'But I was with you on the path, and Durwin was already dead,' Hermitage said.

'Hm.' Burley sounded worried that this was all Hermitage's fault somehow.

'The connection is obviously not a monk, is it?' Wat was

impatient. 'Not even Hermitage, who has to deal with death quite a lot. The connection is obviously this business of yours. Unless there are more people in the shadows, there were seven of you involved in this to begin with; the three peasants, the Alurics, you and Durwin. And now two of them are dead. Stabbed in the back, no less. If anyone is a curse around here, it's you.'

'What are you saying?' Burley asked, although Hermitage thought it was pretty plain.

'That I think we'll leave you to your business now. You and Lady whatever-her-name-is can go to the meeting with the church. We'll head off home. You know, before someone stabs us in the back as well.'

'You can't,' Burley pleaded.

'Erm,' Wat thought about it for a moment. 'Yes, we can.' He pointed back down the road to indicate the direction in which they could do it.

'We need to find out who's doing this and stop them.' At least Burley seemed to accept that two of his companions being murdered was a bit more than a coincidence.

'Investigate, you mean?' Cwen asked.

'What the devil does that mean?'

'From the Latin, *vestigo vestigare*, to track. You want to track the killer.'

Burley gave her a very odd look. 'Not really. I want him to stop. What's the Latin for stop?'

'Perhaps *prohibere*?" Hermitage offered.

'Yes, that. That's what we want to do. Prohibere him killing anyone else.'

'Most specifically, you,' Wat said.

'That would be good, yes.' Burley's eyes narrowed slightly as a fresh motivation for their assistance in this

A Less Than Dignified Death

occurred to him. 'And it's no good you going home anyway. You're involved now. You found Durwin and you've just seen Aluric. If this killer is going through the members of our associamus...,'

'Consociatio,' Hermitage corrected quietly.

'You're in it as well now. You could be next.'

Hermitage hadn't considered that properly until now. They were outside of this horrible scheme, just looking in, but whoever was doing the stabbing might not know that.

As he pondered where all this might lead, he thought he spotted a movement off in the woods of the forest. Probably a deer or something. At least deer didn't carry knives; well not the ones he'd ever seen. Mind you, the King's Investigator was in their woods now so goodness knew what they'd be getting up to.

Caput XIII

Back on The Road Again

Hermitage considered it most unfair to be threatened with death over something he didn't even understand properly. He had been threatened with death plenty of times, but on those occasions it had been because of his investigations. That was still entirely unreasonable to his mind, but it was some sort of explanation.

He could never really put himself in the mind of a murderer, but he imagined that if one was being investigated, he would rather it would stop. And, being a murderer already with some obvious expertise in the area, getting rid of your investigator by the same means was only logical.

The whole thing was completely unjust; but then murder tended to be unjust most of the time.

At least this situation gave them a good excuse to continue with their tax investigation. Burley didn't need to know that they had a motive of their own. What could he call it? A more distant motive, perhaps? The Latin, *ulterior* seemed to lend itself perfectly. Yes, he had an ulterior motive. That sounded quite exciting.

'I think,' Cwen spoke up, 'that we could simply run away.' She gave Hermitage a private wink to indicate that she was deliberately suggesting this to draw Burley out. Hermitage thought she might have got a bit of tree in her eye.

'This individual with a knife and a good eye for backs obviously has an interest in what you're up to. If we're

Back on The Road Again

miles away, it would probably be for the best.'

'Ah, but you won't know, will you?' It was rather worrying that Burley sounded as if he had done this sort of thing before. 'It could be they want to finish me off first, but they'll probably come for you afterwards. And if you try to leave now, they might do you straight away.'

'Sounds to me like you know who they are.' Wat folded his arms and faced Burley, demanding some sort of explanation.

'Absolutely not. You know me, Wat. I'm all for a bit of risk in business, but not with my own life.'

Wat shrugged that this was probably true.

'What do we do then?' Cwen asked. 'Carry on to the meeting? Unless the man from the church has already been murdered of course.'

'We'll find out when we get there.' Burley nodded. 'But what about Lady Aluric?' He tipped his head over towards the path where the lady stood, quietly fretting.

'If we're still on her land, she could go home,' Cwen said.

'On her own through the woods?' Hermitage asked. 'With a killer on the prowl? I don't think she'll be very keen on that.'

'She'll have to come with us then.' Wat took a step towards the path but was brought up by a cough from Hermitage. 'What?'

Hermitage simply gave him an expectant look and accompanied it with a nod towards the body of Aluric.

Wat's shoulders sagged. 'Not again? Why do we have to keep covering up the bodies?'

Back on the path, Lady Aluric made it perfectly plain that she was not going anywhere on her own; probably ever again. She would rather they escorted her back to

135

The 1066 From Normandy

safety, but as Burley said they could not delay the meeting any further, she agreed to go along.

'Do you know what Lord erm, Hendor's plans for the meeting were?' Burley asked as nonchalantly as he could.

'I have no idea,' the lady replied. She made it clear that such matters were so far beneath her that she wouldn't even relieve herself on them. 'I do not trouble myself with such matters. Al.., erm, Hendor dealt with all that sort of thing.' She stifled a shaking in her chest. 'And once this meeting of yours is completed, you may take me home.' She quickly walked away from the group.

Hermitage felt very sorry for her, alone and unable to share her grief with those around her; mainly because she thought they were all peasants. She seemed to exude an unapproachable aura, as if none of her travelling companions were the sort of people she liked to talk to in any circumstances.

He wondered about offering her the traditional words of comfort; how her husband would be with the Lord in heaven now, but he had his own doubts about that.

His other thought was that she would likely be best comforted by female company, but as the only option they had was Cwen, he quickly dismissed the idea. He didn't want to make things worse.

She kept herself apart from the rest of them as they walked on, obviously deep in her own thoughts. She still released a quiet sob every now and again but tried her best to maintain the dignity that went with her station.

The death of Aluric/Hendor had cast a pall over the whole party and there was no conversation at all. Speculation about who they were going to meet was absent and there wasn't even any planning of who would say what once they got there.

Back on The Road Again

As Hermitage considered their destination, he began to fret about what might happen. It could be that some very high-up figure of the church would be in attendance and he would have to offer his obedience. As this whole situation was as mired in sin as it was possible for anything to mire itself, the experience could be quite difficult.

Instead of being able to head due north towards Chesterfield, the path they trod wound steadily away towards the east. Hermitage was quite proud of his local knowledge as he reasoned that they would soon join the main Roman road heading out of Derby towards the far northern reaches and York. Where it went beyond that was a mystery; if it went anywhere at all. Hermitage assumed Scotland would be next.

Sure enough, they emerged from the winding track of a Saxon drover's path onto the sort of broad highway that the Romans seemed to need to get anywhere. This arrowed to north and south, and Hermitage felt a gentle tugging inside himself that he should turn right and head back to the workshop. His mind told him that north was the only option. There were murders to be solved and a king to be placated; neither of which would be achieved if he were hiding under his cot.

As the five travellers spread out along the path, each absorbed by their own thoughts, Hermitage noticed that Cwen and Wat now drifted towards him.

'We need to think about this meeting,' Wat whispered when the three of them were close.

'I'm glad someone is going to,' Hermitage said. 'Burley is offering no information at all. If he even has any.'

'Probably not. It's all been suggestions and schemes so far. Now's the time for things to start happening.'

'As if they haven't already. I'm sure two dead people

137

The 1066 From Normandy

weren't included in the plan.'

'Which is why we need to prepare for every eventuality before we get to Chesterfield.'

'Such as?' Hermitage couldn't think of many eventualities that came out of a pre-arranged meeting; apart from the meeting.

'What if there's a small army of them?'

'Small army of who?'

'Church people. Important, influential ones, who might even know who Wat the Weaver is.'

'If they're as dishonest as the people we've come across so far, it's almost certain,' Cwen commented.

'Very helpful.' Wat sniffed. 'And what if they also know who the King's Investigator is?'

'That's hardly likely, is it?' Hermitage didn't think anyone would know who he was.

'The Castigatori, for instance?'

'Oh, them.' Hermitage swallowed. They did know who he was. Their awful leader, Father Dextus, was a most difficult fellow and had no time for Hermitage. He was also a very big fellow, young and in his prime and not at all averse to a spot of violence; deplorable in a man of the church, but he didn't seem to worry about being deplored either.

'And the Castigatori don't think much of Wat the Weaver,' Cwen pointed out.

'They do not,' Wat admitted. 'If we get a sniff of them, we disappear, yes?'

For a moment, Hermitage wondered how they were going to smell the Castigatori, but quickly saw what Wat meant. 'How do we explain that to Burley?'

Wat shrugged. 'Do we care? Him or the Castigatori, which would you choose?'

Back on The Road Again

'Your point is well made.'

'And if there's no one we know?' Cwen asked.

'Still a risk. They may still know us. After all, if they're the sort to engage in depriving the king of his tax, they're probably going to be well connected.'

Hermitage voiced his latest worry. 'If they know us, the first we'll hear about it could be when they ask what the King's Investigator is doing in their midst.'

'Could be.' Wat bit his lip in deep thought. 'Does that matter?' he asked slowly.

'I should think so.'

'You're not here on official business. The king hasn't sent you to investigate a murder. What you do in your own time is your own business.'

Even Hermitage thought this was a stretch. 'And they won't worry about having a king's appointee in the middle of their scheme to rob the king?'

Wat didn't have an answer to that.

'We just run for it if there's trouble.' Cwen sounded as if this was her plan all along. 'Fight our way out if we have to.'

'Fight our way out?' Hermitage was aghast.

'I fight our way out,' Cwen corrected.

Hermitage was happier with that; and quite confident that she could do it.

'That's the other problem,' Wat said. 'One that I didn't really want to raise.'

'Another problem.' Hermitage's voice was heavy. 'Do we have the room?'

'What if the church is involved in all this?'

'I don't understand. We know they're involved; we're going to meet them. It would be a bit of a surprise to get to a meeting that's been arranged with them only to find out

139

The 1066 From Normandy

they don't know why they're there.'

'Not the meeting,' Wat hissed his concern. 'Involved in the deaths.'

Hermitage couldn't follow that reasoning at all. 'Involved in the deaths? Are you suggesting that the church killed Durwin and Aluric?'

'It's a possibility.'

'No, it isn't. People of the church do not go round killing other people.' Hermitage was quite insistent upon this point.

'Not sure you're right there,' Cwen said. 'They may not do it themselves, but I'm sure they can arrange for it to happen. And look at Odo, Bishop of Bayeux and the king's brother. Killed more people at Hastings with his club than most did with a sword.'

'I'm not sure he's truly representative of church folk. They can't all be brothers of William.'

'More and more of them are his appointees. He probably thinks getting the church to kill people is only spreading the work around a bit.'

'To what end?' Hermitage was feeling quite frantic in his objection to the suggestion that the church was full of killers. 'Here we are, involved in this frankly ludicrous scheme to move money round in a circle, and the church is key. Why on earth would they have the people on the other side of the deal murdered?'

'Could be a whole host of reasons,' Wat said.

'Can you give me one?'

'They knew too much.'

'Who knew too much?'

'Durwin and Aluric.'

Hermitage couldn't help but feel bemused at this notion. 'As far as I can see, no one knows very much at all. How

140

Back on The Road Again

anyone could know too much in this situation, let alone be murdered for it, is beyond me.'

'Durwin might know who in the church he was going to meet. Aluric was obviously a wealthy fellow who escaped the battle at Hastings. He'd be keen to ingratiate himself with the new king, perhaps he was going to betray them and had to go.'

Cwen sounded enthused by this option. 'Just like we're expected to betray them to the king.'

Hermitage didn't find that a helpful remark. 'I'd be surprised if Durwin actually knew where Chesterfield was, from what you've said of him. He hardly seems to be the type to have secret knowledge. And he hadn't even left before he was murdered, what could he know? And wasn't Aluric the one with all the money? Why would they kill him?'

Wat looked disappointed that his ideas were going nowhere. 'They want to keep all the money themselves?'

'They haven't got their hands on any of it yet.'

'They're the only other ones who know what's going on,' Wat persisted. 'Burley's hardly likely to do it, not when he's organising things in the first place.'

'Could be they want to impress the king themselves,' Cwen suggested. 'They heard that some horrible people were planning to rob the king of his rightful taxes, and so they had them killed; wasn't that nice of them?'

Wat seemed to think that was a reasonable option.

'The church does not go round killing people,' Hermitage insisted. 'It's ridiculous.'

'I still think we need to be on our guard.' Wat grumbled.

Hermitage certainly agreed with that and they walked on Hermitage suspecting that Wat and Cwen were simply concocting even more bizarre possibilities.

141

The 1066 From Normandy

After a while, Cwen voiced her next thought. 'There's no telling that the murders are connected. Just because two people are stabbed in the back doesn't mean the same person did it. As you said, Wat, stabbing in the back must be pretty common. Could be that Durwin was done by someone he's crossed in the past, and Aluric was just a robbery gone wrong.'

Wat held up a finger as Cwen's idea set off some thoughts in his head. 'Someone he's crossed in the past.'

'Yes, you know, someone whose property ended up in Durwin's possession; probably in the middle of the night.'

'Right idea; wrong person.'

'Who, then?'

'Aluric.'

'Aluric robs people in the middle of the night?'

'No. Probably in broad daylight.'

'Explain please?'

'Aluric of Yelling, the minor landowner who went off to Hastings and came back alive. The one who changed his name in the process and became his own cousin, Hendor. The minor landowner who now appears to have a major fortune.'

Hermitage thought this all sounded very interesting but largely unhelpful.

Cwen was nodding though, for some reason. 'Where did that come from?' she asked.

'Exactly. Not his own money, that's for sure. Not from a place like Yelling.'

'And now he's keen to see it disappear through a very dubious trade in lead.'

'Supposedly to keep it out of the king's hands.'

'But it could also be to keep it out of the hands of its rightful owner.'

Back on The Road Again

Hermitage looked back and forth between the two of them. He was happy that they seemed to be making some sort of progress and was confident that they'd explain it to him in due course.

'Dying at Hastings could have been just what he needed,' Wat went on.

'Or maybe dying at Hastings was the source of his riches?' Cwen suggested.

'How?'

'Lots of dead nobles lying about in a field. All of them carrying their wealth at their side. Purses full of gold, jewels in case they need ransom. How were they to know that William was a different sort of victor, and would simply kill them all?'

'I like it,' Wat nodded.

Hermitage didn't. The shout he wanted to release had to be contained to a very harsh whisper. 'Are you seriously suggesting that Aluric of Yelling robbed the dead at Hastings?'

'Someone would, why not him?'

'Because the very idea is disgusting.'

'No more disgusting than getting your head chopped off by a Norman on a horse.'

Hermitage would prefer to consider one disgusting idea at a time.

Wat was clearly taking the thought seriously. 'And Lady Aluric greets him home saying, "I heard you got killed", to which he says, "No, I got rich." "Ah, welcome home, my Lord," she says. Now someone has found out what Aluric was up to and wants to exact revenge, or punishment, or something...,'

Hermitage quickly remembered the movement he had seen in the woods. Could that be connected? No, of course

143

The 1066 From Normandy

not. Deer didn't do revenge.

Cwen took up the tale. 'Or his enemies just think it's a bit odd that a cousin, who looks just the same as the dead man, has turned up with a trunk full of treasure.'

'Time to make sure the curse of the Alurics lands on the cousin as well.'

'And the messenger who's on his way to Chesterfield. The worst thing to happen would be the church getting their hands on the treasure. No one would ever see it again.'

'In which case, Burley was right.' Wat had come to a clear conclusion, which Hermitage thought would doubtless be very helpful.

'We are next.'

Caput XIV

Into the Bushes

Before they could reach Chesterfield itself, Hermitage decided that he really needed to visit the bushes for his own business. Knowing how well it went for the last person to venture off the path had made him hold it in for far longer than was comfortable.

'I just need to, erm, go behind a tree,' he told Wat and Cwen.

Cwen shook her impatient head at such nicety.

'Not on your own,' Wat said.

'I beg your pardon?'

'Look what happened to Aluric. If there is someone out there with plans for the spots on our backs where the knife goes, you don't want to be on your own.'

'Don't look at me,' Cwen said. 'I'm not going with him.'

'I hadn't asked if you would.'

'Why can't he just do it on the side of the road like normal people?'

'The habit is a different garment from leggings,' Hermitage explained.' The whole thing needs to be got out of the way and...,'

'Yes, yes, fine,' Wat interrupted. 'I'll come. I could do with it anyway.'

Alerting Burley and Lady Aluric that they were stopping for a moment, Wat led the way off the path. Finding a suitable tree, the two men took position on opposite sides.

Hermitage shuffled around a bit so he could at least see the edge of Wat's arm. If someone was going to sneak up

The 1066 From Normandy

behind them with a knife, he would know it fairly quickly. Of course, he'd know it even quicker if he was the victim.

With no stabbing pains to record, he finished and got this habit back in order. He stepped back around the tree, just as Wat adjusted his leggings and they both headed back to the path.

'Better?' Cwen asked.

'Much, thank you,' Wat smiled. 'Just let me know when you want to go, and I'll pick us a nice tree.'

Cwen ignored him and turned back to the road where Burley and the lady were waiting. They were waiting several feet apart and weren't talking to one another.

'Well,' Wat said. 'This is a happy band, isn't it? What are we going to do when we get to Chesterfield?'

'Let me do the talking,' Burley said.

'I hope someone knows what they're talking about.'

'Of course.' Burley was offended that his expertise in whatever it was they were doing, was being questioned.

This exchange did nothing to relieve the atmosphere of mutual distrust, suspicion and despair. Lady Hendor was clearly in no mood to deal with any of this and simply wanted to get it over with.

After a considerable time walking, Hermitage started to have some doubts they were going the right way at all. 'How far is this Chesterfield place?'

Burley shrugged. 'Should be there by the end of the day.'

'End of the day? I thought it was just up the road.'

'Yes, just up the road, about a day away.'

'That hardly counts as just up the road.'

'I suppose we could ask for it to be a bit nearer, but I don't think we'll have much luck.' Burley shook his head in a rather irritated manner and walked on ahead of them.

Far from easing Hermitage's worries that they were

Into the Bushes

about to turn a corner and bump into some bishop or other, he now realised he had more time to worry about the whole business.

One thought occurred to him that was quite attractive on the face of it. He considered that the others might not see it that way, but then his head came up with a very good reason why they would.

'Perhaps,' he began, keeping his voice down for Wat and Cwen's ears only, 'when this meeting takes place, I should hang back and keep out of sight.'

'Oh yes.' Cwen sounded as if she'd been expecting this idea for some time now. 'And why would that be?'

'Well. For one thing I am a monk.'

'That you are.'

'And despite the fact that you tell me I am to play the part of a monk of dubious virtue, would it not be easier if there was no monk at the meeting at all? That way no explanation is required.'

'Go on,' Cwen said.

Hermitage was disappointed that she hadn't leapt at the idea with only one reason to go on. Wat hadn't even said a word but was looking at the clouds for some reason.

'Secondly, it is possible that I will be recognised. This church official, whoever they are, may have had some dealings with De'Ath's Dingle, or any other of my monasteries, or abbots, come to that. He may simply know my face. That could make things unnecessarily awkward.'

'Hm.' Cwen was sounding a little more convinced.

'Thirdly, if this official does know the King's Investigator, it really would be best to keep my face out of the way. Yes, we can offer an explanation, but it would surely be safer not to have to?'

'Anything else?'

The 1066 From Normandy

Hermitage thought that a "thirdly" ought to be enough for anyone, really. But then he came up with a fourthly. 'I could stand ready to come to the rescue.'

'Come to the rescue?' Cwen sounded quite aghast at Hermitage's fourthly.

'Absolutely. If the meeting descends into trouble I can come forward.'

'To the rescue?'

'That's right.'

'I never had you down as the coming-to-the-rescue type.'

Hermitage had to admit that he hadn't either, until just now.

'If there's a big fight,' Wat said. 'You know, the Castigatori are there and decide that destruction is the better part of valour. You're going to come to the rescue?'

Hermitage considered this one. 'I could fetch help,' he offered.

'Run to fetch help?' Cwen checked.

'Of course.'

'I suspect your motives, Brother Hermitage,' Wat said very seriously.

Hermitage held his breath.

'But it's not a bad idea.'

He let it go again.

'A monk might well confuse the situation,' Wat mused.

'Hermitage certainly could,' Cwen said.

'All right,' Wat agreed. 'When we get within sight of the meeting, you take to the woods and get close enough that you can keep an eye on us. You never know, you might recognise the churchman, that could give us a useful advantage. You'll just have to give us a secret signal.'

From simply hanging back and not getting involved in the meeting, Hermitage was now expected to sneak

Into the Bushes

through woods and give secret signals. That wasn't what he'd had in mind at all. His plan had required sitting in the woods until they came back and explained everything. He wasn't even sure he could give a secret signal.

'Ho, Burley,' Wat called, before Hermitage could explore the signalling options.

'What?' Burley turned back to them, sounding quite gruff and cross for some reason. Perhaps proximity to Chesterfield was making him nervous.

'We think Brother Hermitage here would be best out of the actual meeting. You know, a monk and a churchman, might cause problems. And he can wait and see if we have any trouble.'

'Him?' Burley gave Hermitage a very disparaging look. 'He doesn't look the coming-to-the-rescue type.'

Cwen managed to restrain her comment to a light cough.

'Still,' Burley shrugged. 'Please yourself. He's not really needed so probably best left out of it.'

Hermitage felt quite disappointed that his plan was now described as "being left out of it". That didn't sound very helpful at all.

'Do you still want us in it?' Cwen asked. 'After all, the church is probably only expecting you.'

'Yes, I do,' Burley insisted. 'Aluric's now dead and Durwin's gone. I've only got the widow left, and if there is some suspicion about the church I'd like as many people at my side as possible.'

'But not a monk,' Hermitage put in.

Burley frowned at him. 'I said people.'

They walked on farther, making the day older with every step, until Hermitage started to wonder if they'd come the right way.

The 1066 From Normandy

'We seem to have been walking for hours now. Is this Chesterfield place nearby?'

'Must be,' Burley said.

'What do you mean, must be?' Cwen asked. 'Have you never been there?'

'Of course not. Why would I?'

'Silly me. There was I thinking that you knew where you were going.'

'I do know where I'm going; Chesterfield.'

'But you're not actually sure where it is or what it looks like, or even if we're on the right road.'

'I know near enough.'

'Near enough, that's fine then.' Cwen was starting to growl a bit, which was never a good sign.

'It's up the old Roman road. Used to be a fort, so it's bound to be along here somewhere.

Most places used to be forts, Hermitage thought. How would they know if they'd got to the right one? After all, you didn't have a sign outside each town displaying its name for travellers. That would be completely ridiculous. He even started to smile at the idea of someone going to the trouble of writing the names down and then sticking them on posts on the side of the road.

Mile markers were quite sufficient. The Romans had put them in, and they were all you needed to know how many miles you'd gone. Gone towards where, would be a complete luxury. They told you how many miles it was back to where the road began, who could need more accurate information than that?

And he realised he hadn't even been counting the mile posts. Nor did he know where this road began, so that wasn't much help either.

Coming upon the crest of a very modest rise in the road,

Into the Bushes

the party drew to a halt and looked forward. There was no sign of anything. Perhaps the church wanted to have the meeting in a bush?

'We've gone wrong,' Cwen said.

Everyone drew to a halt. Even Lady Aluric, who had walked ahead of everyone all this time, wandered slowly back. She did look tired, Hermitage thought. This had been a long journey and her day had obviously been worse than most.

'How can we have gone wrong?' Burley retorted. 'This is a Roman road; they don't go wrong.'

'Then we're on the wrong one.'

'We are not on the wrong one,' Burley mocked the idea. 'We'd have to be on the other side of the country to be on the wrong one. How many roads do you think there are?'

'I don't know, do I?' Cwen snapped.

'Ah, well,' Burley now sounded quite interested in his topic. 'In this particular part of the country there are three main thoroughfares.'

'Really?' Cwen didn't sound at all interested.

'Oh yes. To the west of here you'd find the route that heads north-west into the hills. Rumour says that it goes all the way to Mancunium, if you can believe that.'

It was now quite clear that Cwen didn't want to hear any more about roads, let alone believe it.

'But if we were on that road, we'd be heading north-west, and of course, we're not.' He nodded towards the position of the sun as it lowered in the west, which showed that they were, indeed, heading north.

'And then of course, you've got the great artery of Ermine Street, going to Lincoln. But that sets off from London and goes far to the east of here. At least twenty miles away, I'd say.'

The 1066 From Normandy

'All right.'

'The fascinating thing about Ermine Street is that's not its name.'

'Oh God,' Cwen sighed.

'No indeed. It's called Ermine Street after the Earningas tribe who lived on its path. No one recalls the Roman name at all.' Burley looked as if this amazing fact should be amazing everyone. It wasn't.

'Probably *via* something,' Hermitage said.

'Don't you start,' Cwen warned him.

'Really?' Burley was intrigued

'Oh yes.' Hermitage had started so he had to finish. 'The Via Appia, for instance. I have no idea where it is, but I have seen manuscripts with reference to it. A road that went from Rome to Appia. Via is simply the Latin word for road. Perhaps we could speculate that the Romans named their roads for the destination.'

'Perhaps we couldn't?' Cwen pleaded.

'In which case, Ermine Street could have been via Lindum, the Roman name for Lincoln? It couldn't be via Londinium of course, because then all the roads would have the same name, going to London as they do.'

'It could indeed,' Burley agreed with an excited nod. 'In which case...'

'SHUT UP,' Cwen shouted.

They all all looked at her with some surprise.

'Will you stop going on about roads and what they're called and where they go? I have never heard anything so boring and pointless in my entire life.'

'Hardly pointless,' Burley began, but he stopped in the face of Cwen's pointing finger, which quickly transformed into a fist.

Even Wat was looking at her in shock at the reaction.

152

Into the Bushes

'They're just annoying me, all right?'

'Lots of things annoy you,' he pointed out.

'Well, I've just discovered that men going on and on about roads is a whole new basket of annoying.'

The habitually blank expression on Lady Aluric's face even said that she agreed with this sentiment.

The men just exchanged looks that said they didn't understand this, and probably never would.

After a short, but very awkward silence, Burley spoke up. Cwen glared at him to make sure it wasn't going to be anything about roads.

'Look, there's a hovel down there.' He pointed down the hill to where a thin wisp of smoke was rising from the roof of a very modest house.

From the state of the place, Hermitage judged that the smoke might be the only thing holding it up

'We can check with them that we're on the right road, erm, path, that is, to erm, Chesterfield.'

Cwen was not looking much happier, but they did make some progress down the hill towards the smoking hovel.

As they drew near, they saw that there was another hovel set close behind the first one. Probably, the children of the first family had left home to make their own way in the world and had made it in their parents' back garden.

Whatever the origin, it was clear that the offspring had taken everything their forebears knew about the construction of hovels and ignored it.

The first place was a disreputable, disgusting and decrepit pile of rotting wattle and failing daub. The grass of the roof looked as it if had grown in a poisonous swamp, and even the holes that constituted doors and windows looked like they'd been taken from something that wasn't supposed to have holes in it.

The 1066 From Normandy

And the second hovel wasn't as good as that. If the decaying and aged trees of the forest had fallen at random, they'd have been ashamed of landing like this. It even looked as if the place had been burned down at least once, and then simply propped back up again.

None of the visitors wanted to even approach this construction for fear that the crack of a twig under their feet would cause the whole place to simply crumble. Not that there was much sign of conscious construction anyway.

Wat risked a light cough to alert anyone mad enough to be inside one of these appalling places that they had visitors.

Hermitage could imagine that the only people coming here would be carpenters. They would bring complaining apprentices who resisted their master's exhortations to accuracy by asking "what's the worst that could happen?" Well, this was the worst that could happen, so they'd better pay attention.

Much to their surprise a figure appeared at the doorway and he looked quite normal. He was obviously a peasant of the land, but he showed no signs of bruising or cuts from when bits of his hovel fell on him.

'Ar?' the man asked. He didn't seem put out by strangers appearing at his door. Not even by Lady Aluric in her fine garb.

'Chesterfield,' Burley said loudly and plainly. 'Are we on the right road for Chesterfield?'

'Ar.'

'There you are,' Burley smiled at Cwen in a rather superior manner.

'How much farther?' Burley enunciated.

'Ar?'

Into the Bushes

'How much farther is it to the centre of Chesterfield?'

The man looked at Burley and then looked back at his hovel. Next he took a step forward and peered around the corner of his own dwelling to the disreputable place that loitered in its shadows.

'Well?' Burley asked.

The man looked thoughtful. 'To the centre?' he asked.

'That's right.'

The man now considered the ground before him and nodded over to the right. 'Be about four feet that way, I reckon. Why do you want the centre?'

Caput XV

Chesterfield City Centre

'This is Chesterfield?' Burley clearly didn't believe it.

'Ar,' the man replied in his customary manner.

'Where's the fort?'

'Over yonder.' The man nodded in the direction of yonder.

Hermitage followed the nod and could see no sign of any Roman construction. Or any sign of civilization at all, come to that. Mind you, there was very little sign of civilization right where he was standing.

'This is the place for the grand meeting with the church?' Wat asked.

'It's discreet,' Burley offered.

'It's disgusting.'

The peasant didn't seem put out by this description of his home.

'Do you have any senior members of the church in residence?' Wat asked.

'What?'

'Any churchmen hereabouts?'

'Oh,' the man understood the question. 'Ar.'

'You do?' Now it was Wat's turn for disbelief.

'Him over yonder.'

'Is that the same yonder as the fort, or a different one.'

'Says he's come for a meeting,' the man reported. 'And of course, we offered to provide him accommodation. As is only right and proper.'

'Same can't be said for the accommodation,' Wat

Chesterfield City Centre

muttered. 'That was very good of you,' he said out loud.

'But he took a look and then decided he'd make camp in the fort.'

'Can't say I blame him. At least that's only a thousand years old and probably has no roof; be much more comfortable.'

'Didn't stop him coming and asking for our food though, did it?' The man was clearly unhappy about that arrangement.

Hermitage could understand. These people obviously had very little, and while a member of church could expect the locals to feed him, it would be a great burden in this case.

The old peasant cackled unpleasantly. 'But one bowl of Marda's stew and he was off back to the fort at a quick run.'

'Was he?' Wat was looking as if it was past time to move on.

'Marda's stew does that to you if you're not ready for it.'

'Lovely. Well, we must be getting on. We'll leave you to whatever it is that you do.'

The peasant shrugged that he really didn't care what they did.

'Do you know who this church fellow is?' Burley asked. He clearly wanted to have as much information as possible in advance of their meeting.

The peasant's replying look said that he didn't really move in ecclesiastical circles. As Chesterfield didn't even have a church at all, it did seem a rather hopeful enquiry.

'Did he have a name, at least?'

'Ar.'

'Well, what was it?'

'Parbold.'

The 1066 From Normandy

'Parbold?'

'That's what he said his name was. And he should know.'

Burley ignored the unhelpful and increasingly impudent peasant and looked to the others for any recognition.

Hermitage gave the name some careful thought, but it wasn't one he'd come across before, so he shook his head.

'After all,' the peasant went on. 'If I wanted to know a man's name, he'd be the one I'd ask.'

'Yes, thank you.' Burley tried to draw the conversation to a halt.

'I've even got one myself, if anyone wanted to know it.'

'No, thank you,' Burley said, and he took the first steps in the direction of yonder and the fort.

As they left, Hermitage gave the peasant an apologetic nod. He got a shrug in return that this was no better than the man had expected.

'Of course, Parbold may not be his real name,' Burley speculated as they crossed onto a small track that hopefully led towards the fort. 'This business is pretty confidential, so people will be reluctant to let the world know names and details.'

Hermitage was quite looking forward to getting some details, they might help him understand how any of this was supposed to actually work. He thought that he'd followed the main principles, dishonest and deceitful though they were, but how was it to be done? Would bags of money actually be handed back and forth? Would there be ingots of lead; or even one ingot perhaps.

'Right, Hermitage,' Wat said as they got into thicker woodland once more. 'Time for you to disappear into the trees.'

'I don't think I want to go again.'

158

Chesterfield City Centre

'Not that, you idiot. The hiding and the watching and the secret signals?' Wat sounded quite exasperated.

'Oh, right, yes.'

'You keep us in sight but stay hidden.'

Hermitage nodded, with little idea of how he was supposed to do that.

'Stand behind a tree and peep around it,' Wat gave explicit instruction.

'Tree. Peep. Right.'

And if you recognise this Parbold character you give us a signal.

Hermitage still had no idea what signal he could give, apart from calling out; which would doubtless meet the signal requirement but would be a bit light on secret.

'Make a bird noise,' Cwen suggested, recognising his dilemma.

'Tweet?' Hermitage suggested.

'Birds don't really go tweet, you know.' She released a soft but tuneful whistle, very reminiscent of a blackbird.

'Oh I say, that's very good.'

'Can you do it?'

'No. I've never been able to whistle. It is a bit frivolous.'

'Frivolous.' Wat now had his head in his hands. 'Just crack a twig, then.'

'Crack a twig?'

'The little bits of tree on the floor? Can you manage that?'

Hermitage nodded that he could.

'Do it loudly. It could be a deer in the wood or something. You'll have to be pretty close, though.'

Hermitage worried again about that deer that had been cracking twigs back where Aluric had been killed. Perhaps he should mention it now, before the meeting began.

159

The 1066 From Normandy

'Are we sure this a good idea?' Burley asked, giving Hermitage a very worried look that their fate could be in the hands of him and his twig.

The moment to mention the deer had passed.

'It'll be fine,' Cwen assured him.

'At least it sounds like there's only one of them,' Burley went on. 'That peasant didn't mention a gathering of church folk. We can handle one if it comes to it.'

A few more paces revealed the first indications of Roman presence. A large, cream coloured stone, completely out of place in its surroundings, jutted from the path. It had obviously been shaped by human hand, but what it was doing just here was a bit of a mystery.

'Probably too heavy to steal,' Cwen noted.

Hermitage now stepped off the path and nodded to them as he moved carefully between the trees to run a parallel path to their own.

Wat and Cwen, Burley and Lady Aluric took two more small corners on the path before the full majesty of the Roman fort was revealed.

And the full majesty was pretty empty of everything, including majesty. A few more of the stones were littered about the place, with weeds growing up and around them. Small trees had grown in what was obviously once a clear space and the outlines of walls, emerging from the ground could be seen here and there.

Hermitage could see all this from his hiding spot which he wasn't sure was quite hidden enough. He considered the site with interest. There was frequent debate between learned folk, about why Roman remains across the country seemed to be largely buried.

The leading theory was that Romans were very small, not much bigger than a badger, and so had to build

Chesterfield City Centre

underground for protection.

Hermitage had some doubts about this, as the statues of Romans that existed showed people of a perfectly normal size; if not slightly larger.

The learned folk replied that if you were only as big as a badger, you'd make your statues pretty huge, wouldn't you?

Hermitage still wasn't convinced, but he didn't have an alternative theory.

The man who appeared among these ruins to greet the arrivals was of a normal size and Hermitage was relieved that he was a stranger. He dropped the twig he'd been carrying, already convinced that it was too small to make a recognisable crack anyway.

At the back of the space, one part of the old Roman wall did rise to some height, and against this Parbold, for this must be he, had pitched his simple tent.

Hermitage chanced a step or two closer so that he could hear the conversation. With a flash of inspiration, he lay down on the ground and crawled forward amongst the leaves. He reasoned that a monk standing on the edge of the woods might be noticeable.

He had a clear view and could see that Parbold was a young fellow, not at all what he'd expected. He wasn't sure what he had expected, but a hideous plan of the sort Burley was executing would surely require some more senior involvement.

If this wasn't the main conspirator, but was some simple messenger, they wouldn't have much of value to report to the king.

Parbold was wearing simple, black clerical garb, and his head was properly shorn into a neat tonsure. Hermitage ran a hand over his own rough cut and felt quite ashamed

The 1066 From Normandy

at how he had let things go. This young man must have fewer summers than Hermitage himself and so was probably only an acolyte of some sort. He carried an intelligent look about him, so might even be a lector, but that was about the best that could be assumed.

'Parbold?' Burley asked.

'Yes.' Parbold said this as if he was bored by being asked his name all the time. Which seemed odd as he must have been camped out here on his own for at least two days.

'I am Burley.'

'It's about time.'

'Yes, sorry about that. There was a bit of a delay.'

'I'll say. I joined the church to serve God, you know.'

'Erm.' Burley sounded confused. 'Good?'

'It is good, or it should be. I did not expect to be loitering in the middle of nowhere, sent on errands I don't understand by people who won't explain anything.'

Parbold did not sound like an enthusiast for the plan, mainly because he didn't actually know what it was. He didn't sound cross or angry about it, he just sounded very, very disappointed. And from his tone one might judge that this was only the latest in the very long line of disappointments that constituted his life to date.

Hermitage worried that they weren't going to be able to find much out for the king if the man from the church didn't know what was going on.

'And who are these people?' Parbold asked. It was obviously bad enough that he had to engage with one person, no one had told him there would be more.

'This is a lady,' Burley nodded towards Lady Hendor.

'You don't say.'

'And these two are weavers, who may be interested in taking part in the scheme.'

Chesterfield City Centre

'Weavers?' Parbold sounded as if the greatest sadness in his life was that he would one day have to meet some weavers; and now he had. Wasn't it awful?

'You say you don't understand your errand and have had no explanation?' Burley did his own disappointment and added some genuine concern.

'Oh, I have instruction. There are questions and answers, but that's all I've been told.'

'What questions and answers?'

'That's for us to discover,' Parbold sighed. 'Apparently.' It was clear that the young man thought he was capable of so much more than this and was dissatisfied with his instructions.

Hermitage drew the conclusion that Parbold spent a lot of his time dissatisfied; probably in between the disappointments.

Burley cast a glance around the others, clearly frustrated that this was a lot less than he had hoped for from the meeting.

'Are we to proceed then?'

'Proceed with what?' Parbold asked. 'That's one of my questions, you see?'

'You mean you don't know?'

'I know something. Obviously not everything, as a simple fellow like me can't be trusted with anything too complicated, can he?' That didn't sound like one of his official questions, more like a heartfelt complaint. 'I ask, and you tell, that way I know that I'm talking to the right person.'

'This is ridiculous,' Burley complained.

'We can agree on that then.' Parbold looked around and found a piece of Roman stone to sit on. He did so as if his life had been one long standing-up until now.

163

The 1066 From Normandy

'The business of the lead.' Burley spelled the words out plainly.

'Right answer.' Parbold even sounded saddened at this, as if the wrong answer would have meant he could go home again. 'And do you have something for me?'

Burley reached into his purse and took out the piece of rock. He stepped over and handed it to Parbold as if gifting the finest jewel.

'What's this?' Parbold looked rather disgusted.

'It is lead.'

'It's a piece of rock.'

'It's got lead in it.'

Parbold examined it closely. 'I can't see any.'

'You have to boil it to get the lead,' Wat spoke up as if he'd got bored with being left out.

'I have to what?'

'Not you personally. The rock has to be boiled to get the lead. Well, there's a bit more to it than that, but that's the principle.'

Parbold considered the rock and unceremoniously dropped it on the floor.

'Oy,' Burley complained.

'You've given me some lead, or so you say. I was told that was supposed to happen.'

Burley nodded slowly that it was all going well so far.

'And next?' Parbold asked.

'Ah, yes.' Burley went back to his purse, delved about in it, and brought out a large gold coin.

A deeper silence fell across the old Roman fort at the sight of such riches in the hand of one man.

'How many of those things have you got?' Cwen breathed.

Wat said nothing but wiped a bit of spittle from the

Chesterfield City Centre

corner of his mouth.

Lady Aluric scowled deeply at the passage of what was probably her pound.

Burley handed the gold over to Parbold, while Wat twitched slightly in the background.

'Thank you for your donation,' Parbold recited his lesson. 'Or, at least I think those are the words.'

'They are. And now?' Burley looked very expectantly at the coin.

'Oh, yes.' Parbold's boredom with this menial process showed no sign of abating.

Now, he took a small knife from his belt and placed the coin on the top of the rock.

Wat averted his eyes as if he couldn't bear to watch.

Parbold had to stand up and dig the point of the knife into the coin and then rock it back and forth to achieve his goal. He even seemed to think that there was a much better way of doing this, but he was only following the instructions of his superiors; who weren't actually very superior. After some considerable effort he cut into the soft metal until a section of it was separated. He handed the remainder back to Burley.

With a broad grin spreading across his face, Burley considered the metal in his hand. 'What's this?' he asked as his smile slumped into a frown.

'Er, that's payment for the lead.'

'Three quarters?' He held the coin up so that everyone could see that a neat quarter was missing.

'Oho,' Wat said in a very knowing way.

Parbold appeared to be considering this carefully. He looked at the small piece he'd cut off, which lay in his own hand, and then looked at the portion Burley was now holding up Eventually, he nodded. 'Yes, that's right. Three

165

The 1066 From Normandy

quarters.'

'I think the church just put their price up,' Wat said.

'You're only supposed to take ten pence worth.'

'Ah, they said you'd say that as well.'

'And?'

'That a quarter is right, take it or leave it.' Parbold showed complete disinterest in his words and could even be heard muttering under his breath; something about traders in the temple, but they couldn't catch it all.

Burley had no words but was obviously building a collection of quite rude ones to release at the right moment.

Hermitage was so engrossed in this development that only when the others had turned to look back at the wood, did he realise that there had been a pretty loud crack of a twig; more like a branch really.

'Probably a deer,' Wat said loudly.

Hermitage turned his head around from his hiding place to see if he could spot the animal. He quickly realised that Wat had concluded that this was the secret signal.

As he caught a glimpse of something between the trees, he saw that the conclusion was wrong on all fronts. He even wondered if that deer near Aluric's resting place had really been a deer at all.

He had to get out of here and warn the others, but felt that if he moved, he could be the first to go.

Caput XVI

Legs

The scene in front of Hermitage's eyes had become a tableau. Parbold was still sitting on his rock, looking intensely bored, if not slightly insulted by the whole carry-on. The others were gathered around Burley who simply stared at the coin in his hand, while the rest of his face struggled with which reaction to show first. Anger seemed to be winning at the moment, but it was clearly being tempered by greed.

This gave Hermitage a few moments to consider what he should do about the feet. Well, the legs, to be more precise. There were legs in the woods. And they wore finer leggings than was normal for a deer. He couldn't see much more, but just assumed that below the legs were feet and above them was a body. It was hardly likely that someone would leave a pair of legs just standing in the woods.

One of the legs moved at that point, which Hermitage took as clear proof that someone was in charge of them.

And the someone showed no signs of wanting to intervene in the business going on in the fort. They were content to stand and watch. He wondered if it might be the peasant, come to see what all the fuss was about, but the leggings were too fine for that.

Of course, this could be some total stranger who just happened to be passing through the woods when he came across a churchman up to something in an old fort. The scene might be good enough for a tale and a mug of ale in the tavern later. Of course, it would help his tale if one of

The 1066 From Normandy

the protagonists turned into a rabbit, or just vanished, but anything remotely interesting would do.

This was too much of a coincidence though. Durwin had been stabbed in the back and left in the water box. Lord Aluric had been stabbed in the back while he was making water. And now there was a figure in the woods watching them. This had to be the killer, just waiting for his next back.

And Hermitage's was just lying there in the leaves.

The legs were only thirty or forty feet away and so he dare not move. He concluded that they must have arrived quite recently, as he certainly hadn't seen anyone around when he'd crept amongst the trees; not that he'd been looking very hard.

He also assumed that the legs had not seen him. A disinterested observer, having spotted a monk lying in the woods, would likely just walk slowly away, politely pretending that he hadn't seen anything at all.

A backstabbing killer, spotting a monk lying in the woods, would likely come over and do some more backstabbing.

And now he was stuck. He couldn't move and raise the alarm with the others for fear of being spotted; and stabbed. But then neither could he lie here interminably.

This was just the situation in which he was supposed to crack a twig. Now even that was out of the question. The legs in the wood would hear the signal and probably act upon it.

Wat's voice snapped the freeze of his dilemma.

'Perhaps we need to discuss this on our own for a few moments?' he suggested to Burley.

Parbold seemed as disinterested in this suggestion as he was about the whole business.

168

Legs

Burley appeared to swallow whatever reaction he had come up with and just nodded at Wat.

Wat gave Cwen a knowing look and nodded his head towards the wood, where they probably expected Hermitage to be waiting, ready to explain his warning twig.

Hermitage now grimaced at the problem. He thought it unlikely that one killer pair of legs would be willing to take on all five of them, but you never knew. He had heard the tales of lone knights defeating hundreds of enemies with one savage blow. But then these enemies had been stabbed in the back, one of them while relieving himself in the woods. That was hardly the behaviour of a mighty knight capable of savage blows.

With any luck, the arrival of the others would scare the killer away. Hermitage could then get up and explain the situation. They might even chase after the killer and hunt him down. Well, Wat and Burley and Cwen might; most likely just Cwen.

Before they could leave Parbold behind, Lady Aluric went over to Cwen and whispered something in her ear. Cwen took a step back after she had heard the words and looked the lady up and down as if unable to believe what she'd been told.

'Again?' Cwen asked. 'You've only just been.'

Lady Aluric did not look happy to have details of her personal habits strewn about the woodland like this.

Wat and Burley had stopped and were looking at the two women.

'What do you want me to do about it?' Cwen asked.

Lady Aluric whispered once more, although this time her face showed a lot more irritation with Cwen.

'Really?' Cwen asked, sounding quite disgusted.

The 1066 From Normandy

'Not exactly *with me*, you stupid girl. But look what happened last time. I'm not going into the woods on my own.'

Cwen appeared to understand the request now, although she still wasn't happy about it. 'Look what happened to the other person who went in the woods with you last time, you mean.'

The men got the idea of what was happening now and turned away to resume a slow stroll towards the cover of the trees.

'We'll catch you up,' Cwen called after them, sounding rather annoyed but resigned to her task.

Pointedly walking away from the men, Lady Aluric and Cwen headed off into the bushes.

Hermitage was slightly worried to note Wat and Burley were heading in the direction of the mysterious legs. Obviously, that's where they thought Hermitage was, having heard the crack of the twig.

He turned his head towards the spot that the legs had been and saw that they were gone. Well, that was good. Or was it? Now that he couldn't see them, he worried that they might be sneaking up on him.

He risked raising himself up onto his elbows and turning to scan his surroundings. No legs. He hadn't even heard the sound of their departure. Mind you, Wat and the others had been making enough noise to cover any escape.

Now Hermitage rose to his knees and then stood, reasonably confident that there was no knife waiting for him. Happy to be still alive and standing, he skipped over to intercept Wat and Burley.

When he came within sight of them, he could hear Burley complaining about his lot and the unfairness of the church.

'A quarter,' he was saying. 'They want a quarter. I might as well pay the king his tax. All this trouble, all these arrangements and they go and put the price up. Who do they think they are?'

'I think they know who they are,' Wat replied. 'That's the problem. They're the church; the only one there is. It's not as if you've got a choice about which church buys your lead from you. They've also got a pretty desperate customer.'

'I am not desperate.'

'Yes, you are. You arranged the meeting; you've sorted out the lead and you've brought a whole pound's worth of gold with you. You look pretty desperate to me.'

'I shall walk away,' Burley dismissed the whole scheme now.

'I'm not sure you'll even have that choice.'

'What?'

'Well, the church knows that you've got lots of money now. They like lots of money, does the church. And I think they'd like some of yours.'

'Well, they shan't have it.'

'Not even if they suggest telling the king that you've been trying to evade his tax?'

'They wouldn't,' Burley only sounded half convinced about this.

'Of course they would. And the king will probably reward them for their honesty and integrity. Most likely by giving half of what was yours to them. While he keeps the other half, of course. You not needing it anymore.' Wat made a helpful slicing gesture across his own throat.

'I'd tell him that they were in on the whole thing.'

'The church?' Wat sounded truly shocked. 'God's own

The 1066 From Normandy

church involved in something so reprehensible? It's unthinkable.'

'Of course it isn't.'

'It is to William. Despite the outward display of having come from one of the more violent places in hell, he loves the church. Probably because he needs to keep the Pope sweet, but it makes no difference. Who shall I believe? He'll say. My own beloved church or this wool merchant who's trying to steal from me?'

Burley appeared to have taken the message.

'Here,' Hermitage called as quietly as he could.

Wat looked up and raised a hand around waist height, glancing back to make sure that Parbold wasn't watching.

Parbold had lowered himself to the floor and now sat with his back against the stone. It looked as if he was ready for a little sleep, this whole affair was so boring.

'Hermitage, why the signal? Do you know Parbold?'

'It wasn't me.'

'What wasn't you?'

'The signal. I didn't make the signal.'

'Oh, right.' Wat looked a bit confused but was prepared to accept that this had been a false alarm.

'There were legs.'

'I see,' Wat said very slowly. 'You haven't been eating any mushrooms, have you? The funny ones with long stalks?'

'Of course not. There were real legs. It was them that cracked the twig. Someone was watching you.'

Wat considered the woods with a serious look. 'You didn't see who?'

'Only the legs. I was lying on the ground, keeping out of sight.'

'And the legs didn't see you.'

172

Legs

'No. And when you started to come up here, they left.'

'Could have been anyone.' Burley dismissed the problem.

'Really?' Wat did not believe this. 'Just a stranger in the woods happens to be standing by while you do your tax evasion with the church?'

'It could be the killer,' Hermitage said.

'It could indeed,' Wat agreed.

That didn't make Hermitage feel any better at all. He'd rather been hoping that Wat would say something like "no, of course it wasn't."

'Or it could be that peasant,' Burley suggested. 'Poking his nose around trying to find out what's going on.'

Hermitage shook his head. 'The leggings on these legs were too good for a peasant.'

'What sort were they?' Wat asked.

'The normal,' Hermitage said. 'Average length, a knee on each one.'

'Not the legs, the leggings, Hermitage, for goodness sake.'

'Oh, yes, Well, erm, I'm not really an expert on leggings.'

'Like mine or Burleys?'

Hermitage looked at their legs. 'Hm, not really.' The leggings before him were very fine. Dark red in Wat's case and dark brown for Burley. They were made of a thick woven material and were tight fitting, emerging from their tunics, to drop all the way down to cover the tops of their shoes.

'How different, then?'

Hermitage cast his mind back. He hadn't expected to comment on legging style. The main worry was the legs that were inside them, surely.

'I think they were leather.'

'Leather?' Wat sounded puzzled at that.

The 1066 From Normandy

'Well, no. Now I come to think of it.'

'Not leather then'

'Yes.'

'Hermitage, you're confusing me. And yourself, I think.'

'I mean they had leather on them. Sort of around them.'

'Binding? They had leather binding.'

'That's it. Sort of.'

Wat looked thoughtful. 'Sounds like a practical sort of fellow. Ready for action.'

'Like killing people,' Hermitage suggested.

'Could be.'

No one had anything more helpful to offer at the prospect of a killer in nice, functional leggings stalking them through the woods.

'What's the problem?'

The men all jumped in surprise at the unannounced arrival of Cwen.

'Don't sneak up on people like that,' Wat said.

'Who's sneaking? What's going on?'

Lady Aluric stopped some distance from them, clearly not interested in engaging with anyone about anything.

'Hermitage saw some legs in the woods.'

'Not mine, I hope.' Cwen sounded quite offended. 'What have you been looking at, Hermitage?'

'Of course not yours. There were legs in the woods while we were down there talking to Parbold.'

'How many?'

'Pardon?'

'How many legs?'

'Well, two. The normal number carried about by one person.'

'You didn't say. There could have been dozens of them.'

'Well there were two. Two legs, one stalker.'

Legs

'Or two one-legged stalkers standing close together?'

'And now they're gone,' Hermitage explained, hoping to keep the conversation on track.

'But they were practical legs. Leather-bound leggings,' Wat said.

Cwen nodded at that information. 'The sort a killer might wear.'

'Exactly.'

'We're back to the question of why anyone would want to kill any of us.'

'I think we need to get some information out of Lady Aluric.' Wat looked in the lady's direction.

'Oh, Wat, you can't,' Hermitage pleaded. 'The poor woman has just lost her husband. Only a few hours ago.'

'And she might lose the rest of her travelling companions if we don't find out what's going on.'

'She's already said that she doesn't know. Her husband dealt with all that sort of thing.'

'True, but he must have mentioned where all the money came from. And she should know who their enemies are, surely. I think Lord Aluric would have told her to watch out for so-and-so, because they want to kill me.'

Hermitage still thought it unreasonable to disturb the lady in the midst of her grief but could see that for the avoidance of being stabbed in the back, it might be unavoidable.

'Lady Hendor?' Wat called.

The lady turned and looked as if she expected someone like Wat to ask for permission before using her name. And it wasn't even her name. She didn't reply, but simply raised an eyebrow. It must have required quite an effort to lift that much weight of disdain.

Wat took a step over to her, the others trying to look

The 1066 From Normandy

nonchalant at his side. 'Your husband's fortune?'

Now the other eyebrow rose up to join the first.

'It could be the reason we're all being stabbed in the back.' Wat was blunt and to the point.

'And the reason you can't go into the bushes on your own anymore,' Cwen added.

'We're being followed,' Wat said quite fiercely. 'Someone in the woods has been watching us, and it could well be the man with the knife. If we know why he's there, we might be able to stop him having another back to play with.'

The lady showed no reaction.

'Now,' Wat went on. 'It may be that this is simply a robber who found that Durwin had a pound on him and thinks there are greater riches to be had from the rest of us. However, your husband was killed, and nothing was taken. That means someone wanted to kill him personally. Why would they do that?'

She did give a mild shrug at this, either indicating that she didn't know, or that there could be a whole host of reasons.

'Did he have any enemies?' Cwen asked.

'Apart from the ones he left behind at Hastings,' Wat said.

Now Lady Aluric looked mightily offended and glared at Burley. Burley took the glare and bounced it on to Wat.

'We're being murdered, Lady Hendor,' Wat was insistent. 'Or should I say, Lady Aluric? Everyone thinks your husband died at Hastings, but we know he survived to become a rich man before being stabbed in some woods earlier today. Who was after him?'

Lady Aluric now appeared to be struggling with her response. It seemed that her natural urge was to tell Wat

176

Legs

to mind his own business and learn not to speak to his betters until he was invited. Countering this, the natural desire to avoid being stabbed to death was persuading her to speak out. She turned her head away.

'He had enemies,' she confessed, still managing to sound annoyed that she was having to speak to people like this at all.

'I bet he did,' Wat agreed.

'He said that we had to be careful, and that it was urgent to move his fortune.'

'Hence the business with Burley.'

Lady Aluric looked at Burley as if it was the last business she would do with the man. After that, she wouldn't even speak to him.

'And our meeting with friend Parbold.' Wat tipped his head back towards the resting cleric. 'Who's the enemy? Who do we think is following us with a knife and some very ill intent? Someone who wants their fortune back? Or who would like a spot of revenge for what happened at Hastings? Perhaps it's even the real cousin Hendor, who hears that he's suddenly rich, but discovers that he's not quite himself anymore.'

'Parbold,' Cwen said.

'Hardly,' Wat replied. 'He doesn't seem to know much about what's going on. And he'd rather be in church praising God.' Wat sniffed as if that was a ridiculous waste of time when there was money to be traded.

'No,' Cwen said. 'I mean look at Parbold. Was he lying down like that a moment ago?'

They all looked over and saw that Parbold had slumped from his position of resting against the stone and was now lying at its side.

'Oh, Lord,' Hermitage whispered. 'Not another one?'

177

Caput XVII

The Uses of a Tangled Web

There could be no doubt that Parbold was another one. The poor young man was lying on the ground, a modest amount of the blood from his back staining it in a dark and ominous manner.

'Oh my, oh my,' Hermitage fretted. 'That's Durwin, a dishonest craftsman; Aluric, an apparently dishonest noble; and now Parbold, a dedicated churchman. Who could want to kill him?'

Lady Aluric gave a haughty sniff at the suggestion that her husband had been dishonest. He was a noble, anything he did was honest; by definition. If you were a noble and you could get away with it, it was fine.

Wat was squatting at Parbold's side and had laid a sad hand on the man's shoulder.

'He didn't even want to be involved in all this,' Hermitage went on, feeling some unfamiliar irritation with Burley and Lady Aluric for bringing all this upon them, and most particularly upon Parbold. 'He wanted to serve God, he told us so. Yet he was sent to deal with dishonesty, and death was his reward.' He even gave a little glare at the two main protagonists. It wasn't up to Cwen's standard, but there was real feeling behind it.

'Except,' Wat said quite slowly. 'In this case the murderer has made one major mistake.'

Hermitage turned his attention to Wat.

'He didn't do the murdering bit properly. Parbold is still alive.'

The Uses of a Tangled Web

'Oh, wonderful.' Hermitage felt true relief at this. It still didn't relieve Burley and Aluric of their guilt, but it was a small ray of light.

'Not that he's very well,' Wat added. 'It's a nasty wound but the knife must have hit the bone of his back, instead of going into anything soft.'

'Where the humors reside,' Hermitage commented.

'Exactly. That would have been the end of him. We all know what a knife in the humors can do. Lucky he was resting against the rock and his attacker didn't have much of a target.'

'We must dress the wound.' Hermitage wanted to act. 'Quick, remove his robe.'

Wat attempted to lift Parbold into a sitting position and got a distant moan of complaint in return.

'Is this really necessary?' Lady Aluric sounded quite offended at the prospect of young men of the church having their robes taken off in front of her.

'I don't think we'll be able to do it anyway,' Wat said. 'We'll only make him worse if we heave him about.' He reached to his belt and took a small knife that he usually used for cutting fruit or bread. He placed it at Parbold's neck and then ripped it down, slicing the robe open from shoulder to waist.

'I don't think he's going to be very happy about that,' Hermitage commented.

'Better to be unhappy and still alive, perhaps?'

Hermitage could see the reason in that.

With Parbold's back exposed, the wound was clear. It was a nasty one, quite broad and deep, but as Wat had said, it had not penetrated far enough to find death at its tip.

'Now.' Hermitage thought quickly. 'Cwen, could you look and see if you can find any honey.'

The 1066 From Normandy

'Honey?' Cwen half laughed. 'Where am I going to get honey from? I haven't seen a bees' nest, and if I had I'm not sticking my hand in one.'

'Of course, of course.' Hermitage accepted that this had been a bit of a ridiculous request, it was just that honey was the first remedy to reach for in the case of a wound. 'Ground shellfish?' He immediately saw that that was hardly going to be common in the Chesterfield area. 'Erm, clay? Betony! Yes, see if you find some betony leaves. We'll use material from his robe for binding and make a salve from the betony.'

Cwen shrugged that she probably could find some betony in the woods and so went off to look.

'See if you can find some spiders' webs as well.'

'Obviously,' Cwen snorted that she wasn't an idiot.

'Burley,' Wat instructed. 'Go with her.'

'Why?' Burley protested.

'Because with the killer still nearby, I'd rather he stabbed you in the back than Cwen.'

'Ah, thank you,' Cwen smiled.

'Oh dear, this is awful.' Hermitage didn't really know how to manage. It was all very well investigating murders and tracking the murderers but to have a murderer tracking the investigator seemed entirely unreasonable.

'It's not good,' Wat admitted. He nodded hard at Burley, who reluctantly set off with Cwen to look for the healing plants.

'I mean,' Hermitage went on. 'We're being murdered.'

'Other people so far,' Wat pointed out. 'Which is lucky. But yes, it looks like our man with the knife has us all in mind.'

'Oh dear, oh dear.'

'We just have to stop him before he finishes the whole

180

The Uses of a Tangled Web

job.'

Hermitage tried to get his thoughts in order. 'I can understand Durwin and Lord Aluric, they were in the thick of all this wrong-doing.'

Lady Aluric managed to stand silently, but did it in a slightly more haughty manner than normal; which was already quite haughty.

'If this killer is seeking revenge for something, or to recover what he thinks is rightfully his, he would kill Durwin and Aluric. But why Parbold?'

'All part of the plan?' Wat suggested. 'The plan to hide the Aluric fortune from the king and anyone else who might think they're entitled to some of it.' He looked up at Lady Aluric but shook his head in disappointment as she seemed to be not listening, or was thinking of something far more interesting.

'Parbold is here for a meeting about avoiding tax and cheating the king,' Wat pointed out. 'I doubt if the killer has a chat to see what his victims are up to before putting his knife to work.'

'But we don't have anything to do with it.'

Wat cast a warning glance from Hermitage to Lady Aluric. 'Not yet, we don't. And having seen how well things are going, I think I'll keep my gold and silver in its current hiding place.'

There was much debate in the workshop about where that hiding place was. As no one had found it yet, it must be a good one.

'And the killer in the woods doesn't know what we're up to. As far as he's concerned, we're probably all as bad as one another.'

'And if he killed a churchman,' Hermitage concluded, 'he'll have no trouble with a monk.'

181

The 1066 From Normandy

'At least we're all in it together.' Wat looked once again at Lady Aluric. 'And I don't think he'll stop at women, either.'

There was still no reaction from the lady.

'Where did the wealth come from?' he asked bluntly.

Lady Aluric looked puzzled; not that she might not know the answer to the question, but that Wat was asking.

'If we knew where it came from, we might know who was trying to get it back or take revenge for its departure in the first place. And if we know who it is, we might be able to talk to them. Talking to them being better than letting them stab us in the back, yes?'

The lady just shook her head slightly, as if Wat was trying to talk about the very latest thing in hawking, when he knew nothing about hawks.

'Maybe it's best if we just leave them to it,' Wat said to Hermitage. 'We patch Parbold up and take him to the nearest church. Burley and the lady here can obviously look after themselves and don't need any help from us.'

'You have had your meeting with the church,' Lady Aluric deigned to speak. 'Now we shall return. You may accompany me.'

'We're only going as far as Derby. After that, you're on your own.'

Before there could be any debate, Cwen returned with Burley and the leaves. She also had a fine ball of spiders' webs held gently in one hand.

'Ah, excellent,' Hermitage took them from her and knelt at Parbold's side. 'Can you get the betony into a salve somehow? Crush up the leaves and mix them with a little water, if there is any.'

Cwen held up her small leather drinking bottle to show that everything was in hand. 'I assume wine will do?'

182

The Uses of a Tangled Web

Hermitage nodded that it would do very well, much better than water, really, which everyone knew was full of disease and dangerous to drink. He would have to wait for later to ask Cwen why she was carrying a bottle of wine instead of a weak ale like normal people.

Hermitage didn't like to examine the wound too closely, but Wat seemed to insist on peering into it in horrible detail.

'While he's out of his senses we need to look and see if there's anything in the wound. Tip of the knife blade, something like that.'

Hermitage considered the spiders' webs while Wat carried out the examination.

'Looks pretty neat. Go on then.'

'Can you cut a bit of the robe off?' Hermitage asked. 'Enough to go right round his chest and hold the betony in place.'

Wat did so and handed the cloth to Hermitage. Using this to wipe away the blood so that he could see what he was doing, he placed the bundled spiders' webs in the middle of the cut and then spread them slightly so that they overlapped the broken skin.

He had known of the medicinal qualities of spiders' webs since he was a tiny boy with a cut knee. He seemed to recall that his grandmother had rubbed some into his wound and told him that it would all be better soon. She showed him the best place to gather the webs, but even then he knew that he stood little chance of standing firm in the face of an angry spider.

With the web in place, Cwen stepped forward and held out a hand full of thick green slime that had once been the betony leaves.

'Perfect.' Hermitage took this and slathered it on the

The 1066 From Normandy

injury, quickly putting the binding on top to press the leaves tight.

'That should ground out most of the evil humors.' Hermitage was quite satisfied with his work.

Either feeling the immediate benefit of his treatment, or fed up with being pushed and poked, Parbold released a groan of pain and moved slightly.

'Some wine.' Hermitage held out his hand for Cwen's bottle.

She handed it over and Hermitage tipped it up to Parbold's mouth.

Most of it dribbled straight back out again, but Parbold did cough once and slowly opened his eyes.

'Ah, master Parbold.' Hermitage welcomed him back to the land of the living. 'You have been stabbed.'

Parbold gave a weak nod that he was aware of this.

'But we have treated the wound with webs and betony. It is not deep, and you should recover, if you take care to have the binding refreshed.'

Parbold nodded once more and croaked out a 'thank you,' before closing his eyes again. This time it seemed to be so that he could gather some strength and he opened them again quite quickly.

'Did you see who did it?' Wat asked.

Parbold wetted his lips, and Hermitage offered him more wine, which he now drank down. He shook his head slightly. 'Behind me,' he half-whispered.

Hermitage assumed that the attacker would be behind him, having gone for the back and all.

Wat stood now from Parbold's side and looked around the ruins of the fort 'We must move from here.'

'I'm not sure Parbold is in any condition to move.' Hermitage worried that any movement would open the

184

The Uses of a Tangled Web

wound and cause more loss of the sanguine humor.

'Put it another way, we can't stay here. There is a killer prowling around out there somewhere, and it won't be many more hours before dark. I know we're in a fort, but there's not much left of it that's any good.'

'Will we get anywhere better?' Cwen asked. 'There's no point going to Chesterfield, is there?' She didn't need to say that the hovels of that place would be worse than camping in the open air.

'Where did you come from, Parbold?' Wat asked.

Parbold took a gentle breath. 'York.'

'Hm.'

'There's no way we're getting to York, or even back to Derby in one evening,' Cwen pointed out. 'Particularly not with a wounded whatever-he-is.'

'Lector.' Parbold had found his voice, although it was still weak and light.

'I thought that might be the case,' Hermitage nodded at his own conclusion.

'Well done you,' Cwen said. 'Very helpful.'

'He will read the lessons in church or in a monastery,' Hermitage explained.

'Lovely. He can read to us while we're being attacked by a killer, then. Oh dear, we haven't got a book, never mind.' She gave him a quite unnecessary look.

'Could we make it back to Crich?' Wat speculated, looking at the sky to see how many hours of daylight they had left.

'Doubt it,' Cwen replied. 'Not with a damaged lectern.'

'Lector,' Hermitage corrected.

'Yes, one of them.'

Wat sighed heavily, reluctantly concluding that Cwen was right. 'Now we have to defend a ruined Roman fort

The 1066 From Normandy

from some wandering killer all night. With no actual weapons of our own.'

'We could always send Burley and her ladyship out on their own,' Cwen said. 'Perhaps the killer would be happy with them?'

'You'll do no such thing,' Burley protested. Even Lady Aluric looked as if she was ready to say something. 'We just have to stick together, that's all. The others were on their own when they were, erm..,'

'Stabbed to death?' Wat offered.

Burley only nodded. 'If we stay together, we'll be safe until morning.'

'You hope. Unless our killer goes off to get some of his friends.'

'That would hardly seem likely. He's been picking us off one at a time. If there was a force, they'd have come by now.'

'Only one person who hates what you're up to enough to kill us all then? That's comforting.'

'We'd better get some wood for a fire before it gets dark,' Cwen said, taking a practical approach. 'Come on Burley.'

'Why me again?'

'Because I don't think the Aluric family dirty their hands with picking up wood. And because this whole situation is your fault.'

'My fault? I only had the idea. Without the Aluric fortune we wouldn't even have got this far.'

'And what a success it's been.' Cwen now shoved Burley back towards the woods.

Lady Aluric watched them go before brushing down her skirt and perching herself on one of the Roman stones.

'You came from York, you say?' Wat asked Parbold.

The young man nodded carefully, still wincing at the

The Uses of a Tangled Web

pain.

'Anyone in particular send you?'

'Ealdred,' Parbold croaked out.

Wat looked to Hermitage.

'The Archbishop?' Hermitage was surprised at that. Surely an Archbishop would have nothing to do with goings-on like these.

'But I'm not supposed to say,' Parbold managed to go on.

Hermitage frowned that if that was the case, why was he saying?

'But then I wasn't supposed to get stabbed in the back. I consider my obligations in this matter at an end.' The anger at his situation seemed to give Parbold some strength.

'Ealdred sent you himself?' Hermitage asked. 'I thought he was a hostage of King William?'

'One of his advisers said it was at his instruction.'

'If you were being held hostage, you might come up with a few ways to get your own back,' Wat suggested.

'But he obviously didn't give you all the details.'

Parbold shook his head and winced at the pain this caused. 'Only what you heard. Someone would give some lead and a coin, and I was to give three quarters of the coin back.'

'And then return to York?'

Another nod.

'So that someone more senior could actually put their head above the parapet,' Wat said.

Hermitage puzzled over the expression.

'The important people only peer over the castle wall when no one is actually shooting at it,' Wat explained. 'Once they knew that things were going well, they'd step in and take over. If it all went horribly wrong, they could deny all knowledge and blame Parbold here.'

'And it has all gone horribly wrong.'

'It certainly has.' Wat gave a rather horrible smile. 'I'd love to see the look on Ealdred's face when he hears about all the bodies.'

Hermitage could only give a weak smile.

'Always assuming any of us are still alive in the morning to tell him.'

Caput XVIII

No Smoke Without Smoke

Cwen and Burley returned with armfuls of fallen wood to make their fire. Hermitage was not surprised to note that Burley was doing most of the carrying while Cwen was issuing instructions.

'Not there,' she snapped when he dropped his burden at the old fort's outer perimeter. 'It's no good over there, is it? We'd have to go and get it whenever we needed to stock the fire. Perfect opportunity for the man with the knife to do what he does best. Bring it over here.' She walked off to the outside of Parbold's humble tent.

'What did your last servant die of?' Burley grumbled.

'Impudence,' Cwen informed him.

She surveyed the area and considered the tent. It wasn't really a tent at all, more a length of canvas propped against the wall with sticks. It would be as much as a man could carry comfortably and was only intended for one anyway. 'Parbold must have the tent, obviously.'

'Really?' Lady Aluric spoke up as if this was not obvious at all. What was obvious was that she should have it.

'He's the wounded one who has taken a knife in the back for the sake of your money.'

The lady looked quite horrified at this. 'I will not be spoken to like that.'

'I can punch you in the head while I do it, if you like?' Cwen smiled as if she was quite looking forward to it.

'She will,' Wat cautioned.

All Lady Aluric could do was breathe very pointedly and

The 1066 From Normandy

look as if the outrageousness of this behaviour would be clear to any civilised person. The problem was that there weren't any of those to hand.

'Better get this started,' Cwen said, looking at the jumble of wood. 'I don't suppose there's anything to eat?'

Parbold nodded painfully towards his pack which lay in the tent entrance. 'I have a little bread and some dried meat. You are welcome to that.'

'No, no. You'll need that for your strength.'

The Lady Aluric's breathing was now positively gale-like.

'What was your plan for the day then?' Cwen asked Burley. 'Pop to Chesterfield and back in one day?'

'I have some bits and pieces,' Burley admitted.

'What have we got in the Aluric household?' Cwen asked, nodding towards the pack that Hermitage had been carrying.

Strangely, Lady Aluric didn't show the least sign of objection to her pack being opened. Probably because she didn't have clue what was actually in it. Doubtless, there was a specific servant who dealt with packing things.

Inside, Hermitage found a fine collection of food and drink. There were meats and fruits and nuts wrapped carefully in cloth, two small skins of what was probably wine and a large loaf of bread.

Lady Aluric looked at it as if only now realising that this was where the food came from.

'Lovely,' Cwen said. 'Light the fire, bread, meat, wine and the avoidance of being stabbed in the back.'

Wat had left Parbold and moved over to the pile of wood. He organised it with a handful of dried grass with kindling at the bottom to larger pieces on top. He then took a flint and a rather nice, shaped metal from his pack.

190

No Smoke Without Smoke

It looked as if it had been specially made for the purpose as it sat so easily in his hand.

Next he took out a small piece of cloth - already charred dry, ready to take the spark. With one simple strike, he had a glowing ember on the char cloth, which he blew gently into life before lowering it to the bottom of the fire.

Ember soon turned to flame, and it wasn't long before the fire had truly taken.

'It's going to be a bit noticeable, isn't it?' Hermitage asked as the first smoke started to rise into the sky.

'I think with two dead and one stabbed, we can assume that our attacker already knows we're here.'

Hermitage didn't take any comfort from that at all.

There was no conversation as they gathered around the fire and ate and drank with little pleasure. Lady Aluric didn't seem to have any objection to people taking the food and drink from her pack. Hermitage suspected that this was because she'd never known what was in there.

As he took another drink from the wineskin as it was passed around, he noticed that the fire seemed to be getting brighter. He looked out and saw that it was the rest of the world that was getting darker. And it was a world that had a killer in it.

Well, it was a world that had several killers in it, truth be told. Probably many. The main focus of his attention was the one who was out there in these woods somewhere; the one who wanted to do his killing on them.

'We need some serious guarding tonight,' Wat said. 'Not the sort of "keeping watch" that really means staring into the fire and nodding off quite regularly. There's someone out there with a knife and he's probably watching us right now.' He looked at each of them in turn - except for Lady Aluric and Parbold - 'When it's your turn for

The 1066 From Normandy

watch, you keep watch, yes?'

Cwen, Burley and Hermitage nodded agreement. Not that Hermitage was quite sure how he'd manage. Keeping watch was so dull that it usually sent him to sleep. Perhaps the very real prospect of death would keep him up.

'And the way to stay awake is to stand up.' Wat seemed to say this specifically for Hermitage's benefit. 'Don't sit down.'

Hermitage nodded.

'Right. It's still early, but it's going to be dark soon. Anyone want to use the bushes before we settle?'

Heads were shaken.

'Good. Anyone feel like sleep now?'

That just made Hermitage yawn.

'You first then, Hermitage. You can help with Parbold though. Better check his wound and settle him in the tent.'

Parbold was already asleep. Doubtless, exhaustion from the wound bolstered by the wine skin had taken his senses.

Hermitage and Wat stood and gently encouraged him to his feet so that they could get him in the tent. Only half-awake, he protested at his treatment but soon settled under the cover and looked to be sleeping peacefully.

'Smoke,' Hermitage said as they returned to the fire.

'Usually unavoidable,' Wat replied.

'No, I mean over there.' Hermitage pointed to the woods away to their west. 'Look.'

Wat did look, and in the gloom of the evening a small plume of smoke could be seen hovering above the treetops. 'That must be less than a mile away.' He frowned. 'Our killer is not the cautious and careful type, is he?'

'What makes you think it's him?'

'Who else? It's in the wrong direction for the people of Chesterfield, if they've even discovered fire yet and what

No Smoke Without Smoke

we saw wasn't their hovel gently burning down.'

'It could be just another traveller making their camp for the night.' Even as he said this, Hermitage didn't believe himself.

'Bit of a coincidence, I'd have thought. Us being harried by a killer in the woods nearby and what do we see? A fire in the woods nearby.'

'Why would he light a fire?' Cwen had stood to join them.

'He's cold?' Wat suggested.

'Very clever. I mean why, if he wants to sneak up and stab us in the back, would he light a fire for any reason?'

'So that while we're busy looking at his fire he can do the sneaking up and stabbing?'

Hermitage spun around, expecting to find some horror behind him at that very moment.

Cwen nodded that this was very sound thinking. 'Either that or he just doesn't care? He's had two of us already. Well, two and a half if you count Parbold the not-quite-dead. Perhaps he's so confident that he can deal with the rest of us that he's settled down to camp for the night. Get on with business in the morning.'

Wat scratched his chin. And then his head. 'He must have seen our smoke.'

'Does he think we've all called it off for the night? You know, a truce.'

'Not likely. If you want to stab people, and don't mind doing it in the back, what better time than the night, when they're asleep.'

'Well,' Cwen didn't have any more ideas. 'Not a lot we can do about it, other than keep watch.'

Wat took a breath. 'Or we could go and have a look.'

'Go and have a look?' Hermitage burst out. Looking at

The 1066 From Normandy

killers when they came to you was bad enough, hunting them out in dark woods was the act of a madman.

'Yes.' Wat seemed to be warming to the idea. 'There's enough of us. One can stay here with Burley and the widow Aluric, the other two have a wander over and see what's going on.'

'Have a wander over towards a known killer, to see what's going on?'

'You are repetitious today.'

'I'm just making sure you understand the words you're using.'

'Think of it as investigation,' Cwen said. 'Only this time it's some real tracking.'

'Not you too? You really think it's a good idea to go off into the dark woods, looking for the camp of a killer.'

Cwen gave it a moment's thought. 'I think it's better than sitting in a camp waiting to see if a killer turns up.'

'There we are then.' Wat rubbed his hands as if it was all agreed. 'Only question is, who goes, who stays?'

'I go, obviously,' Cwen said.

'It's not obvious at all. We've got to have someone capable staying at the camp in case the smoke is a distraction and our man is on his way over right now.'

'You'll be excellent.' She patted Wat encouragingly on his shoulder. 'Hermitage and I can go through the woods and see what we can find.'

'Me?' Hermitage hadn't for a moment thought that he would be going anywhere.

'Of course. It needs two of us, in case there's trouble.'

'And Hermitage will be good with trouble in the woods, will he?' Wat asked.

'Leaving him here to defend the camp while you and I go is a better idea, is it? If the killer does turn up, Burley will

No Smoke Without Smoke

probably run away and Lady Aluric would tell him how rude he was being while he stabbed her. Hermitage could pray for them, I suppose.'

'How about no one goes?' That seemed a much more sensible idea to Hermitage.

'This could be our chance to catch the man before he does any more damage.'

'Or get caught by the man so he can get on with it more quickly.'

'Come on, Hermitage. We're only going to have a look. It may be nothing. Could be a simple traveller, as you said.'

'Hermitage is right, it could be dangerous.' Wat showed real concern for Cwen.

'Certainly could. But then so could staying here. Let's be honest, no sensible killer is going to light a campfire just down the road from his victims, is he? Would you if you were trying to sneak up on people?'

'Well, no.'

'There you are then. All we'll find when we get there is an empty camp. You'll have to be on your guard for when the knife man turns up here. Good that's settled, off we go, Hermitage.'

Before Hermitage could say another word, Cwen had pushed him out of the old fort and back towards the track. Wat stood and looked, clearly torn between whether he should let Cwen walk into danger or stay and have it come to her.

'Just keep the noise down,' Cwen instructed. 'And when we get close, don't go strolling in as if you're meeting a bishop.'

'I hadn't been going to,' Hermitage hissed at her, still very confused about what he was doing here and why.

The track back to Chesterfield bent round to the south

The 1066 From Normandy

after a few paces, and so Cwen cut away due west, into the thick of the wood.

'We're going to lose sight of the smoke,' she told Hermitage. 'We'll just head west and see what we can pick up.'

It was really quite dark now. Full night had not arrived, but it was that period at the end of dusk that seemed to be the most difficult in which to see anything.

'It's a still night, but we might pick up a scent of the fire.'

Hermitage stepped carefully forward, trying not to break twigs under his feet and alert anyone to his passage. At least his habit was dark and would hide him from sight to a degree.

As they moved farther into the woods, the trees seemed to grow thicker and a lot more intimidating. They towered over Hermitage looking ready to swat him from their presence at any moment.

'We must be getting close now,' Cwen whispered. 'Stick to the trees.'

Stick to the trees? What on earth did that mean. Why would he want to stick to a tree? Then he saw that Cwen was now moving from tree to tree instead of walking through the open spaces in between.

She was also crouching slightly, making herself a smaller target for any watcher.

He followed suit and crouched and scurried from one huge tree trunk to the next.

'There.' Cwen had stopped at one particularly aggressive looking Ash tree and was sniffing the air.

Hermitage did likewise and there was a definite tang of wood smoke.

Cwen moved her head around, trying to determine the direction of the fire to the best of her ability. Reaching

No Smoke Without Smoke

some sort of conclusion, she gestured to Hermitage that they should head towards the chosen spot.

Only now did Hermitage wonder what they were going to do when they arrived at the fire. It was a bit late to start thinking about that, but he hoped that Cwen had something in mind. If it was the sort of thing Cwen usually had in mind, it was all likely to get very difficult.

Sneaking very slowly forward now, Cwen crouched even lower and tip-toed her way across the ground. Hermitage's following was slightly distracted by worry now, and so he sneaked right into the back of her.

'Hermitage!' she hissed.

'Sorry.'

'Get down.'

'I am down.'

Cwen lowered herself to lie on the floor, waving urgently that Hermitage should do the same. When he was down in the leaves at her side, she pointed forward and nodded that he should look.

Now he could actually see the smoke of the fire. It was full dark in the wood, but their eyes had got used to it. The night sky had lit with its full complement of stars, and a thin moon hung somewhere out of sight, adding to the illumination; which, to Hermitage's mind was all rather ominous.

'Can you see anyone?' Cwen whispered.

Hermitage peered through the trees but couldn't even see the source of the fire. He shook his head.

'Me neither. Let's get closer.'

That hadn't been his reaction to the situation.

Cwen crawled forward on her stomach very slowly, while Hermitage wondered if he should hang back slightly. If there was trouble ahead, it would be no good if both of

The 1066 From Normandy

them were in it. He wasn't sure what good it would be if Cwen was in it and he was back here watching, either. He would probably be expected to leap forward. Or go back for help, perhaps.

As he pondered his dilemma, he detected that Cwen had almost frozen solid. Her forward motion had stopped but she also seemed to be staying as still as she possibly could.

He worried that this was not a good sign.

The very slightest movement from her hand indicated that he should go forward to join her but do so very carefully and very quietly.

This hardly seemed the time to make any alternative suggestions, so he did as he was instructed. He did it so slowly that Cwen looked around to see where he had got to.

Eventually, he arrived at her resting place, and followed the silent instruction that he should look towards the fire.

Fortunately, there was quite a substantial bush of some sort between them and the small camp, so they were well hidden from view. Between the leaves and branches though, Hermitage could see the fire itself and the simple scattering of goods around the place to indicate that someone had settled for the night.

A canvas cover was slung over a lower branch and secured into the ground with wooden stakes selected from the forest floor.

A pack sat on the far side of the fire, looking mostly empty now.

Most alarming to Hermitage was the large sword that rested on the pack. Wrapped in cloth at the moment, this was not the sort of thing an innocent traveller would carry. It was also the sort of thing that very effectively stopped Hermitage moving. He had no idea how they were going

No Smoke Without Smoke

to get out of here. He dare not move a muscle for fear of that sword being picked up and used on him.

He felt a nudge in his side and looked to Cwen, to see that she was nodding towards the left-hand side of the fire. He peered that way and in addition to his muscles not working, his blood now froze.

He managed to swallow, but felt as if had been the loudest swallow the world had ever heard and was sure to bring destruction down upon them.

At least they now knew what sort of person was killing people in this neck of the woods. A very efficient one.

Caput XIX

Killer in The Night

They had to get back and warn the others, but that would mean moving and Hermitage was pretty sure that he couldn't manage that.

Cwen appeared to have less trouble and had started very slowly shuffling backwards.

Hermitage could not believe that they weren't going to be spotted at any moment now. Surely, someone as practised in the ways of murder would not let himself be observed without taking some action. And people creeping through leaves was exactly the sort of noise people like the killer would expect.

After a few moments of complete stillness, he felt a tap on his ankles and took the risk of peering around. Cwen was quite a way back now and was gesturing urgently that he get a move on.

There was no sign of activity from the figure by the campfire; perhaps he had gone to sleep. Hermitage risked the very slightest movement of his left foot. To him, it felt as if he had stood up and danced naked in the woodland shouting "here I am, come and get me".

Nothing happened, and so he chanced his other foot. Still no reaction, and now he very cautiously put his weight onto his elbows and levered himself backwards.

He froze once more as the figure stood and went over to poke the glowing pile of the fire. He stepped to the far side of his small camp site and returned with two fallen timbers, which he threw on the embers, encouraging them into life

Killer in the Night

with a gentle push from his boot.

When things settled again, Hermitage realised that if he hadn't buried his head in the leaves, he might have been able to see who this figure was. He wasn't sure how that would have helped, but it was always nice to know who you were dealing with.

As things quietened once more, he felt a positive pull on his ankle. He glanced down and saw that Cwen was looking quite impatient and a little angry. Her silent encouragement, accompanied by the noiseless indication of what would happen to him if he didn't move, got him shuffling back once more. He was still very slow, and stopped every time he heard a leaf crackle under him, but he did find himself a few feet away from the camp site, with Cwen's head at his side.

'What are you doing?' She whispered. 'Let's get going. We need to tell the others.'

Hermitage thought he was still far too close to their assailant to risk conversation, so he nodded and sped his shuffling up a bit.

By the time they had reached the shelter of a young tree some thirty feet from the fire, Hermitage was still unable to believe the man they'd been avoiding wasn't going to pop up and ask them what they thought they were doing.

'Go, go,' Cwen urged, looking back towards the killer in his camp.

Their "go-going" was still very slow and thoughtful, but at least they were on their feet now. There was no question of running, that would surely demand attention like the blowing of horn, but their steps were carefully placed and moved them successfully out of range of anything sharp that might be shot at them.

At last, Hermitage thought that he might be allowed to

201

The 1066 From Normandy

breathe again. 'I can't believe we got away,' he said to Cwen as they increased their pace back towards the fort. 'Surely the fellow would have been expecting some action?'

'He may be nothing to do with this,' Cwen replied.

'That hardly seems likely. A man like that, just here when we've got people being stabbed in the back with alarming regularity?'

'Could be your simple traveller.'

'You mean there's another killer out here somewhere?' Hermitage shook his head. 'It's too much of a coincidence. A man like that, with a sword like that, in close proximity to an increasing list of people with knives in their backs. It must be him. In which case why is he so relaxed that he would make camp and just sit there?'

'He obviously doesn't think we're a threat of any sort.'

'He could be right.' Hermitage noted Cwen's reaction. 'Well, you'd be a threat quite clearly, but Burley, Lady Aluric and me? Hardly. And Wat looks too well-dressed to risk get anything dirty at all, let alone stained with blood.'

Cwen nodded that she accepted this.

'But what do we do? It could well be that the man is simply taking a rest before he comes to finish us all off in the middle of the night.'

'That would be reasonable.' Cwen was thinking carefully. 'Or, he could be waiting until he can pick us off one at a time again.'

'Why bother? With a sword like that he could do at least two of us with one blow.'

'I know, so why doesn't he? Why dump Durwin in the water box? Why get Lord Aluric when he was behind a tree doing what people do behind trees? Why stab Parbold in the back at all? He could have simply walked up to him

Killer in the Night

and taken his head off.'

Hermitage found thoughts of investigation bothering his head. Motives and methods and opportunities swam around trying to make it to the island of sense. They failed, of course, but something did occur to him.

'He doesn't want to be discovered.'

'Why? If he's going to kill us all, it will hardly matter if he introduces himself.'

'It's the only explanation. The man is clearly big enough, and strong enough and well-armed enough to deal with us all directly. Why doesn't he? Why sneak around stabbing people in the back without being seen? So that he can do it without being seen.'

'You mean someone might know who he is?'

Hermitage hadn't thought of that, just that the killer might not like to be seen. 'Could be.'

'Lady Aluric and Burley,' Cwen concluded. 'This is all to do with their fortune. This could be someone they know.'

'Who might find it a bit awkward to stab them in the front?' Hermitage couldn't see that anyone who did stabbing of other people was going to be too concerned about the niceties.

'Someone who might turn up to take the fortune once everyone else is out of the way. If they were suspected of being the killer, that might be a bit difficult.'

'Not if everyone's dead,' Hermitage pointed out.

'Maybe not everyone is going to be. Could be just the conspirators. Lord and Lady Aluric, Burley and Parbold. We haven't been involved in any of this. And he might know that, if he's been following their progress.'

Hermitage quite liked the sound of that. Obviously, it was terrible if everyone around him got stabbed to death, but as those around him didn't include him, there was

203

The 1066 From Normandy

something to be said for it.

They'd escaped from the woods completely now, and re-joined the track back to the fort. It only now occurred to Hermitage that if there was another killer in the woods, he might have come visiting while they were away.

He breathed a great sigh of relief as he re-entered their camp and saw Wat sitting by the fire. Lady Aluric was off to one side, just sitting and staring into the flames. Burley was pacing back and forth and presumably Parbold was sleeping in his tent.

When he saw them arrive along the path, Wat jumped up and stepped quickly to Cwen, wrapping her in his arms and lifting her from the ground. 'What was I doing?' he said. 'I should never have let you go on your own.'

'I had Hermitage with me,' she smiled and laughed at his relief.

'Like I said, I should never have let you go on your own. No offence, Hermitage, but if you had been attacked…,' he left the sentence unfinished.

'I'd have been as much use as a sparrow-feather quill.' Hermitage accepted his limitations.

'Erm, yes, right. And what did you find?'

They walked up to the fire and Burley joined them to hear the report.

'We found our killer.' Hermitage announced.

'Really? Who is it?'

'Erm, we don't know.'

'But you found him.'

'We did.'

'And you saw him.'

'That's right.'

'What was he doing?'

'Sitting by his campfire.'

204

Killer in the Night

'Hm,' Wat said. 'Very suspicious.'

'But you didn't recognise him, he was a stranger?' Burley checked.

'Well, we didn't actually see his face.'

'I see.' Wat was starting to sound a little wary of their revelation. 'But he's definitely the killer.'

'Absolutely. He must be.'

'Must be?'

'A man in the woods with a great big sword? What else would he be?'

'Just a man in the woods with a great big sword?' Wat suggested. 'Have you any reason to believe he's the killer other than the fact that he's in the woods and he's got a sword? The people so far having been killed with a knife, after all. Did he have a knife?'

'Bound to have done.'

'Bound to have done, eh? But you didn't actually see one?'

'No, but everyone's got a knife, haven't they? Even ordinary people have knives for ordinary things. Being a man with a sword, he's even more likely to have a knife.'

'And he's just sitting there? This man with a sword who's bound to have a knife.'

'He is.'

'Not actually bothering about us at all. Does he even know we're here?'

'Funnily enough, we didn't stop to ask,' Cwen stepped in. 'As he specialises in stabbing people in the back when no one's looking, he's hardly likely to stroll into camp waving his sword about. We have thought about this.'

Wat held up his hands in surrender. 'All right, all right. If you say so, he's the killer.'

'And we think he probably only wants to kill Burley,

205

The 1066 From Normandy

Lady Aluric and Parbold.'

'That's good then.'

'Hardly,' Burley said.

'And he needs to stay out of sight because he'll want the fortune once they're gone.'

'And you got all this from just spotting him by his campfire.' Wat nodded appreciatively, until Cwen kicked him on the shin.

'You think that the woods out here are full of killers, do you?' she asked. 'When the entire population of Chesterfield could fit in the one hovel? We've got people being attacked and we find an armed man in the woods.'

'Fair enough. He's the killer then. What do we do about it? It doesn't sound like he was making plans for an attack?'

'That's because he doesn't want to be seen,' Cwen repeated impatiently.

'Excellent. If we just stay here, and he just stays there, none of us will get killed.'

'He's obviously going to wait until late in the night,' Cwen explained.' Or even the morning, when we're on the move again. Then he'll start picking us off. Well, picking them off.' She tipped her head towards Burley.

'He's not making much effort to hide himself,' Wat said. 'For someone who doesn't want to be seen, I mean. Lighting a fire?'

'He's confident. He knows we're no threat.'

'And we think he's probably known to Burley and Lady Aluric,' Hermitage added. 'If he showed himself, they'd recognise him.'

'Someone I know wants to kill me?' Burley asked.

'Can't be the first time, surely?' Wat said.

'I think fewer of my customers want to kill me than those of Wat the Weaver.' Burley retorted.

206

Killer in the Night

'Now then, boys,' Cwen interrupted. 'Let's just carry on as planned. We keep watch through the night and see how Parbold is in the morning. We then head back for Crich and get him to a physick if he needs it.'

'We need to get word to his superiors,' Burley said. 'About the lead.'

'Really?' Cwen sounded very surprised. 'You really think that this scheme of yours to steal from the king is still alive? It's got more knives in its back than all the dead people put together. You're going to be lucky to get out of it with your breath, never mind any money.'

'I do think your best chance is to give up the plan,' Hermitage advised. 'After all, its pursuit seems to lead inevitably to death.'

'And see what her ladyship thinks,' Cwen suggested. 'It does seem to be her money you're playing about with. She's already got a dead husband out of it and just wants to go home.'

Burley looked to be really torn, which was disappointing to Hermitage's eye. Two people were dead, one cleric had been attacked and there was a killer waiting for the rest of them in the woods. Still this man wanted to press on with his scheme to avoid paying the king his tax.

At least the end of this would be an end to the investigation. It might still all work out for the best; not for the dead people, obviously, but the king could be placated. Hermitage would be able to report that the evasion of William's tax was now stopped. And none of the people involved would be any the wiser about Hermitage's involvement. Would he really get away with neither side being angry with him?

There was still the problem of the killer. It could well be that he wanted the Aluric fortune, but that wasn't a

207

The 1066 From Normandy

problem that Hermitage had been asked to solve. That sort of thing probably went on all the time amongst rich folk. He was sure they'd be able to sort it out between them.

Not that any of this rational thinking did anything for his ability to sleep. Knowing that the killer was out in the woods meant that rest was impossible. Even if that killer was sitting comfortably by his fire, he was still a killer. If he only wanted to kill Burley and Lady Aluric, and probably finish the job on Parbold, he would still have to come this way. And surely, if he were spotted, he'd have to kill the rest of them as well?

All of these thoughts gathered in a corner of Hermitage's head and made up gruesome tales of how his end would come. There was no way they were going to let him get any rest at all.

It was quite a surprise to be woken by Cwen in the morning.

'Up you get, Hermitage. Time to head off.'

'Have we survived the night, then?' Hermitage asked through the blur of his sleepy head.

'Well, I have. You'll have to decide for yourself.'

'I thought we were going to take turns at watch?'

'We were, but Burley couldn't sleep for some reason. Probably the fact that there was a killer in the woods over there who wanted his back. He took most of the watch, and Wat did the rest.'

Hermitage found his senses and sat himself up from the uncomfortable spot on the ground he had slept in. He realised he was quite cold as well, and so shuffled over to the remnants of the fire.

'And everyone else is well?'

Killer in the Night

'Seem to be still alive, at least. Even Parbold is in a reasonably good state. The quick application of the betony must have done the trick.'

'That is good news.'

'Absolutely. All we've got to do now is make it back to Crich without any more of us being picked off along the way.' She gave Hermitage a hearty pat on the back, as if this was just the sort of journey she'd been looking forward to.

Caput XX

Escape Alive?

𝔓arbold was indeed in a reasonable condition for a man who'd been stabbed in the back only yesterday. He still couldn't manage to take down his tent or pack his belongings but that was entirely fair. He winced when a movement in the wrong direction twinged his wound, but he was as keen as anyone to get away from this wretched spot.

His robe was now tied around his shoulder from its loose ends, and with his pale face he did not really look in any condition to be making a journey, but his spirit was clearly willing.

'Will you return to York?' Hermitage asked him as they made final preparations to leave.

'Once we've got out of this alive?' Cwen suggested from where she was gathering her belongings.

Parbold looked as if he thought that would be a good idea. 'I suppose I must. But at least I can report that this business is a hopeless one.'

'I wouldn't say that,' Burley called from where he was putting his pack together. 'Just a hiccough, that's all.'

'Pretty deadly hiccough,' Cwen said. 'And there could be more of them before we make Crich, never mind York. Not that we're going to York anyway.' She obviously wanted to make it clear that Parbold was on his own after Crich.

'Do you recall anything of your attack?' Hermitage asked, remembering that there were some deaths to explain.

210

Escape Alive?

Cwen and Burley returned to their work.

Parbold shook his head. 'I was resting against the stone while you had your discussion. I suddenly felt a sharp pain in the back and thought I must have been stung or bitten. A snake, perhaps. I jumped up and immediately fell to the ground, the injury being suddenly more painful that I could imagine.'

'And no sound or sight of anyone?'

'Not a thing. I heard no one behind me, that's why I thought it must have been an animal.'

'It was probably the stone that saved your life. The killer could not get a clear aim at your back and so only struck near your shoulder.'

Parbold nodded at this. 'And I must thank you for your prompt action in saving me from death.'

'Oh, I'm not sure it would have come to that.' Hermitage was modest. 'Just a small wound in the back. It would not have been fatal.'

'Undressed and untreated I am sure that it would have been.'

Hermitage shrugged. He had to acknowledge that even the most minor wound could easily lead to death if the foul humours got into it before any healing balm.

'You are bound for Crich, then?' Parbold asked.

'We are from Derby, but Crich was where we met Burley.'

Parbold nodded slowly at this, but clearly had other things on his mind. 'And you are, erm, engaged in Burley's, what can we say, adventure?'

'Me, oh heavens no.' Hermitage was so anxious to make sure Parbold understood his innocence, that he didn't really think about what he was saying.

'It is a delicate situation,' Hermitage gave no explanation

The 1066 From Normandy

at all. 'I am, erm, how can I put it, with Wat and Cwen.'

'Yes,' Parbold said very slowly. 'I am intrigued to know what a brother of your obvious learning and piety is doing with Wat the Weaver.'

'Aha,' Hermitage squeaked a bit. 'You know him, then?'

'Of course not. But a weaver introduced as Wat who shows all the signs of wealth and comfort? As well as a finely embroidered belt.'

'Oh, heavens. Don't call his weaving embroidery. He gets terribly upset.'

'But he is Wat the Weaver.'

'Well, yes.'

'And you are a monk, I assume. Not wearing some sort of disguise.'

'I am a monk, yes. I have been a brother of various establishments, most recently De'Ath's Dingle.'

Parbold crossed himself very quickly. 'De'Ath's Dingle? My God.' He immediately looked apologetic for the oath.

'And it was there I met Wat.'

'You met Wat the Weaver in the monastery at De'Ath's Dingle?' Parbold clearly though that this was simply unbelievable.

'That's right. And since then I have lodged with him.'

'Really?'

'And diverted him from his lurid works of old. He now only produces tapestries of a decent and appropriate nature.'

'If you say so.' Parbold did not look convinced. 'And Wat is involved in Burley's scheme?'

'Not exactly.'

Parbold considered all that Hermitage had told him. 'For a monk who is guiding Wat the Weaver, and a weaver who is not exactly involved with Burley, you are spending a

Escape Alive?

lot of time in his company. And just at the moment that he is trying to arrange a dishonest trade with the church.'

Hermitage thought that not answering this at all might be best.

'And Cwen?'

'Mistress Cwen is also a weaver.'

'This is all very confusing.'

Hermitage could only agree with that.

'Right, we're ready,' Wat reported. He hoisted his own pack onto one shoulder and lifted Parbold's onto the other. 'I don't think you're in any condition to be carrying anything.'

Parbold nodded his gratitude.

Lady Aluric simply stood looking at her pack as it sat on the ground, until Hermitage gathered it for her. There wasn't even the hint of a suggestion from the woman that she would lend any help at all.

'Now,' Wat instructed. 'We stick together, right. If anyone has to go into the bushes, or simply wanders off on their own, they might not be coming back. Doubtless the man with the sword in the woods will be following our every move. Give him an opportunity and he'll take it. Yes?'

He looked to everyone in turn and they all nodded. Even Lady Aluric acknowledged that he had said something.

'Come on then. Keep up a good pace and we'll be back in Crich well before evening.'

The strange party headed back towards the centre of Chesterfield and the Roman road that would take them south.

Hermitage was still worried, as normal, and walked alongside Wat. 'Are we sure that even Crich will be safe? After all, there's only the peasant's house there. It's not

The 1066 From Normandy

much better than Chesterfield.'

'I know,' Wat said quietly. 'I'm seeing how our pace is with Parbold, who may not be able to travel quickly because of his wound, and Lady Aluric who may not be able to travel quickly because she doesn't want to. If we get to Crich in good time, we can press on to Derby. We know we'll be safe back at the workshop.'

Hermitage felt a huge relief at that. It would still leave the problem of the king and the tax and all, but at least he would be home. 'If the others will come with us?'

'If we get back to the workshop, who cares. Dear old Burley and Lady Aluric can deal with their own problems as far as I'm concerned. The three of us and Parbold are the only innocents in this sorry business. We're the ones who deserve to escape alive.'

Hermitage was shocked at this rather heartless reasoning. 'And the king?' he whispered

'Oh yes, I'd almost forgotten about him.'

'He's probably got people watching for our return.'

'Could be. In which case we tell him what we've found.'

'Deliver Burley and Lady Aluric into his hands?' Even though they were fundamentally dishonest and greedy, Hermitage thought giving them to William was a bit harsh.

'And Parbold, probably. William will be very keen to know who in the church is involved in all this.' Wat could obviously see the concern on Hermitage's face. 'Look, Hermitage, there's a killer in the woods, yes? One who might not have anything personal against us but would still put his knife in our backs. And whose fault is that? Burley and the Aluric family.'

'And Parbold?'

'Yes, well, that is a shame. He seems a decent sort. If I

214

Escape Alive?

was him, I'd betray my seniors to the king as quick as a Saxon finding the best road out of Hastings.'

'I suppose we do know that William is generally supportive of the church.'

'Even when they're stealing from him?'

Hermitage didn't like to speculate about King William's behaviour. Whatever he assumed would probably be wrong.

This conversation had taken them back onto the Roman road, passing the hovels of Chesterfield, where the peasants didn't even emerge to see them go by.

The width of the road gave Hermitage some comfort. It would be much harder for anyone to jump out of the trees and stab someone without being noticed. There were even other travellers on the road, who exchanged nods with the party as they passed by.

The security of company was taken by Lady Aluric as an opportunity to move slightly away from the awful people she was having to share her journey with.

Hermitage frequently glanced backwards to see if the woodland killer had the temerity to simply follow them openly. That would be unlikely if he really was known to Burley and Lady Aluric. Unfortunately, he couldn't imagine the man letting them reach safety without taking some sort of action. The last thing he would want would be Lady Aluric making it back to Yelling where she could consolidate her position and have her people defend her from any attack.

He took to examining every passing traveller on the road in detail, suspecting that the killer might have dressed as a peasant or trader, and would simply gather his next victim as he walked past.

Most of the passing travellers on the road looked away

The 1066 From Normandy

from the strange monk who was staring at them. Strange monks who stared at people were generally to be avoided. They had very peculiar ideas and frequently wanted to do even more peculiar things. At least this one wasn't muttering to himself at the same time.

'I am sorry, my friends,' Parbold said after a little while. 'But I fear I must rest for a moment.'

'Of course,' Hermitage said. He guided Parbold over to the side of the road, where they could sit without obstructing the way.

'We've stopped,' Cwen called after Lady Aluric who was still walking on.

The lady turned, released a great sigh at the inconvenience and came back to join the others.

They all gathered in a protective ring around Parbold as he lowered himself gingerly to the ground.

'Let me examine the wound,' Hermitage said.

Parbold gave no objection and so Hermitage put Lady Aluric's pack down before gently moving the robe to one side and lifting the edge of the binding.

'It looks good,' he said encouragingly. 'I think we could do with fresh betony when we find some, but I see no signs of devilment.'

Parbold nodded slowly.

'But I am sure it is painful.' Hermitage opened the top of the pack and took out one of the wine skins. 'Here.'

Parbold contentedly took a swig of wine. 'That's better, thank you.'

They all waited a few more moments before Parbold indicated that he was ready to stand once more.

Another of Lady Aluric's disappointed sighs indicated the resumption of the journey and they all stepped along again.

Escape Alive?

'Well,' Wat said quietly, as he drew up close to Hermitage's side with Cwen at his arm. 'That was helpful.'

'How so?' Hermitage didn't know what was supposed to be helpful about what.

'Our little stop for Parbold confirmed that we're being followed.'

'What?' Hermitage barely controlled his squeak. He looked ahead to Lady Aluric who had not noticed anything. Burley was closer to the middle of the road and was out of earshot as well.

'We're being followed.'

'How do you know?'

'Because someone's following us.' Wat clearly wondered how else anyone was supposed to know they were being followed.

'Who?'

'No idea.'

'Then how do you know?' Hermitage repeated the question. He chanced a look back up the road to see if he could spot their pursuer.

'Everyone on the road is moving, yes?'

'Well, yes.'

'And as we walk along you can just feel everyone moving with you.'

Hermitage would have to take his word for that.

'Those going in our direction and those going the other way.'

'Yes?'

'When we stopped, someone else stopped as well. Further back up the road there was just less movement all of a sudden. Then, when we moved again, it all got back to normal.'

'That is a bit vague, if you don't mind me saying.'

The 1066 From Normandy

'How far back do you think?' Cwen asked.

'Quite a way. They obviously don't want to get too close, in case we spot them. There's just a body back there that's following us instead of walking along like a normal person. They aren't getting closer and they aren't moving away.'

'What do we do?' Hermitage asked. 'Go faster so we can identify them?'

Cwen and Wat frowned at him.

'If we go faster, the person following would have to go faster as well. Then we might see who they are.'

'Clever,' Cwen said, as if she'd never have thought of that.

'Or we could stop again and look to see who stops?'

Wat looked a bit unsure about this. 'Let's assume that it's the killer, shall we?'

'Ah, yes.' Hermitage now thought that actually exposing them might not be such a good idea.

'And I don't think Parbold can go any faster than he is now.'

'Do we just let him follow on, then?'

'Not sure what else we can do. At least we know he's behind us. That's got to be better than not knowing where he is.'

'I could hang back,' Cwen offered. 'You all walk on and I'll slip backwards and see if I can find them.'

'And then what?' Wat asked. 'Enquire of the killer if he'd very much mind not following us?'

'Scare him off. He obviously doesn't want to be spotted. If I can get an eye on him, he might think better of it and go away.'

'Or he might take advantage of having you on your own to do some more killing?'

'In the middle of the road? He can have a go.' Cwen

218

Escape Alive?

clearly had no concerns about her plan.

'Let's just head for Crich and see what happens,' Wat said. 'If we can get to the peasant's home again, we can rest there and see what our follower does.'

'Probably vanish into the woods again,' Cwen suggested. 'In which case we're no further forward. It's only one killer for goodness sake. There are six of us.'

'There are,' Wat agreed. 'One wounded cleric, a monk and Lady Aluric being three of them. And I don't think Burley's going to be much help.'

Cwen looked most unhappy that they weren't prepared to go on the offensive. 'We can't just walk all the way to Derby being followed. We've got to find out who it is at some point.'

Wat glanced back up the road again and seemed to be considering the options. 'He's gone.'

'Gone?' Hermitage looked up the road again and couldn't see any difference from the last time.

'Someone's missing.' Wat considered the length and breadth of the road. 'They must have realised they'd been spotted.'

'Where have they gone?' Hermitage looked at the other travellers nearby, thinking that one of them might be about to jump on them.

'Who knows? Could be backwards, could be off the road.'

'Could be trying to get ahead of us,' Cwen suggested. 'We have been talking quite loudly about going to Crich.'

'And in order to do that, we have to cut off the road and go back through the woods,' Wat pointed out.

'Why don't we stay on the road and head straight for the workshop?' Hermitage suggested.

'I don't think Parbold will make it that far.' Wat nodded

219

The 1066 From Normandy

towards the cleric who looked very frail. 'We have to stop somewhere, and at least we know Crich.'

'And he might try something before we get there.' Cwen seemed to think that was worth waiting for.

'Really?' Hermitage's voice trembled.

'Of course.' Now she was positively looking forward to the prospect. 'Whatever he's up to, he won't want his targets to get away. If it is Lady Aluric and Burley, he'll need to get them before they get home.'

'And us?' Hermitage asked very quietly.

'We'll just be in the way.' Cwen shrugged. 'In which case he'll probably need to do us as well.'

'Perhaps he's gone to get some friends,' Wat said.

'To wait for us on the road to Crich,' Hermitage said. 'Marvellous.'

Caput XXI

A Creeping Killer

The turn for Crich came far too quickly for Hermitage's liking. He could only imagine that the moment they set foot on it, bushes by the side of the road would turn into murderers. And then who would investigate the murder of the King's Investigator? Most likely, King William would just shrug and get another one.

Lady Aluric and Burley had not been made aware of their follower. Wat thought that Burley would only panic and Lady Aluric would demand that someone do something about it. Better let them find out when the time comes, he had said; which did not help Hermitage in his anticipation of the time coming.

Treading along the path as if he was tiptoeing through a field of sleeping wasps, Hermitage made very slow progress.

'Come on, Hermitage, for goodness sake,' Cwen pleaded. 'The quicker we move the sooner we'll get there.'

Hermitage did move but couldn't avoid looking to left and right for any movement in the trees.

'And if we all stay together, our killer is hardly likely to leap out on us, is he?'

'What if there's more than one?'

'What if there is? What's creeping along the path going to achieve? They'll catch you even quicker.'

If Cwen thought that she was helping Hermitage, she wasn't. He did speed up a bit though and made sure that he was in as close a huddle with the others as was decent.

The 1066 From Normandy

'This really is the most ridiculous situation,' he said to her when he was sure the others couldn't hear. 'We've had to deal with killers time and time again and we've never been hunted like this. And it's all about money.'

'Popular stuff,' Cwen said.

'Most popular amongst people who've already got more than enough.' He nodded his head towards Lady Aluric and Burley. 'If they were penniless peasants one could understand them coming up with a scheme to put a few coins in their purse; or even to get a purse in the first place. The Alurics have a fortune, Burley is a trader, yet they put all this effort into keeping just a portion of their wealth out of the king's hands.'

'Rich people do tend to behave worse about their money than people who haven't got any,' Cwen agreed.

'And now two people are dead, and another is wounded. And him a man of the church.' Hermitage felt the injustice and unfairness of the situation. Any sympathy he had for those being hunted by a killer was rapidly dissipating. Unfortunately, he seemed to be one of them; which was even more unfair.

'You know, if and when we get back to Derby, I am inclined to report fully to the king.'

'Really?' Cwen didn't sound too surprised.

'Lady Aluric and Burley have done nothing to persuade me that they do not deserve to be held to account for their behaviour. I think we should tell the king what we have discovered and let him deal with them.'

'The way that William tends to deal with people?'

'They're rich,' Hermitage pointed out. 'He won't kill rich people, he'll just take them hostage, or help himself to their money.'

'Oh, they won't like that.'

222

A Creeping Killer

'Quite.' Hermitage's natural charity and fellow-feeling for one and all had been sorely tested over the last days. And now he felt as if it had broken. 'It's all got to come out anyway.'

'What has?'

'The whole business. Whoever this killer is, they clearly aren't going to stop until they get what they want. Another attempt on Parbold's life is quite possible, followed by the rest of us. If the king gets involved, the whole business will be exposed and there'll be no point in killing anyone else.'

'Unless our killer just likes killing people.'

Hermitage ignored that horrible idea. 'If this is all about Lady Aluric's ill-gotten fortune, it is best that the king makes a decision. If our killer does want to take it, or claim it, he can present himself to William.'

'Hm, not sure that's likely.'

'Exactly.'

This conversation had taken Hermitage's mind off the dangers of the road, and as he looked around he saw places that he recognised from their previous journey. They must be close to the mine once more, and poor Durwin's resting place. The thought of the very first victim simply hardened his resolve.

Naturally, he wasn't hoping that the murderer would appear and deal with Lady Aluric and Burley, but he was determined that they should not simply walk away from this disgraceful behaviour. He was fairly sure that if this scheme had to be abandoned, they would only come up with another one.

He had managed to plead for Wat and Cwen to be spared when this all began; he was sure that he could prevent William being too harsh.

The mine appeared through the trees now, and

The 1066 From Normandy

Hermitage couldn't help but look over to the water box. He concluded that the killer must have dealt with Durwin and put him out of sight on purpose. He would then be able to pursue the others without suspicions being raised.

Murdering Lord Aluric as he had was quite a drastic step though. No hiding that away so that no one would notice. He must have grown bold, or seen that success demanded action. He did puzzle about why this killer might have done that. It was very obvious, while Durwin's death had been very discreet. And then the attack on Parbold while they had all been standing there. That was positively brazen.

And hadn't they decided that Durwin knew his killer? How did that help? Durwin probably knew lots of people.

They all walked on down the road from the mine back towards the peasant's house. Or not a peasant, as Cwen had pointed out. The gethis was now a landowner, thanks to the dishonesty that ran through this whole situation. Well, Hermitage would also make sure that the old man retained his land and his rights. It was only just and fair. And it was about time that something was.

There was no indication that anyone was going to kill anyone else before they made it back, and Hermitage felt a weight lift from him as the home of the gethis came into sight.

There was no activity, but then it was getting late in the day and so the folk would be out finishing the work in the fields or tending their animals. Doubtless the old man would be there to receive them, being apparently incapable of doing anything useful.

Lady Aluric looked disappointed to be back here once more, or perhaps it was melancholy. The last time she had been here her husband had been alive. Despite her

A Creeping Killer

appalling behaviour, Hermitage couldn't avoid a feeling of sympathy.

Burley was clearly cross that they were back here again, nothing having been achieved.

Parbold appeared to be hugely grateful that this was somewhere he would be able to rest.

Wat led the way back to the door of the house and pushed it open, calling out as he did so. 'Surprise, surprise, it's us again. Well, not quite all of us anymore.'

He disappeared into the interior and there was no further noise; no greeting in return, no repetition of the greeting from Wat. Nothing.

Hermitage thought that was a bit odd. And it remained odd when Wat did not reappear. He exchanged glances with the others, suddenly concerned that the killer may have got here before them and was lying in wait. Lying in wait was one of the things killers probably did very well. Had Wat already fallen?

The look on Cwen's face said that she shared his concern. 'Wat?' she called out, stepping towards the door carefully, in case there was some hideous shock preparing itself.

Before she could get there, the door opened, and a shape emerged. It wasn't Wat's shape. And it held a sword out in front of it, which Wat had most definitely not taken in with him.

Hermitage recognised the sword from the campfire. There couldn't be two huge weapons like that in this neighbourhood. Especially not possessed by someone who seemed so interested in them.

His heart and stomach both sank together as he considered the weapon, and the fact that Wat had just walked into the trap. For one ghastly moment, he found

The 1066 From Normandy

himself looking at the blade to see if it had any fresh blood on it. Thankfully, it did not.

Then the holder of the sword stepped fully out of the house, and Hermitage was almost sick on the spot.

Thankfully, there was some relief as Wat appeared once more, standing at the side of the new arrival.

'Hermitage,' Wat chided gently. 'Fancy you going all the way to the campfire last night and not saying hello.'

Hermitage didn't dare swallow, in case the movement caused his stomach to make a break for it. If he had got close enough to recognise the figure at the campfire, he would have given them all away for sure. The best he could do was put his mouth in the rough shape of a smile, all the time keeping his lips clamped firmly shut to prevent any escape.

'Good God,' Cwen said. 'It's you.'

'As astute as ever,' the swordsman replied.

'Do you, erm, know this fellow?' Burley asked, trying to sound as innocent as a newborn lamb that was the result of a virgin birth. If he didn't know the man, he knew what he was. The clothes and the hair gave it away.

'We do,' Cwen said. 'Allow me to introduce Lord Le Pedvin. He's a Norman, you know. Quite an important one.'

'Excellent,' Burley squeaked a bit.

Even Lady Aluric's usual disdain had been replaced by a look of genuine worry.

At least Hermitage knew who'd done the killing now. He still didn't know why or how, but he was sure that would come. His feelings were very mixed at the moment; under the overarching terror which tended to dominate everything.

What on earth was Le Pedvin doing here? He and

A Creeping Killer

William had sent them off on this mission in the first place. What was the point of that if he was going to sneak along behind them killing people?

But then he saw that they had simply been used. William and Le Pedvin had sent them off to find the tax evaders. Le Pedvin had simply followed along and as soon as they found one, he killed them.

Obviously, he didn't want to do them all in one go, he needed Hermitage to lead him to all the conspirators then he could do them one at a time without scaring the others away.

He must have got ahead of them to do Durwin. Or Durwin did something stupid to draw attention to himself. Lord Aluric in the woods was a bit blatant, and then the attempt on Parbold. That wasn't like Le Pedvin at all; attempted murder. Hermitage was pretty sure that when the man attempted it, he succeeded.

The wounding of Parbold was deliberate then. Now he could be interrogated to find out who else in the church was involved. Then they could be killed as well.

Hermitage couldn't help but think that this was all his fault somehow. If they hadn't pretended to be interested in the scheme and gone along with the Alurics and Burley, Le Pedvin wouldn't have had anyone to kill.

And now that they'd started heading home again, there was no reason for Le Pedvin to stay out of sight.

'A Norman, you say?' Burley enquired lightly, it being perfectly obvious that Le Pedvin was about as Norman as you got.

'King William's right-hand man,' Cwen said, with some unhealthy glee and a horrible smile for Burley.

'Aha, the king,' he laughed pathetically. 'Our noble king.'

'He certainly is,' Le Pedvin confirmed. 'And the noble

The 1066 From Normandy

king is most interested in what you and the lady here have been getting up to. Why don't we all go inside and have a nice talk about it.' This wasn't the sort of invitation that accommodated a polite refusal.

Burley was obviously trying to look as if it was his fondest wish to sit down with Le Pedvin, but he wasn't doing it very well.

Lady Aluric wore a look of resignation. Hermitage thought that her natural aloofness would not let her show any of her real emotions, but with her husband dead and Le Pedvin here, there was probably no point in worrying; things really had got as bad as they could possibly get.

All Hermitage could hope was that Le Pedvin didn't decide to kill Burley and Lady Aluric right now. Or question Parbold, come to that. Not that the wounded cleric would hesitate in betraying the confidences of his superiors. Surely it was enough that the conspiracy had been uncovered. The king's tax would be safe, wasn't that what all this had been about?

Hermitage was actually a little bit thankful that Le Pedvin had turned up. Now he didn't have to go and report to the king, it would all be done for him.

There was still the problem that Burley in particular, might want to discover how Le Pedvin knew they were here at all. If that was revealed, the role he, Wat and Cwen had played in all this would come out. Agents of the king. He could not imagine that would go down very well.

Mind you, he thought that Burley looked in no state to ask Le Pedvin anything. Abject, sycophantic surrender seemed to be the order of the day. It could be that the Normans were having all the rich people followed, just to see where they'd got their money so they could steal it. Fair enough.

A Creeping Killer

Burley obviously wanted to be the first to offer his complete cooperation to the king's right-hand killer with the big sword, and so he almost skipped over to the house.

'Always happy to help the king in any way that I can,' he bleated.

'Yes,' Le Pedvin agreed. 'You will be.' He beckoned that the others should join them. 'Come on, monk.'

Hermitage nodded his polite nod, still keeping his mouth firmly clamped shut, just in case.

'You're the what-do-you-call-it.'

Hermitage knew what he called it. 'Investigator,' he managed to say without throwing anything up.

'That's the one.'

Lady Aluric did give him a slightly quizzical look at this.

'You can explain what the devil is going on here,' Le Pedvin instructed.

'Aha,' Hermitage said, wondering where on earth Le Pedvin had got that idea.

Caput XXII

Revealed; All

'Well?' Le Pedvin asked when they were gathered in the peasants' hovel.

The peasants had wisely decided that it was nicer out of doors today; out of doors and as far away as possible, if they had any sense.

'Well,' Hermitage repeated, now feeling rather confused about why Le Pedvin was asking him. Was he really expected to lay bare their subterfuge in front of the very people who had been deceived? It could be; the Normans were a devious lot.

Le Pedvin had taken the old peasant's comfortable seat, clearly content that no one in this room was a threat to his little finger. He even laid his sword on the table, ready for someone to take it up and strike him dead.

Everyone looked at it as if it would rise up and strike them dead all on its own.

'Explain,' Le Pedvin instructed.

'Explain. Just so.'

Le Pedvin sighed and moved in his chair. Hermitage twitched as he expected the sword to be brought into the conversation. Instead, the Norman just stretch his legs.

'Right then.' Hermitage glanced pleadingly at Wat and Cwen, who looked equally puzzled why Le Pedvin was asking him. Surely, Burley, Lady Aluric and Parbold should be the focus of the enquiry.

'Call yourself an investigator?' Le Pedvin asked disparagingly.

Revealed; All

Well, no, Hermitage didn't call himself an investigator. Other people kept calling him one, most notably the king. But when the king called you something that was probably what you were.

And there hadn't really been much investigation to do, after all. He'd just followed people and watched their increasing and desperate dishonesty, along with the deaths that littered their path. He'd only done what the king had instructed. He'd found the tax evaders; well, Wat had really, and so now the king could get his tax. What else was there to explain?

And then he suddenly saw what else there was to explain.

'Aha,' he said.

Wat and Cwen looked at him with some surprise.

Hermitage looked at himself with some surprise as well and he was on the inside and should have seen it coming.

Horrible thoughts were almost dancing in Hermitage's head, as if let free from some smothering power. They all seemed to be saying "I told you so", and reprimanding Hermitage for being so unobservant.

In his defence, he considered that the thoughts were so horrible they deserved to be smothered; preferably at birth. He would never have dreamed of such things if the awful Le Pedvin hadn't prompted him. There you are, it was his fault.

'Yes?' Le Pedvin drawled, clearly not wanting to wait here any longer that was necessary.

'The king wants his tax,' Hermitage said.

'Well, yes.' Le Pedvin simply shook his head sadly. His consistent observations that Hermitage was an idiot were being confirmed.

'From the wealthy people.'

The 1066 From Normandy

'No point taxing the people who haven't get any money, is there?' He glanced to Wat as if asking whether this was the best they were going to get.

'So why kill the wealthy people?'

'Exactly.' Now even Le Pedvin looked a bit lost.

'I keep forgetting how, erm,' Hermitage searched for the right word. Well, he knew what the right word was, "horrible". It just wasn't the right word to use in these circumstances. All the others that sprang to mind, "heartless", "greedy", "self-interested" and "cruel", for example, were equally out of the question.

'Single-minded,' he came up with. 'I keep forgetting how single-minded the Normans are. If someone is going to pay you tax, you'd want them alive to do it.'

'You can tax the dead,' Le Pedvin explained nonchalantly. 'It just takes a bit more effort to threaten the relatives, and then they only tend to pay the once.'

'And if someone had come by their fortune in a dishonest manner, would that really concern you?'

'As long as they pay their taxes.' Le Pedvin was not troubled by dishonesty, but then Hermitage hadn't expected that he would be.

'All you wanted to do was find the people who were cheating the king of his tax and get them to pay.'

Le Pedvin's familiar sigh said that no one could really be this stupid, but that Hermitage was managing it somehow.

Wat and Cwen were frowning now as they tried to follow what on earth it was Hermitage was talking about.

Burley was doing his best to look absolutely fascinated by any comment that Le Pedvin made.

Parbold was in too much discomfort to pay much attention and was resting in a chair at the table. Lady Aluric was at his side and looked as disinterested in other

232

Revealed; All

people as usual.

'First we had Durwin.' Hermitage needed to get all of those horrible thoughts of his in some sort of order. 'Done to death in the water box.'

'And who was in the water box with him?' Wat asked.

'I shall come to that,' Hermitage said, hoping that when he got there it would make some sense. 'Then there was Lord Aluric in the woods.'

Lady Aluric took a sharp intake of breath at the name being used in front of the Norman.

Le Pedvin didn't seem to notice.

'And finally, poor Parbold here, stabbed in the back.'

Le Pedvin did raise his eyes at that, as if people stabbed in the back was a particular interest of his.

'I did wonder about that. Why would Lord Le Pedvin stab someone in the back and not kill them?'

Le Pedvin nodded at this truth of nature.

'Of course, it could be an intentional wound, just to make sure that Parbold told all he knew.'

Parbold looked as if that was exactly what he would do once he got the strength.

'But there is another option.'

'And that is?' Cwen asked, sounding a bit impatient that this was all taking too long.

'It wasn't him.'

'Not him?' Wat sounded surprised. If there was a room full of people and Le Pedvin was in it, it wouldn't be hard to spot the killer.

Hermitage shook his head, wondering if he dare release his conclusion. 'It couldn't have been, not if it was Lady Aluric.' Oh dear, he'd said it.

Lady Aluric only lifted her eyes for a moment, before dismissing whatever it was this monk had said.

233

The 1066 From Normandy

Burley was looking around the room at everyone else to see what their reactions were. Whichever was the most popular, he would join in.

'Her?' Cwen sounded quite disappointed.

'It was she who alerted us to the death of her husband.'

'Well, yes, but then she found him.'

'She did find him, but only because she stabbed him.'

The lady was now shaking her head in the gentle manner people do when they want to convey that they are being faced with the most monumental stupidity.

'She did seem upset,' Cwen said.

'Of course. She couldn't kill her husband and then behave as if it was a great success.'

'Why did she kill him?' Wat asked.

'The fortune. As you said, Aluric of Yelling was supposed to have been killed at Hastings.'

'Oh,' Le Pedvin spoke up. 'That Aluric, eh?' He didn't seem concerned that the man wasn't dead after all.

Hermitage carried on. 'But then Aluric turns up, quite alive and with a new fortune.'

Wat nodded slowly as he saw the possibilities. 'Her husband is supposed to be dead, but here he is with a lot of riches. If he really was dead, all the riches would be hers. And how could she be accused of killing someone who was already dead?'

'But he had the idea of becoming his own cousin, Hendor, and carrying on as if the fortune was his.'

'While Lady Aluric would much rather be widow Aluric than Lady Hendor,' Wat concluded.

'She stabbed him in the back while he had his leggings down?' Cwen seemed to think that this was a rather underhand way of going about things.

'He wouldn't be able to chase her,' Wat pointed out.

Revealed; All

'Where's her knife?' Cwen asked. 'I haven't seen her using one. Not even sure she'd know how.'

'Ah, yes,' Hermitage felt a bit embarrassed about this bit. He had hoped that no one would ask. 'It was something you said, Cwen.'

'Me? What did I say?'

'That it must have been difficult for Lady Aluric to, erm, find anything under all her skirts.'

'I did say that,' Cwen agreed, as if she'd suspected all along that that was where Lady Aluric kept her weapons.

'I think there would be plenty of room in all that material to hide a knife.'

'Shall we have a look?' Cwen suggested.

Lady Aluric did seem a bit alarmed now. It was the first reaction she'd shown.

'I don't think that will be necessary,' Hermitage urged.

'Not sure I want her sitting there with a knife tucked away.'

'Perhaps you could get it later?'

Cwen nodded that it was actually quite a good idea and she was looking forward to it. 'What about Durwin though?'

'That, I am not so sure about,' Hermitage admitted. 'We know he had a pound in gold on him.'

'And where is that now?' Le Pedvin asked.

'Gone.'

'Really.' It sounded as if he had Hermitage's next investigation all lined up for him.

'It could well be that Lady Aluric did not want that pound going anywhere, and so she went to get it back. Durwin could easily have believed that she wanted a private word with him, perhaps as a deception of the others. She lured him into the water box and then killed

235

The 1066 From Normandy

him.'

'I can't really see her ladyship crawling into a water box.' Cwen looked at Lady Aluric as if that was only one of her failings.

'She might if the need were desperate,' Hermitage went on. His eyes widened as another thought occurred. 'Those extra footprints in the silt weren't of someone on tiptoe, they were of someone with small feet. Like a woman.'

'And it wasn't me,' Cwen explained.

'Quite. But there is another disturbing option,' he said as he thought of another disturbing option.

'And what's that?'

'Distraction.'

'It would be quite a distraction, getting stabbed in the back.'

'A distraction from the plan all along, which was to kill her husband. She killed Durwin first to make people think it was all to do with the tax cheating.'

Cwen snapped her fingers. 'And while she was supposedly off in the bushes, she did Parbold for the same reason.'

'Just so. Except of course, she didn't manage to finish him off.'

'I knew she couldn't have wanted to go again so soon. After all, we'd had nothing to drink.'

Hermitage was quite keen to move on from that area of discussion.

'Makes a bit of a habit of it, doesn't she,' Cwen mused. 'Pop behind the bushes for a quick murder.'

'We would all think that this was some killer out to steal from the tax cheats. We'd never conclude it was all just to murder Lord Aluric for his fortune.'

'You did,' Wat pointed out.

236

Revealed; All

'Well, yes.'

'But then you are the King's Investigator,' Cwen pointed out.

'He's what?' Burley asked in a bit of a shriek.

'And what do you have to say to all this?' Le Pedvin directed his question at Lady Aluric.

She glanced up as if she hadn't really been paying attention. 'All complete nonsense,' she said. 'I don't know what a monk's doing here anyway.'

'But you are the wife of Aluric of Yelling, yes? The one who died at Hastings?'

Lady Aluric nodded acknowledgement of this fact.

'And this dead fellow in the woods was him as well?'

'I don't know where people get their ideas,' Lady Aluric sighed her disappointment at people. 'That was Lord Hendor, Aluric's cousin.'

'Who is now also dead.'

A slight inclination of the head indicated that Lady Aluric agreed with this assessment of Hendor's current state of health.

'And you married him as well.'

'Just so.'

'Can't afford to loiter, I suppose. And we're told you have a knife hidden in your skirts.'

Lady Aluric arranged those skirts, making it quite clear that this was one fact they were not going to check.

'Let me just get this straight.' From Le Pedvin's manner it was clear that this was something for everyone else to get straight, rather than him. 'You have now inherited the fortune of Aluric of Yelling as well as that of his newly dead cousin.'

Another modest nod indicated that this was, unfortunately, the case.

237

The 1066 From Normandy

'Being in possession of a fortune, you will doubtless be paying all the king's taxes as soon as they are demanded.'

Lady Aluric seemed to have frozen. Perhaps her knife was cold.

'I don't think we've sent a contingent of men to Yelling yet,' Le Pedvin mused. 'They tend to make such a mess of places when they turn up. Places and people. Still, at least whatever they find ends up belonging to the king.'

'Taxes,' Lady Aluric managed to squeeze the word out. 'Of course.'

'And you,' Le Pedvin turned to Burley. 'Whoever you are.'

'Oh yes,' Burley agreed that he was whoever he was.

'You'll be paying your taxes as well.'

'Never in doubt,' Burley agreed.

'As for the church,' Le Pedvin looked at the pale and uncomfortable Parbold. 'This might be a message to them that engaging with anyone on plans to evade the king's tax, tends to go badly.'

Parbold's slow nod said that he quite agreed.

'The king may have a soft spot for the church, but me? I'll find their soft spot and put something sharp and pointy in it.'

Parbold took the message.

'Well.' Le Pedvin rose from his seat and reached out for his sword. 'I'm glad that's all ended well.'

'Ended well?' Hermitage let his irritation show. 'Lady Aluric has murdered her husband; both of him.'

'The one that already died at Hastings?'

'Erm, well, yes. But she may have killed Durwin and tried to kill Parbold.'

Le Pedvin didn't look very interested in that. 'She's going to pay her taxes though.'

238

Revealed; All

'Is that really all that matters?' Hermitage put as much sincerity into the question as he could.

'Yes.' Le Pedvin looked confused that there could be anything else.

Lady Aluric stood from her seat, sniffed at them all, and walked to the door. 'Burley,' she said. 'You may accompany me back to Yelling.'

Burley nodded and smiled and shook his head and frowned all at the same time.

'Burley, eh?' Le Pedvin said with an awful smile. 'I must remember that name when the time for taxes comes around.'

Burley nodded that he looked forward to it but did seem a bit stunned at the same time.

'Right, you lot,' Le Pedvin addressed them. 'You can get back to wherever it is you go when you're not wanted. Take the churchman with you.'

No one had any response other than cooperation.

'You followed us,' Hermitage managed to let some of his annoyance take voice. 'You set us off on an investigation, under threat of death, when you had no intention of letting us investigate anything.'

'Of course. We never really believed you knew anything about tax or would be able to deal with it when you found it. You're an idiot. How you resolve murders is a mystery.'

That was Hermitage's view as well.

'Sorting out tax is way beyond your capabilities.'

'Erm.'

'The best you could do would be lead us to whoever was up to whatever it was they were up to. And you did.'

Hermitage would have to think about that sentence later.

'And now we've sorted them out. Well, I have. I

The 1066 From Normandy

wouldn't have trusted you to do that.'

Le Pedvin took a moment to consider Hermitage's confused expression. He glanced at the others who clearly didn't want to say anything.

'You really are an idiot.' Le Pedvin sheathed his sword. 'But sometimes even idiots have their uses.'

'You threatened us all with death,' Hermitage complained. 'You even said you were going to kill Wat and Cwen there and then.'

'Who?' Le Pedvin asked. 'Oh, those two.' He deigned to acknowledge that the other two might be called Wat and Cwen. 'I threaten to kill a lot of people; you can't expect me to keep track of them all.'

'And you had me dragged from my bed in the middle of the night.'

'Best time to be in your bed.'

'Couldn't you have found an easier way of doing this?'

'Not easier for me, no.'

'You're letting a killer go free.' Hermitage nodded towards Lady Aluric, who now seemed quite keen to be in Burley's company.

'A tax-paying killer,' Le Pedvin corrected. 'And as far as I know she hasn't killed any Normans.'

'Not yet,' Cwen put in. 'But there were none standing between her and her fortune.'

'I'm sure that she wouldn't dream of harming a hair on a Norman head.'

Lady Aluric nodded that this was indeed the case.

'There you are. Now,' Le Pedvin sounded as if this was going to be his final word. 'Unless you three want me to find something else for you to do, I suggest you go.'

Lady Aluric had managed to start looking down her nose at them again.

240

Revealed; All

'Oh,' Cwen said, as if she'd just remembered the stove was boiling over. 'We can confirm that the owner of the mine knew nothing about any of this.'

Le Pedvin frowned and Lady Aluric was very still.

'He's an old servant of the Saxon kings. Ancient old boy, but the mine is in his name and the Alurics just seemed to be using him.

The words on Le Pedvin's lips were "why do I care?"

'Just in case anyone claimed that the place was theirs, for instance.'

'I really don't care who claims what. It all belongs to us now anyway.'

'Oh, quite right too. It's just that this mine is the local thegn's, not the Alurics'. It'll be good to know when the king gets round to that big book of his with a note of who owns what.'

Hermitage could almost hear Lady Aluric's teeth grinding.

'Please yourself,' Le Pedvin said. 'Now get out before I really do have to kill someone.'

'Well done, Hermitage.' Cwen gave him a friendly pat on the back as they walked back down the road to Derby.

Parbold had asked if he might accompany them, as he didn't see either Lady Aluric or Le Pedvin as terribly sympathetic to a wounded cleric.

Even then, Wat had made it clear that there was only room for one monk in his workshop, and as far as he was concerned a lector still counted.

They all felt a lot lighter somehow, probably because Le Pedvin wasn't pressing down on them anymore. 'Fancy it being Lady Aluric all along. I would never have worked all that out.'

The 1066 From Normandy

'Well.' Hermitage was modest. 'It was only a case of putting the facts together and seeing which fitted the situation.'

'We're lucky Le Pedvin only kills people properly,' Wat said. 'Otherwise we'd have just assumed it was him.'

'How could she kill her own husband?' Cwen asked with a shake of the head. 'And like that?'

'Found him annoying?' Wat suggested.

'I find you annoying, but I wouldn't put a knife in your back.'

'Thank you very much.'

Hermitage was still feeling a sense of confusion, as if some feature of events was still not sitting in its proper place. It clearly showed on his face.

'What is it, Hermitage? You didn't say "aha" about the wrong person did you?' Wat asked.

'No no, it's not that. It's just that, well, I don't really even know how to ask the question.'

'Give it a try.'

'All this tax business and the lead and the money and so forth.'

'Yes?'

'Can you tell me what was going on?'

FINIS

Brother Hermitage's trials do not end there. Oh, no.
Read the opening of the next instalment below;
The 1066 to Hastings.

The 1066 to Hastings

By

Howard of Warwick

Caput I

Descended Upon

The people of Derby came out of their various houses, hovels, taverns and other people's houses to watch as the procession went by. It was usually a saint's day when there was so much activity in the street and the people were worried that they'd forgotten one and that the priest would punish them; again.

They knew that Saint Everilda was coming up. Or was she the one they'd just done? It was hard to keep track sometimes. Perhaps this was Saint Alkelda.

They enjoyed Saint Alkelda's day, when the ladies of the town could re-enact the saint's strangling by Viking women. There was always a healthy competition about which of the women folk would play the Vikings and which the saint. As enthusiasm for the part frequently got out of hand, the competition was usually around not playing Alkelda. With no one putting themselves forward, the Viking women had to spend the day strangling one another.

'Where's the relic?' One small boy called out in disappointment.

Some of the adults now noticed that there was no relic being carried high, so this couldn't be a saint's procession. Saints had to have relics, otherwise what was the point? It was the highlight of the day, seeing a box with a finger in it or even a whole arm, sometimes.

Of course, they didn't actually have any decent relics in the church of Derby, they had to rely on visiting bits and pieces. On very special days, some really important relic

Descended Upon

would be taken around the country for everyone to see and marvel at; and pay a coin to get close to.

The priest at Derby did his best, but following a stick that once poked the body of a dead ass that might have carried a saint's luggage wasn't the same at all.

Satisfied that this was not a saint's parade, the locals speculated about what on earth was going on.

There was a cart in the middle of the road flanked on each side by half a dozen men in uniform of some sort. They marched like soldiers but hadn't killed anyone yet, so perhaps they weren't. It was a grand cart as well, more like a small hut on wheels. It was solidly built and obviously well maintained. Whoever was inside this thing must be someone of great import.

The small boy wondered if it might be a living saint, hence the absence of relics. While this was an admirable piece of thinking, his elders and betters pointed out that all saints had to be dead, didn't they? And a cart like this would be no use to a dead saint would it?

Most remarkable of all was the fact that the thing was being pulled by horses; two of them. The people of Derby hadn't see two horses at the same time for as long as they could remember.

Old Jeb reckoned he had seen two horses go by once, but most agreed that he'd seen one and then saw it coming back again.

The main vehicle was followed by a gathering of men and women, all of whom walked with upright demeanour, ignoring the common folk of Derby completely.

'They must be Normans,' someone said to widespread agreement.

There really wasn't anyone who would be parading anywhere these days if they weren't Norman.

The 1066 To Hastings

As this clearly wasn't a church procession it had to be a noble of some sort. And everyone knew that the only nobles still standing were Norman. The fact that they hadn't been nobles when they arrived at Hastings was irrelevant; now they were, having very effectively separated the previous nobles from their nobility; and their heads, in many cases.

'They don't look like Normans,' an observant woman pointed out, sounding quite bitter about the fact. This was Margery, whose skill as a Viking strangler was so renowned that the sheriff had banned her from three years of Alkeda days, a punishment about which she still nursed resentment.

Mistress Wenna had nursed a bruised throat for three weeks and hadn't been able to talk for a month.

But it was true, those marching along the street of Derby did not look like Normans. For one thing, the men did not have the ridiculous Norman haircuts that looked as if the owners had gathered the local population of hedgehogs and persuaded them to stand still in the middle of their heads.

They also lacked the horrible helmets, hideous swords and the long shields that could knock a man senseless on their own.

For another, they displayed completely the wrong attitude for Normans. These folk were marching along in silence, ignoring anything around them. They weren't threatening the locals with death or stealing anything they could get their hands on.

No one had been punched, kicked, robbed or simply taken away for some awful purpose, never to be seen again. Definitely not Normans, then.

But who else could they be? Someone suggested Scots,

Descended Upon

but as no one had ever seen a Scot, they didn't know what signs to look for. These people had one head, two legs and two arms. Scots were bound to have more of one or the other, so probably not Scots either.

The word "Spaniard" was whispered about, to much alarm and trepidation. A worried pall fell over the crowd as they gaped in wonder, until it was noted that these people were walking and everyone knew that Spaniards could fly.

Every known nation of the world was now thrown into the mix, and dismissed just as quickly. French was only another name for Norman, apparently, so that didn't count.

The Welsh would have brought a dragon with them, the Cornish were all pixies and the Irish could appear and re-appear at will, so why would they have a cart at all?

Eventually, having no more names to come up with, someone shrugged and said, Saxons?

That really did throw a silence across the street. The crowd considered the passing horde with new eyes, eyes that found recognition after what felt like years of hardship under their cruel new rulers.

Saxons. Yes, these were Saxons. Saxon nobles marching up a street in their own land. Armed and mighty, well, unarmed but still quite mighty. With two horses and a cart. Joy of joys.

Word of the identification spread and the crowd was soon cheering the return of the Saxons. Perhaps King Harold was in the cart, not having been killed at all. The Normans had been lying all this time; they hadn't won the battle. Typical bloody Normans.

Wild speculation soon became fact as it was reported categorically that Harold had been raised from the dead by

The 1066 To Hastings

Saint Alkelda and now had the miraculous power to strangle a Norman with a single glance. That would stop them bothering humble folk.

Old Jeb disappointed everyone by reminding them that the Saxon nobles had been just as good at stealing and threatening with death.

Ah, but they were our own Saxon nobles, was the reply. It was perfectly right and proper to be robbed by your own people. Having some foreigner come over here and do it was simply not on.

The people in the procession did not react to the cheers and encouragement of the crowd, but simply continued on their way.

'Where they going then?' a voice called out.

'To get rid of William,' the reply came, to more wild cheering.

'Put Harold Godwinson back on the throne,' another cried.

This got a cheer that was a little bit more muted, as people started to recall what the Godwinsons had really been like.

'Where's the headman?' Ern, the landlord of the tavern asked. 'He should be dealing with things like this.'

Someone found the headman, loitering towards the back of the crowd and pushed him forward.

'There you go,' Ern encouraged. 'Find out who they are what they're up to.'

'They're nearly gone now,' the headman said, sounding as if he wished they'd called him earlier.

'Well run then,' Ern suggested, sounding as if the headman had been hiding at the back on purpose.

By the time the headman had made it into the street, the last stragglers of the procession were passing by. These

Descended Upon

were the most humble looking servants, maybe even slaves; the ones who probably weren't allowed to walk with the main contingent as they made it look bad. By their appearance, their main employment would be cleaning things; things that were disgustingly dirty to begin with.

'Where you off to then?' the headman enquired.

One of the most revolting of the men or women, it was hard to tell which was which, sniffed revoltingly and looked surprised to be spoken to.

'Just passing though, is it?'

The man looked around to check that it was him being spoken to. 'How would I know?' he said in the sort of voice that belonged to someone who had to do horrible things for his living.

'You're in the gathering.'

'You don't think they tell the likes of me where we're going or what we're doing, do you? All I have to do is clean it up afterwards.'

'Where have you come from, then?'

The man nodded his head back down the road. 'That way,' he explained.

'Oy,' a voice called from further up the road. 'What are you doing talking to him?'

A very smart looking fellow strode back from the main body of the train. He looked ready to issue instruction to all and sundry.

The headman held his ground.

'I am the headman of Derby and I want to know what's going on.'

'And you talk to the likes of him about it, do you?'

'I don't know what the likes of him is, do I?'

'You can smell what the likes of him is.'

'Perhaps someone who isn't the likes of him would care

The 1066 To Hastings

to explain then?'

'Certainly not. And stop obstructing our passage.'

'I'm not obstructing anything. It's you obstructing my street.'

'Well, we'll be off your street just as soon as we can. Wouldn't want to loiter here.' The man looked up and down the street of Derby and clearly did not like what he saw.

'That's good then. Pass along quickly now.'

'We shall pass along as quickly as we please.'

'Are you Saxons?' The small boy had wandered over and was gazing up at the smart dressed one.

'Of course.' The man had more time for a small boy than he did for the headman.

'Cor. We thought all the Saxons was dead.'

'All dead? You're a Saxon and you're not dead.'

'All the important ones, I mean.'

'No, no. There are plenty of important Saxons still alive.'

'What you doing here then?'

'We have come to meet someone very special.'

'What? You couldn't tell me that?' the headman complained.

'You didn't ask politely.'

'Who you come to meet then?' the boy enquired.

'The new king's own high appointee.'

'The what who?'

'King William? You've heard of him?'

'We've all heard of him. You haven't got strangling Harold in your carriage then?'

'Strangling Harold?' The man looked a bit lost now, and was regretting that he'd stopped to talk to anyone at all.

'King Harold. Come back from the dead to get rid of the Normans.'

Descended Upon

'Oh, I see. No, I'm afraid not.'

'Shame. I'd like to see Harold strangling some Normans.'

'You'd better be on your way then,' the headman instructed. 'There's no king's high pointers here.'

'This is Derby, you said so yourself.'

'Yes, it's Derby.'

'Then we have arrived. As it happens, you may give me directions to the one we seek. I imagine he resides in a manor house nearby.'

'Manor house? There ain't no manor house in these parts. Not any more.'

'A castle then.'

'A castle? I don't know who you're looking for, but I think you might have the wrong Derby.'

'The man we seek must be a significant personage in these parts.'

'If you told me who you was seeking, I might be able to help.'

The man looked a bit doubtful about whether he wanted to share this information with the headman. Or with anyone else for that matter. 'There is the question of confidentiality.'

'Not very confidential, you lot marching down the street with a cart and two horses, is it? And the whole town gathered to watch you go by.'

The man took the headman by the elbow and steered him away from the boy. 'We seek,' he looked up and down the street to check no one was in earshot. He even dropped his voice to a whisper 'We seek the King's Investigator.'

'Ha,' the headman shouted his amusement.

'Quietly.'

'Quietly? There's no point you being quiet about the

251

The 1066 To Hastings

King's Investigator. We all know him and where he is.'

The man looked a bit disappointed by this. 'Well, I suppose he must be a most influential figure in the town. Just direct me to his dwelling.'

'Direct you to his dwelling? Oh, yes, I can do that.' The headman smirked as he said this. 'Well, I can tell you where he lives.'

'Good.' The smart Saxon was showing growing signs of impatience with this impudent headman.

'And he's called Brother Hermitage.'

'Who is?'

'The King's Investigator. Young fellow. And his name is Brother Hermitage.'

'Odd name for a monk.' The man appeared to be quite surprised by this.

'Well, he looks like one and he talks like one, but you can make your own mind up.'

'I see. I suppose he must be a learned fellow. That would make some sense.'

'Oh yes, definitely learned. Not sure what he's learned about but there's lots of learning in there. None of it's much use to anyone, but he seems happy enough.'

'And where is his home? In a holy community nearby? A monastery?'

'Not exactly.'

'Not exactly? What does that mean?'

'I suppose I should say exactly not. He lives somewhere that is exactly not a monastery. Har har.' The headman was enjoying his moment.

'Tell me, or I shall ask some of the guards to come and help you out.'

'Wat the Weaver,' the headman said and burst out laughing for real.

252

Descended Upon

'Wat the Weaver?' The man went rather pale and looked quite offended at the same time. 'What has Wat the erm, that man have to do with anything?'

'You've heard of him then?'

'I may have come across the name.'

'Seen any of his works?'

'How dare you? Certainly not. I wouldn't dream of even glancing at anything of that nature.'

'No, of course you wouldn't. There's lots would though.'

'I can imagine.'

'I'm sure you can. Well, that's where the King's Investigator lives. If you want Brother Hermitage, you'll have to speak to Wat the Weaver.'

The Saxon was having trouble taking this in. 'The King's Investigator, King William's own investigator, lives with Wat the erm...,'

'Weaver. That's it. The one who did all those naughty tapestries of people without their clothes on. That's the one.'

The smart Saxon man's mouth was hanging open now, which gave the headman another good laugh.

'And young Cwen,' he added to the obvious confusion.

'Cwen?'

'She's a weaver too, she makes sure we're very clear on that.. They all work together.'

'Wat the Weaver, a woman and the King's investigator? I don't believe it.'

'You don't have to. Just knock on the door and you'll see for yourself. Mind you, Wat doesn't do the rude ones anymore. It's all pious now, apparently. I blame Hermitage. He ruined a perfectly good weaver.'

The man now looked as if he was wondering whether this was all some sort of trick.

The 1066 To Hastings

'You got a murder, then?' the headman asked.

'A murder?' The Saxon didn't seem too surprised by this suggestion.

'Yes. That's what Hermitage does, murders. Well, he works out who did them, he doesn't do them himself. Mind you, if he wanted to, he could probably do a good one. What with him knowing all the ins and outs.'

'A murder? Erm, there is a matter we want him to look into.'

'He's just the man then. Never fails, they say.'

'Do they?'

'But you just get along to the workshop of Wat the Weaver and ask for Brother Hermitage. He's so clever, he's probably expecting you.'

'Yes.' The man now appeared to be deep in his own thoughts. He looked towards the cart that was still rumbling slowly up the road, and was obviously wondering how on earth he was going to explain that they had to go and see Wat the Weaver.

An interminable number of further chapters of *The 1066 to Hastings* will be available soon.